Lexie hurried to escape. . .

Stirred to admiration, James Graham, Marquess of Stormaston, watched her trim figure making its hurried yet graceful retreat, a small, satisfied smile on his fine lips. Did she really believe that he had not recognised her? He had done so the moment her eyes had lifted and widened in recognition. No man could mistake those beautiful green orbs in the elfin beauty of her small face. He had felt her allure all those years ago when she had captured poor old Amber. She had been out of bounds to him then, but now. . .

Sarah Westleigh has enjoyed a varied life. Working as a local government officer in London, she qualified as a chartered quantity surveyor. She assisted her husband in his chartered accountancy practice, at the same time managing an employment agency. Moving to Devon, she finally found time to write, publishing short stories and articles, before discovering historical novels.

THE OUTRAGEOUS DOWAGER

Sarah Westleigh

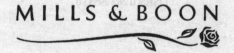

MILLS & BOON

All the characters in this book have no existence outside the imagination of the author, and have no relation whatsoever to anyone bearing the same name or names. They are not even distantly inspired by any individual known or unknown to the author, and all the incidents are pure invention.

MILLS & BOON, the Rose Device and LEGACY OF LOVE are trademarks of the publisher.
Harlequin Mills & Boon Limited,
Eton House, 18–24 Paradise Road, Richmond, Surrey TW9 1SR

© Sarah Westleigh 1996

ISBN 0 263 79533 0

Set in 10 on 12 pt Linotron Times
04-9604-78105

Typeset in Great Britain by CentraCet, Cambridge
Printed in Great Britain by
BPC Paperbacks Ltd

CHAPTER ONE

LONDON seethed with joyous, cheering crowds celebrating peace. With Boney safely incarcerated on Elba, twenty years of war had ended. The day before, on June the sixth 1814, six weeks after the last shot had been fired, the Allied Sovereigns had landed on English soil, come to visit the people who, by their unflinching determination to oppose Napoleon, had contributed so much to the allied victory.

At the port of Dover, detachments from the most famous regiments of the British Army had been there to greet Czar Alexander of Russia and the King of Prussia, the latter accompanied by his young sons and old Field Marshal von Blücher, his Chancellor. Prince Metternich, the Chancellor of Austria, was among other famous names to come ashore with them.

Today they were due to arrive in London as guests of the Regent, and the people of the capital thronged the streets to cheer them. Coaches, carts and wooden stands lined the route from the south-east suburbs to St James's Palace. Word went round that the Regent's scarlet-and-gold-clad postilions would not be needed, for the exuberant, swamping multitude planned to unhorse the coaches and drag them in triumph over London Bridge.

Lexie had not ventured into the suburbs to view the procession but the seething excitement in the capital proved too much for her and, ignoring the protests of

5

Mrs Caroline Baldwin, a remote cousin by marriage who lived with her, she had donned her oldest and plainest garments, intending to walk from her house in Bruton Street to St James's to see what she could see.

'Really, Alexia!' Mrs Baldwin had exclaimed. 'I sometimes think you quite forget your position! What your poor dear husband would have said I cannot imagine!'

'Amber would have understood,' Lexie had retorted as she tucked the last wisp of her fair hair out of sight beneath an old chip bonnet and tied the black ribbons beneath her determined chin—coupled with the washed-out grey muslin gown she had worn in the garden at Porthewan, the Earl of Amber's estate in Cornwall, it rendered her inconspicuous.

Colourless might have been a better description, she had mused wryly, with her pale skin and fair eyebrows and lashes. All the better. She had had no wish to be recognised. As a finishing touch she had fastened a plain white fichu about her shoulders, since the neckline of the dress was a little low for walking out and it would not be prudent to carry a parasol to protect her from the sun.

She could have been sitting in one of the stands erected for the privileged, but she hadn't wanted that. What she craved was freedom from the constraints of convention, the opportunity to take risks. Amber had understood that—why else had he bought her a sporting curricle and a splendid pair of matched blacks with which to race about his cliff-top estate?

He had watched and applauded her expertise with the ribbons and, despite his age, had accompanied her on many of her more sedate excursions. She had heard it said that it was better to be an old man's darling than a young man's slave. Certainly, it had not been unpleasant to be the first but she had no intention of ever becoming the second. If and when she married again—

'Well, I do not!'

Cousin Caro's usually fluttery voice cut firmly across her thoughts. She must be upset, thought Lexie with a secret smile. It took little to agitate the elderly widow whom she had discovered living in reduced circumstances. Lexie had needed a gentlewoman like her cousin, related however distantly to the Earl, to give her establishment respectability, and so had installed her as her companion.

Cousin Caro fluttered about making life more comfortable for her young cousin and made few demands. But she did have strict ideas about what was and was not done in polite society. Mixing with the noisy, sweating mob was something that was definitely not.

'Why you wish to expose yourself to molestation by those common people I cannot imagine!' went on Mrs Baldwin when Lexie did not reply.

'Because they are so joyous, so excited, and are truly enjoying themselves for once,' Lexie explained soberly. 'It is not often they have a holiday. I would like to share in their happiness. They will not harm me.'

'I sincerely hope not,' sniffed Mrs Baldwin. 'I would not trust myself—'

'But you are not me,' Lexie pointed out. 'If you are to be happy here with me, Cousin, you must learn to accept my rackety ways. I cannot live the restricted life convention demands. I did during my come-out year and I loathed it after the freedom I had enjoyed in Ireland. For years I have been incarcerated in the depths of Cornwall and more recently have been forced to lead a retired life in mourning for Amber. Now I intend to live a little. He told me I should, and left me the means to do so.'

Cousin Caro shook her grey head in its elaborate lace cap and sniffed again. 'I would not have thought it of my cousin!'

'He understood me,' said Lexie dreamily, remembering the indulgent peer, old enough to be her grandfather, who had recently lost his only son. She had been coaxed into marrying him because he was an earl and could offer her security. She had not managed to provide him with an heir but he had not held it against her, admitting that it was probably his fault, he was too old to beget a child.

Because he had loved her, he had left her the unentailed estate of Merryfield in Hertfordshire and the town house in Bruton Street—from which she was about to depart on her adventure—not to mention more than enough money invested in the Funds to enable her to live exactly as she liked. His nephew, the new earl, had been furious to see so much of his uncle's fortune left elsewhere.

'At least take Chalker with you,' pleaded Cousin Caro, referring to Lexie's personal maid, Florence Chalker. 'She knows London better than you do!'

'She never liked it in Cornwall and was glad to return,' grinned Lexie. 'She has already gone out. I sent her off an hour or more ago.'

'Then I must—'

'No, you must not, Cousin.' Lexie regarded the

plump figure of her companion with tolerant affection. 'You would become faint in the heat and be of no use at all. Wait for me here. I shall not remain out for long.'

She left Mrs Baldwin reclining on the *chaise longue* in a flutter of anxiety and made her way from her house by the servants' entrance. Most of the staff had already been given permission to go out to join the celebrating crowds, leaving Mrs Walker, the cook, and Mr Dymock, the butler, to look after things.

She managed to make her way to St James's without too much trouble, for she knew the nearby streets well by now, having lived in London for several weeks. The King of Prussia, with his sons, arrived almost as Lexie joined the throng outside the palace. The cheers, she felt certain, would be heard in the City.

Not that the King seemed to appreciate them much, his air of gaunt melancholy never lifting. He left the coach before the doors of the palace. His short coat and white pantaloons enabled the distant, straining crowd to admire his large bottom. The princes, fair, upstanding youngsters, followed him down.

But where was the Czar? Patiently, the good-humoured crowd waited, calling, shouting, laughing and singing.

They did not yet know it but, in the face of the size and enthusiasm of the unpoliced populace, the coaches had scattered before crossing London Bridge. The Czar's coach had skirted London to the south, crossing the Thames by Battersea's wooden toll bridge.

Word spread like wildfire that he had entered the capital by the turnpike at Hyde Park Corner and had gone straight to the Pulteney Hotel in Piccadilly, where his sister, the Grand Duchess of Oldenburg, was already installed. And, once there, he had refused to travel on to the state apartments reserved for him in St James's Palace, declaring that his sister had persuaded him to remain with her for the duration of his visit.

A heaving mass of spectators began to flood along St James's street towards the Pulteney, Lexie swept along in their midst. A stout, sweaty woman caught at her elbow as Lexie stumbled and would have fallen.

'Must keep on yer feet, ducks,' she advised, revealing blackened teeth as she grinned.

Lexie nodded and smiled, not trusting herself to speak for fear of giving herself away by her accent. For the first time she felt fear. Had she fallen she would have been trampled to death. But fear simply hardened her resolve to remain upright and to see her adventure through to the end.

She arrived at last before the hotel, deafened by the cheers and calls for the Czar to show himself. At length he did, waving from a first-floor window, a round-faced individual in bottle-green. His head rose from the high gold collar of a tunic so padded and laced that he had difficulty in moving his arms beneath the gold epaulettes.

But he was the greatest Russian of all, leader of the soldiers whose defence of Moscow had led to Boney's disastrous retreat from which his army had never recovered. The cheers echoed all the way back to St James's Palace and beyond.

But suddenly, distant jeers could be heard as a lavish coach, escorted by outriders wearing the red and gold uniforms of the Regent, attempted to force its way along St James's Street towards the hotel. The Prince, who had been waiting on his own ground to greet the Czar, had been forced to make his way through a hostile throng of his father's subjects to pay his respects to his important visitor.

But the crowd thwarted his intention. Lexie could hear the hoots and cat-calls, the cries of 'Where's yer wife, then, Prinny?'

'Serves Prinny right,' howled the stout woman who, somehow, still remained at her side. And although he would never hear her, she screeched abuse at the royal personage now being forced to turn back.

Lexie felt sorry for a man she knew to be lonely and unhappy. His marriage to Caroline of Brunswick had been forced on him for political and financial reasons. Of course, he should have resisted more strongly before entering into the disastrous alliance, for he was already wed to Mrs Fitzherbert at the time. But the Crown and Parliament refused to accept the legality of that marriage.

He had hated Princess Caroline from the start and tales of his mistreatment of his wife abounded. Having met that stout, crude woman, Lexie did not blame him. But on the other hand, having married her and begotten a daughter by her, he should have treated her more kindly.

'Can't even fight for 'is country,' the woman was screeching. 'Not fit for nuffing 'e ain't, 'cept finking up new uniforms!'

Lexie opened her mouth to defend the Regent, but thought better of it. Prinny, she knew, had pleaded to be allowed to fight with the army but the Constitution would not allow the heir to the throne to risk his life.

So he had comforted himself by designing uniforms, wearing one himself when he went to inspect his own regiment, the 10th Hussars. It was the nearest he would ever get to action, but through no fault of his own.

However, she soon forgot the discomforts of the Regent in her own. The press and stench of unwashed bodies in the heat, the foul breath of the woman who seemed glued to her side, had begun to overcome her. She wasn't used to it, that was her trouble. Lexie knew she must escape the crowd and began to edge her way to its fringes. Easier said than done, she found, progress was slow, but eventually, by a determined effort, she did reach a spot where the crowd had thinned. She paused for a moment to draw deep breaths of the slightly less malodorous air.

That proved a grave mistake. Two rough-looking men noticed her fighting for breath and, friendly enough, asked her if she was all right.

She nodded and incautiously answered, 'I'm feeling better now, thank you.'

'Cor, a nob!' They glanced at each other and then looked her up and down, reaching out to feel the quality of her gown, evident despite its age, and eying the snowy whiteness of the fichu about her shoulders. 'Wot yer doin' 'ere, yer 'ighness, mixing wiv the loikes of us?'

'The same as you are,' said Lexie, keeping calm. They did not mean her harm. 'I wanted to greet the Allied Sovereigns.'

'Did, did yer?' The leader and spokesman's eyes suddenly gleamed. 'Nice bit of gold. Werf a bit, that.' Lexie's hand flew protectively to the pin fastening her fichu. Another mistake she'd made. Amber had given

it to her on her twenty-first birthday and she valued it
for sentimental reasons. But she should not have worn
so finely chased and valuable an article on the streets.

'Got anyfink else under there?'

A great dirty paw shot out to grasp the thin muslin
and tear it off her. Lexie gasped and struggled to
escape but the second man, smaller but wiry, held her
arms from behind while his companion carried on
unimpeded.

'Let me go!' shrieked Lexie, beginning to panic.

'Shut yer gob,' hissed the big man, his hand still
clutching at her fichu, 'or it'll be all up wiv yew. Nice
sport it'd be, taming yew afore we cuts yer throat.'

'No!' she cried. 'Take the brooch and let me go!'

Her last words became a muffled croak as the man
behind clasped a grimy paw over her mouth, making
Lexie heave with revulsion. One or two people glanced
in their direction but their interest was slight. Such
incidents took place every day and it was best not to
interfere. The girl might be the man's wife or daughter
and it wasn't wise to get mixed up in family quarrels.

Lexie began to struggle in earnest. The good humour
with which the incident had apparently begun had
turned sour. The men were determined to have her
brooch and her, too, if she read them correctly. That
such a thing could happen in a crowded street without
anyone coming to her rescue! She would never have
believed it!

She stamped on the foot of the man behind her but
her soft shoe failed to make any impact—he scarcely
seemed to notice. The big man had torn the fichu from
her shoulders and was taking the opportunity to reach
down the neck of her dress, hoping to find something

valuable, if only a coin, nestling between her breasts. When he failed he began to fondle her flesh instead, sending tremors of disgust streaking through Lexie.

'We'd better get going,' suggested the man behind her. The big man nodded. 'Find somewhere's quiet.'

Lexie made a supreme effort to tear herself free and managed to emit a strangled scream.

The effect seemed instantaneous, though afterwards she realised that help must already have been on its way. The big man took a cracking blow on his chin; a thin cane inserted between his legs tripped him up and he collapsed at her feet. A long, blue-clad arm flashed past her ear to land a bunched fist on the smaller man's jaw. His grip on her broke as he slid to the ground.

'Oh!' gasped Lexie, trembling and almost giving way to the waves of faintness washing over her. 'Thank you! I called, but no one else. . .'

'Come,' said her rescuer brusquely, bending down to retrieve her torn fichu, the pin still attached, and scanning the crowd quickly as he rose again. 'The mob may turn upon us. Besides, these men will revive in a moment and it would be better if we were not around at the time. Come, miss. Take my arm.'

Lexie had recovered slightly. For the first time she looked at her deliverer. Her eyes widened before she quickly lowered her head.

Lord Stormaston! It surely could not be! Where had his lazy drawl and languid manner gone?

But she knew that it was, and remembered him and his reputation when she had known him seven years ago. How scornful she had been of his excessive indulgence in all the so-called gentlemanly pleasures of wine, women and gambling. She had not had occasion to speak to him since her return to Society but she had heard the gossip which always surrounded his activities.

The years had moderated his behaviour somewhat: he drank and gambled rather less than of old, but he kept an actress in a love nest near Drury Lane and had lots of other willing women available when he felt like it. He was also rumoured to visit Jackson's gymnasium to practice the noble art of self-defence. After his recent performance she no longer doubted the truth of that information.

It was indeed Stormaston, but a different man from the one who frequented the salons and ballrooms of polite society.

He had given no sign of knowing her. She desperately did not want him to recognise her. It was so many years since they had last met and she had changed. She was no longer the unsophisticated young girl who had been brought from Ireland by her parents to secure a husband. She was now a widow, a mature woman of experience. He would think her a foolish child still if he discovered that the erstwhile Lady Alexia Hamilton had got herself into such a stupid predicament.

She had not taken his arm as requested and kept her head bent as she felt herself dragged unceremoniously from Piccadilly into a less frequented side-street.

'That's better,' he commented as he slowed his pace, released her arm and began to massage his broken knuckles. 'I could deal with two of them by taking them by surprise, but I would not back myself to win a brawl against both together. How are you feeling, Miss. . .er. . .?'

'Much better, thank you,' murmured Lexie, ignoring

his hanging enquiry as to her name, staring steadily at the silver button fastening his cut-away coat at his midriff. 'I am most sensible of the service you have rendered me. . .sir, but I shall be all right now. If I may have my fichu. . .?'

'Ah, yes, your fichu.' He stared down at the piece of cloth in his hand as though seeing it for the first time. He inspected the gold pin through narrowed eyes and Lexie resolved never to wear it in any company of which he might form a part.

But next moment, startled, she was looking up into that dark, dangerous face she remembered so well, at the livid scar which scored his cheek, a mere thread now, which scarcely marred the symmetry of a remarkably handsome face dominated by a long, finely chiselled, arrogant nose.

He swung her fichu aloft on the end of his cane. His black brows lifted and with them his lazy lids, revealing brilliant blue eyes which blazed down at her filled with mischievous merriment.

'I think I deserve a prize for delivering you from those rascals and recovering your property, my dear.'

His words had caught her off guard. But she might have expected such unchivalrous behaviour from a man with his reputation! Especially as, despite the gold pin, he probably thought her nothing more than a lady's maid, dressed as she was.

A strange smile curved his lips as she jerked her head up in response to his taunt. His free hand came out to tilt her chin, so that he could study her features more closely. But still he did not recognise her. At least, she did not think he did, for the smile became a grin as, still holding her property out of her reach, he lowered his face towards hers.

'A kiss, I think,' he murmured, and before she could protest he had covered her mouth with his own.

He held her only by that hand under her chin yet Lexie stood paralysed as he tasted her lips, gently at first, teasingly. Then as, involuntarily, hers began to respond, he deepened the kiss, stirring strange, foreign feelings in Lexie's mind and body.

Abruptly, as quickly as it had begun, it was over, leaving her bemused. He seemed rather breathless as he handed her her fichu, the precious brooch still firmly stuck in the material.

'An ample reward, my dear,' he murmured. 'Would you accept my escort home? It would be safer for you.'

'No!' gasped Lexie, coming to life again after her stunned acquiescence to the kiss. And added a belated, 'Thank you. I shall be perfectly all right now. The crowd has moved off and I do not have far to go.'

He bowed, correctly and yet somehow mockingly. 'They have gone to mob old Blücher, I believe. If you are certain I can be of no further assistance we must part. A pity, my dear. I feel we might deal well together were you—'

'Oh, no! No, please. I must go. Goodbye.'

In her confusion Lexie almost stumbled over her own feet in her hurry to escape. She knew the way but did not want to make straight for Bruton Street. He might try to follow her. But although she looked over her shoulder several times on her way back she saw no further sign of the disreputable Marquess.

* * *

Stirred to admiration, James Graham, Marquess of Stormaston, watched her trim figure making its hurried yet graceful retreat, a small, satisfied smile on his fine lips. Did she really believe that he had not recognised her? He had done so the moment her eyes had lifted and widened in recognition. No man could mistake those beautiful green orbs in their nests of gold-tipped lashes, the elfin beauty of her small face. He had felt her allure all those years ago when she had captured poor old Amber. She had been out of bounds to him then, but now...

Now, Lady Alexia Hamilton was the Dowager Countess of Amber and an unconventional countess, too, it seemed: a young woman of spirit not given to swooning at the least thing. He should have realised her gallant, imprudent nature, given that he had watched her galloping indecorously in Hyde Park, indifferent to the scandalised gaze of other ladies of fashion who never went faster than a trot, and had seen her driving her curricle about town, quite unescorted apart from a youthful tiger up behind.

Amused, he had observed her as she fielded the attentions of half a dozen eager suitors and an even greater number of gentlemen with more dubious motives for their pursuit. He had not joined the throng surrounding her, preferring to watch and wait, to study the way she coolly but charmingly held them all at bay, to attempt to discover the chink in her armour.

He had done that today. She liked to be free from constraint, would take a risk, rise to a challenge. Were they not the very reasons he himself had left his grandmother and sister sitting in a window overlooking the route, had decided against returning to his own window overlooking St James's Street and had skirted the edge of the crowd to discover what was going on at ground level?

Lady Amber had ventured into the midst of the crowd. Even he had not dared that much, dressed as he was in a superfine jacket, pantaloons and shining beaver, until the sight of a young woman being molested had drawn him deeper into the throng to attempt a rescue. Jackson had told him he possessed a useful bunch of fives; today he had proved it.

Absently, he rubbed his sore knuckles again, watching as Lady Amber glanced over her shoulder before turning a corner. Had he not known where she lived he would have followed her to find out, as she no doubt feared. But he had discovered something else about the delectable Countess.

That kiss, stolen more to punish her for her instant withdrawal, her refusal to acknowledge their acquaintance—did she still hold him in the disdain which had so diverted him all those years ago?—had been a revelation. Lady Amber's cool looks and charm hid depths of passion he had contrived to stir. Her response had been instinctive, untutored—what the devil had Amber been about all those years?—and had shaken her as much as it had him.

He grinned to himself as she turned not into Berkeley Street but into Clarges Street; and he began to cover the distance to the corner with long, far from languid strides which quickly ate up the distance. He would follow her on her devious route anyway, keeping out of sight, to make certain she met with no more trouble.

He now watched from the corner where Bruton

Street entered Berkeley Square, saw her descend the area steps of her house and vowed that, before long, the Dowager Duchess of Amber would become his new mistress. Once, of course, he had dismissed Miss Hermione Green, the pretty little actress who currently occupied the discreet flat he owned in one of the less fashionable areas of London.

When Lexie arrived back she took a last look over her shoulder before descending the area steps but could still see no sign of Lord Stormaston. He did not appear to have followed her, for which she was thankful. She would never be able to face him again if she thought he knew who she was.

She lost no time in going up to her room, passing by the door to the small drawing-room where she had left Mrs Baldwin, on tip toe to avoid being heard. Cousin Caro was bound to notice the state she was in, spot her torn fichu, and she felt in no condition to answer her cousin's questions at the moment. She was still trembling as a result of the assault. Stormaston's kiss could have nothing to do with her state, for she was no green girl who had never been kissed before.

On the other hand, she had never been kissed quite like *that* before, in a such a way as to lead her to kiss him back without meaning to. She blushed at what he must have thought. No delicately brought up young lady would have dreamed. . .

But no delicately brought up young lady would dream of doing half the things she did, she reminded herself. For a start, they would never have defied convention by entering St James's Street, where so many gentlemen of the Town had rooms and where no lady of repute would be seen driving, let alone walking unescorted or masquerading as a servant in the midst of a crowd.

What was a kiss, after all? No more than the rather intimate touching of lips, which, on the rare occasions when a suitor had dared to kiss her in the past, had meant nothing or had filled her with faint distaste. Amber's caresses had been fatherly, warm and affectionate, rather than passionate.

Stormaston's kiss had roused new and untried feelings to swamp her mind and body and render her weak and helpless while it lasted. Even to herself she could not deny that she had enjoyed the experience. But it was never likely to be repeated, thank heavens, for surely if it was he would know it had been she whom he had rescued.

Though, on second thoughts, why should he? All women were the same to a man like him. To him that kiss had been nothing more than a momentary diversion. She need not flatter herself that the effect for him had been as shattering as it had been for her.

She roused herself enough to rise from the blue brocaded cover of her four-poster bed on which she had sunk on entering the room, and crossed to sit before the satinwood kneehole table that served for both dressing and writing to look in its mirror.

She scrutinised her face carefully before deciding that, however much she felt it must, her recent experience did not show. Even her lips, which felt tender to the touch, showed no sign of excessive pressure: they were always full and faintly pink. But she could not sit trembling and staring at herself for ever. She must pull herself together and dress for dinner.

Luckily Chalker returned as she was attempting to divest herself of the old gown. 'Oh, my lady,' she panted, flinging off her bonnet and rushing forward to help her mistress. 'I'm sorry to have been so long, but the crowds were that thick! There now, that's the last hook undone. Will you be taking a bath? Shall I ring for hot water?'

'Yes, I need one.' A slight shudder passed through her as she remembered her ordeal before Stormaston had come to her rescue. Chalker did not know how much she needed to rid herself of the feel of those awful creatures who had molested her. Only Cousin Caro knew she had gone out into the streets alone, though Chalker had wondered at her choosing to dress herself so dismally. 'Did you see the King and the Czar?'

'Oh, yes, my lady!'

As Chalker undressed her, Lexie heard all about her maid's adventures, which it seemed had been far less exciting than her own. By the time she had bathed, dressed, and descended to the drawing-room to await the announcement of dinner, she was able to greet her cousin quite naturally and give an entertaining if expurgated account of her sighting of the King and the Czar.

'And no one recognised you?' demanded Mrs Baldwin anxiously.

'No, Cousin, you need have no fears for my reputation!' Lexie assured her gaily. 'I would not have missed the experience for the world!'

Strangely enough, now she had completely recovered, that pronouncement was true.

If she dreamed of strong arms and gentle, firm lips that night it was, she assured herself next morning, much better than suffering a nightmare involving her attackers.

CHAPTER TWO

NOT belonging to the most exalted ranks of the nobility, Lexie had not received an invitation to the
banquet at Carlton House the following evening, given
by the Regent in honour of the victorious allied
leaders. Instead, she had attended a rout, a poor affair
since all the chief exemplars of the *bon ton* were
necessarily absent.

At least, she had consoled herself, it saved her from
the embarrassment of meeting Lord Stormaston so
soon after their encounter. But she would certainly
have to endure the sight of him the next evening, at
his sister's coming-out ball at Downshire House.

His lordship's brother, Lord Hugo Graham, had
been at the rout, but not his sister Fanny. Fanny, Lexie
had surmised, could not venture out into Society by
herself and the Duchess, like the Marquess, would be
at Carlton House. She could have come with me, she
had thought with a wry smile, relishing the idea that,
as a dowager, she would be considered a suitable
chaperon.

The esteem in which Lexie held Lord Hugo was
considerably lower than that in which she held the
Marquess. For all his gazetted wickedness, Lord
Stormaston had an engaging manner that his demeanour only served to enhance.

Green young ladies, flattered and excited by any
attention he showed them, ignored as far as possible

the admonitions of mamas and chaperons who were forced to snatch their charges from his dubious company—for to become embroiled with the Marquess of Stormaston would shred a girl's reputation beyond repair.

The mamas would have taken Lord Hugo's attentions to their charges no less seriously but, in fact, found no need to warn the young ladies against him, for they held *him* in abhorrence. For one thing, he was possessed of neither title nor fortune but, crucially, he lacked his brother's aristocratic address, his charm and the natural authority the dangerous Marquess exercised with such ease. He also lacked his looks and taste, thought Lexie, dispassionately eyeing Hugo across the room set aside for the younger set to dance.

One of a group of noisy, extravagantly apparelled young men whose striped waistcoats dazzled the eye and whose extraordinarily high collars prevented their turning their heads, Hugo had his hair brushed up *á la Brutus* and held a quizzing glass to his jaundiced eye while a cynical smile sat uncomfortably on his rather plump features.

Like his face, his figure spoke of excessive indulgence in food and wine. He had a name for attempting to outdo his brother's deplorable reputation, whoring and gambling with reckless abandon. Some went so far as to brand him profligate and depraved.

Yet no one had ever considered Lord Stormaston either profligate or depraved. Disreputable, disgraceful, scandalous, but not depraved. Despite his faults he was well-liked; besides, his ascetic features and athletic build denied the truth of any real descent into depravity.

Whereas Stormaston's popularity could not be denied, his brother's was doubtful even amongst his cronies. They, it was rumoured, tolerated Lord Hugo as a hanger-on rather than because they liked him.

Thank goodness she had no need to acknowledge him, thought Lexie, for although she had recently exchanged cards and visits with his grandmother and sister, he had not been present. And unlike his elder brother, he had not been in Town seven years ago when she had her come-out.

Earl St Clare, an older admirer who was waiting to escort Lexie into the concert room, followed her gaze and shook his head. 'Young fools,' he grunted, 'making such cakes of themselves. There they go, confound 'em, can't think why they had to annoy us with their presence in the first place. Wouldn't receive 'em myself.'

'They are all scions of impeccably noble families,' Lexie reminded the widower drily.

'Should still be ostracised,' grunted his lordship. 'Off to some gambling hell, no doubt, where young Graham will attempt to restore his fortunes.'

'Does he play that deep?' wondered Lexie.

'Pockets to let, last I heard. Depend upon it, someone will have to settle his debts and honour his vowels soon or the world will fall about his ears.'

'That badly fixed, eh?' murmured Lexie as they walked through to take their seats in the music room. 'Surely he has an allowance and the Duke would. . .?'

'Don't want the Duke to know,' she was informed. 'Scared of the old fellow, I gather; besides, it's Stormaston he wants to annoy. Storm will have to settle his brother's debts if he wants to save the family name from disgrace.'

'I rather thought Lord Stormaston had done quite enough himself to sully the name of Graham—'

'Not badly, never got into a scrape he couldn't get himself out of. His fortune is so vast—'

It was Lexie's turn to interrupt this time. 'That does, of course, colour people's perceptions,' she commented drily, 'but gentlemen have squandered larger fortunes.'

'True, Lady Amber, but Storm never threatened to be such a halfwit as to do anything of the kind.' There was amused affection in his lordship's voice as he ushered Lexie into a seat and sat in the one beside her. 'A little wildness is to be expected in a young man who escapes the bonds of tutor and trustees to find himself master of his own destiny and possessions. There never was any real harm in Storm.'

That had not been the impression Lexie had gained seven years ago. However, since his lordship's own son, Felix, Viscount Dexter, was one of Lord Stormaston's closest friends and every bit as much of a rake, she declined to argue with her partner. She merely remarked, 'But why should Lord Stormaston feel obliged to settle Lord Hugo's debts? Surely it is for the Duke to rescue the family name?'

'Storm was made his guardian you see, until the boy reached his majority.'

'Not the Duke?' queried Lexie, rather surprised.

'No. Young as he was at the time, Stormaston was named guardian to both his younger siblings in his father's will. The Marquess didn't expect to die while his heir was so young, you see.'

'But his son needed a guardian himself!'

'Had trustees instead. The Duke and Duchess and a firm of solicitors. They looked after it all, of course. But once Stormaston reached his majority, Lord Hugo became his problem. Lady Fanny, too. He has to see her settled.'

'I do not envy him,' murmured Lexie.

The musicians struck up at that moment and, since the subject of the conversation was no longer in view, Lord Hugo faded from Lexie's mind. Thoughts of facing Lord Stormaston the next day she found more difficult to banish. To her increasing annoyance she found them disrupting her enjoyment of the evening.

Lexie took great care over her appearance as she dressed for the Downshire ball. It seemed important that she should in no way resemble the dowdy individual Lord Stormaston had rescued from the mob a couple of days earlier.

Eschewing the pastel muslins fashionable amongst the hopeful young ladies enjoying their come-out Season, she had chosen to wear a gown made of jewel-like silk in a shade of emerald that enhanced the colour of her eyes. Over it floated a gauze of a lighter, softer green, ruched and gathered at the hem and decorated with intricate pink and silver embroidery. The low neckline, similarly embroidered, revealed the swell of her breasts, emphasised by the gathering-in of the high waistline. Long matching evening mittens reached above her elbows towards tiny puff sleeves. Diamonds set in filigree silver graced her slender throat.

A circlet of pink silk flowers with silver leaves surrounded the soft, smooth, fair knot arranged on the crown of her head. The use of curling-irons had coaxed the wisps of fine hair about her face into becoming ringlets. Lexie hoped they would retain the curl all the evening but if they did not Chalker would be on hand to restore them.

Chalker put the finishing touches to the coiffure and stood back to admire the effect.

'Thank you, Chalker,' smiled Lexie. 'A touch more powder to cover my freckles, perhaps. That Gowland's lotion does not a scrap of good!'

'You should not have ventured out into the sun the other day without a parasol,' reprimanded Chalker with a smile as she dabbed a puff over Lexie's nose and cheekbones.

'I wore a bonnet,' grumbled Lexie. 'Thank you. You had better bring the powder and curling-irons with you. I fear I may need both before the evening is over.'

She rose and went down to the small drawing-room where Cousin Caro reclined in her favourite position on the *chaise longue*; draperies, which suited her vague manner but not her plump figure, trailing to the floor. She held a piece of neglected needlework in lax fingers.

'Will I do?'

Caro's several chins wobbled as she nodded approval. 'You look fit to be a duchess!' she declared.

'You prefer me looking this way?' teased Lexie, remembering Cousin Caro's criticism on that other occasion.

'It is as you should look, my dear Alexia. You will be the belle of the ball—'

'No,' denied Lexie quickly, allowing a slight frown to mar the perfection of her brow. For a moment she wished she had not taken so much trouble over her appearance. 'Lady Fanny must be that. She is such a sweet child.'

And how did Lord Stormaston come to have such a delightful sister? she wondered rather sourly. Fanny's excellent if rather unassuming looks were understandable since she was very like him, but her character was altogether more admirable. She would never take advantage— But she would not think of that.

Quelling her unruly thoughts and her consequent attack of nerves, 'You will be all right while I am gone?' she asked her cousin. 'You could have accompanied me, you know.'

'I much prefer to remain here, my dear. Maria Seacombe is coming round once she is free. We shall enjoy a comfortable coze.'

'And exchange all the latest scandal, if I am any judge!' teased Lexie.

Mrs Seacombe was in a similar position to Cousin Caro and the two older ladies had become friends. Neither hankered after the excitement and glitter of the occasions which Lexie adored. They would have found full participation in the social round too exhausting. Only occasionally did Caro encase her plump figure in a fashionable gown, cover her greying hair with a pretty lace cap and take her place amongst the matrons and chaperons to listen to a recital.

The butler knocked and entered to announce the arrival of the carriage.

Lexie nodded. 'Thank you, Dymock. I'll see you tomorrow,' she said, turning to Caro and planting a kiss on her round cheek. 'Not before nuncheon, though!'

Dymock took her cloak from Chalker, who was

waiting quietly nearby, and Lexie allowed him to place it around her shoulders. He then led them downstairs and opened the front door for her himself, since the two footmen were both on duty outside with the coach, dressed in the impressive Amber livery of blue and silver, powdered wigs and all. They escorted their mistress to her carriage. Chalker, knowing her place, hurried ahead to squeeze herself into the far corner. One footman helped Lexie to mount and removed the step, the other indicated to the coachman that he could move off. The groom released the horses' heads and both he and the footmen quickly mounted the swaying vehicle as it moved off.

Lady Amber was making a show that evening. And Lady Amber knew that she had taken extra trouble over her appearance and ordered the two footmen in full fig and a groom as well as Jethro Pascoe, the coachman, both wearing black topped by tall hats, to escort her, simply because she wished to impress a certain marquess with the difference between the shabby young woman he had rescued and the wealthy Dowager Countess of Amber. Not, she surmised, that he would see her arrive, he would be too busy inside. But he would be bound to hear the gossip.

She smiled up at Jethro as she descended from the conveyance at Downshire House. Jethro it was who had improved her riding skills and taught her all she knew about driving a curricle. He was, she supposed, in his forties and had gladly left Cornwall to accompany her to London.

'I shall probably be leaving at about two,' she informed him.

'I'll be waiting for your call, my lady,' he assured

her, with a dignified inclination of his head. But his eyes twinkled down at her as she stood, illuminated by the last rays of the sun. He was enjoying himself in London, not least because his spirited young mistress was so evidently blossoming into the great lady he had always considered her.

In the busy receiving cloakroom Lexie greeted acquaintances while Chalker removed her cloak, brushed a tiny speck of dust from her silver sandal and tweaked a recalcitrant curl back into position. The ball would probably go on until dawn but she felt fresh and energetic. She anticipated an enjoyable evening and might stay even later than two. In which case Jethro and the other servants had a long wait. But they had their own ways of passing the time.

By now Lexie was used to arriving at this kind of function alone. It did not concern her in the least; she had made no close friend as yet and would rather that than join some party of acquaintances she would feel obliged to remain with all the evening. It left her free to circulate, to sit with anyone she liked between dances. She never lacked for partners and usually became the centre of a throng of gentlemen jostling for her attention. Some considered her a flirt but that did not concern her either.

Lexie was enjoying herself and knew she was not seriously breaking any hearts. Her success did, however, diminish her popularity with some of the hopeful mamas and their charges. Young men who should have been offering for the young ladies' hands sighed instead over the undisputed charms of the flighty Dowager Duchess of Amber.

Slowly, one step at a time, Lexie mounted the

marble staircase, moving beneath the glittering chandeliers towards those waiting to receive her. Like most
others she had arrived neither early nor late and the
queue stretched before and behind her, which meant
that the guests were being passed quickly along the
receiving line just inside the ballroom.

It was ridiculous to feel so nervous. Lord Stormaston
would scarcely look at her. She wished he would not
be there but he must be, since he was Lady Fanny's
guardian and standing in for his absent grandfather as
host.

She knew neither those above nor below her on the
stairs and could not therefore enter into conversation
with either party. But she had to keep her mind
occupied, so she studied the marble of the entrance
hall and staircase, the wine-coloured drapes, the gold
fringes and tassels, the paintings of august Downshire
ancestors, which reminded her uncomfortably of the
present heir, and the brilliance of the huge chandeliers.

All this splendour would be his one day. Did he
deserve such an inheritance? The indolent rake of
salon, ballroom, card room and gambling hell, in her
opinion, did not. Perhaps responsibility would change
him.

And then she remembered the strong, athletic, far
from indolent gentleman who had snatched her from
the hands of two thugs in the middle of what could
have turned into a hostile crowd, and wondered. *That*
Lord Stormaston had been alert, resourceful, forceful,
full of vigour. And, she reminded herself before she
forgot, instinctively touching with her folded fan lips
which still remembered his kiss, just as loathsomely
rakish as his reputation had painted him.

That encounter had spoilt everything for her. She had been enjoying the Season so much. Her come-out, apart from a natural seventeen-year-old's enjoyment of parties and balls, had proved a wretched experience, for the need to secure a husband had been hanging like a threat over her head, with her mother nagging her unmercifully and her father taking little interest in proceedings, just wanting her off his hands with a favourable settlement.

And she had met no one really suitable, certainly no one who had offered for her. She had so hoped to fall in love! Her parents, of course, had scoffed at that idea and reminded her of her duty. So she had accepted Amber.

Dear Amber. He had been the kindest of husbands yet she had never felt able to call him Edward. It would have been like calling her father—even her grandfather—by their given names.

This time she was free to please herself, choose a husband or not. Of course, she had grown up in the interval and no longer cherished romantic dreams about marriage, but she would not wed simply for the sake of it again. She had security, the will to enjoy life to the full, the flattering attention of many admirers. What more could she want?

Affection, companionship, a family. And why not love? asked a plaintive voice in her head.

She shook it impatiently. Love! Was it love that had made her tremble when Stormaston had kissed her? Certainly not! That had been a purely physical reaction over which she had had no control. Lust, then? She had not believed herself capable of that. Yet that single kiss had stirred her in startling ways, ways the consummation of her marriage never had.

And the memory of it made the thought of coming face to face with the Marquess again unsettling to say the least. For she could not be absolutely sure he had not recognised her. If he had, would he be base enough to mention their encounter? And, she thought ruefully, in future there would be no escaping Lord Hugo, either. Since he was family they were bound to be introduced.

At last she approached the double doors opening into the ballroom. Her turn soon. She kept her eyes firmly fixed on the throng milling beneath yet more grand chandeliers, saw pale gauzes and butterfly colours counterpointed by the darker garb of the gentlemen and enlivened by more scarlet coats than she had ever seen gathered together, except on a parade ground.

The presence of some green coats of the Rifles and blue of the Dragoons confirmed that Wellington's battered but victorious army was already returning from the Peninsula, although the newly created Duke had himself still to arrive in London.

She was next in line. She settled her gauze scarf more neatly across her forearms, fidgeted with her fan, opened it and snapped it together again. Then she was curtsying before the Duchess who was regal in purple silk despite her tiny size, though the feathers in her headdress added a good foot to her height, and being greeted warmly, even kissed, by a radiant Fanny floating in a cloud of white, and passing on to curtsy formally to a black-clad Lord Stormaston at his most top-lofty and impressive.

He took her hand and bent over it. Lexie had to know. She looked up, trying to catch any gleam of recognition in the blue depths of his eyes.

There was none. His lids drooped, almost obscuring them. 'Enchanted, Lady Amber,' he drawled. 'Delighted to renew our acquaintance. . .after so many years. Recognised you immediately.'

Lexie inclined her head, lowering her eyes quickly to prevent his seeing the uncertainty in them. Had he really hesitated? Did his words hold a double meaning? 'Thank you, my lord,' she managed to say without allowing her voice to quiver.

'Devilishly sorry to hear of your loss, don't you know.'

'Everyone,' said Lexie, 'has been most kind.'

'Must present my brother.' His lordship waved a limp hand towards a stout figure resplendent in blue satin. Since he could not turn his head because of the height of his collar, Hugo turned from the waist, his quizzing-glass before his eye. 'Lord Hugo Graham. Hugo, may I present Lady Amber. We were introduced years ago—' he lifted a negligent shoulder '—before you came to Town, my dear fellow, and before she became a countess.'

He was, if anything, more languid than ever. Except that, with a speed which denied his lazy air, while she and Hugo were making their devoirs, he had taken her dance card from her nerveless fingers and scribbled his name thereon, using the little pencil attached.

Hugo made an elaborate leg. His plump, moist hand held hers while he uttered some extravagant compliment to which Lexie made an abstracted reply.

'Grandmama is becomin' quite *risqué* in her old

age,' Stormaston confided as he returned her property, a slight smile lifting one corner of lips whose touch had had such a devastating effect on her. 'Allowed a couple of waltzes to be included, in honour of the Czar, who is exceptionally fond of the dance. You can waltz, I collect?' His voice held an intolerable undercurrent of boredom as he made the enquiry.

'Of course,' said Lexie as haughtily as she knew how, sweeping past Hugo before the next in line trod on her heels and he, too, demanded her card and stole a dance.

Because the insufferable Marquess *had* stolen a dance. She would never have agreed to stand up with him had he afforded her the chance to refuse. Given five minutes in the ballroom she could have protested her card to be full. It probably would have been, too. Her hand was shaking—with rage—as she looked down to see where he had written. And then she nearly exploded. He had claimed two dances, both waltzes! One before supper and one much later, in the early hours.

He had never taken the slightest notice of her until tonight. Had kept his distance while even his friend Felix St Clare, Lord Dexter, had often solicited her hand for a dance and spent its duration shamelessly flirting with her, to her amused enjoyment.

Now, suddenly, he was making a spectacle of her. People would begin to talk, for to stand up twice with her, and both of the dances waltzes, must suggest that he was paying her marked attention. And marked attention from the Marquess of Stormaston was un-desirable to say the least. She must make her displeasure plain or she would quickly be tarred with the same brush as he!

Quietly seething, she greeted her usual court of admirers as they and others gathered round to initial her card, keeping her smile bright and her voice light, laughing and flirting as she always did, until one youthfully persistent and disappointed suitor voiced his displeasure.

'Divine Lady Amber! How can I bear it? I was countin' on leading you out for a waltz! Storm don't usually dance with you at all, do he?' protested the young man, who had not yet reached his majority, in a rather less dramatic but more truculent tone. 'Doin' it because he's host tonight, I collect, doin' the pretty by his guests. But he oughtn't to waltz with you *twice*! I shall strike his second initial out!'

'No!' Quite why she stopped the Honourable Oswald Cresswell from inserting his name instead of Stormaston's, Lexie could not have said. To cover her impatient denial—for dancing with Oswald would be more of a trial than with Stormaston and perhaps that was why—she made a joke. 'He might take exception and call you out, and you know his reputation with pistol and blade!'

Oswald paled. He had forgotten the Marquess's superior rank, how high in the instep he could be, how easily he climbed up on his high ropes and, lastly, how much most men feared being called out by him. Oswald considered himself a poetic young man to whom violence was anathema. Courage was not his long suit.

'Well. . .' He hesitated.

'Put your name against this one,' suggested Lexie

pacifically. Slender and poetic Oswald might be, but he had clumsy feet and a country dance with him as partner would be much more the thing.

Others were clamouring to claim her hand and Oswald reluctantly gave in, muttering that he could not even claim the supper dance, either, as he passed the card to a young Captain of Hussars.

As Lexie had anticipated, every dance on her card had been initialled long before Lord Stormaston was able to relinquish his post at the door. As the orchestra struck up, he took his sister out to open the ball. Dancing with one's sibling was, of course, considered bad form but when had the Marquess ever considered form? In any case, since he was standing in for their grandparent, all would be forgiven.

Lexie could not help but notice the easy grace with which he executed the steps and bows of the minuet, the proud, fond smile he bestowed on his sister as she curtsied. Flushed and glowing with excitement, Fanny's looks had improved out of all recognition. Her latent attractions had surfaced. She was undoubtedly the belle of this particular ball.

Not long after this a great stir ran around the ballroom and a cheer went up from the younger members of the company. The Czar himself had arrived, together with the elderly Marshal Blücher. Both men, epaulettes and stars gleaming under the candles, were immediately besieged. Fanny's come-out had become a glittering occasion.

Although she danced and laughed and enjoyed herself, chatting with friends between the dances, the prospect of her waltz with Lord Stormaston hung heavily over Lexie's head. As usual, his lordship's social behaviour was impeccable—tonight he was the perfect host. Lord Hugo's loud-mouthed cronies, she noted, were not present. He himself had disappeared to the card room almost immediately.

Most of Stormaston's own friends, however, had been invited. Despite their high spirits and bouts of devilry, which they kept well away from ball or drawing-room, they were welcome guests, gracing any assembly with their exquisite presence and impeccable manners.

Although some had already repaired to the card tables, others remained in the ballroom, Lord Dexter, among them, presumably to lend their friend moral support in the doing of his duty. Dexter had secured the supper dance with her and she quite looked forward to it. She found him an entertaining, relaxing companion. She liked Felix St Clare, despite his dubious reputation, and had no qualms about dancing with him.

For some reason she did not hold him in the same disgust as she had always held Stormaston, perhaps because, being almost as young as herself when first they had met seven years ago, his reputation had still to be earned. While Stormaston, enjoying his freedom after reaching his majority a couple of years earlier, had already managed to make himself notorious and had therefore become a gentleman to be shunned.

Dexter was dancing a cotillion with Fanny at the moment, Lexie noticed, she blushing and confused but looking extraordinarily pretty. It was not unusual for the attentions of such men to cause green girls to colour and simper, but Fanny must know Dexter, since he was her brother's friend. Although perhaps not.

Fanny had only recently come to town and Dexter had no reason to do more than leave a card at Downshire House since Stormaston did not reside there. Lexie wondered, and wondered too whether the Duchess had noticed Fanny's reaction to Lord Dexter's attentions and whether she would be warned against him.

Thank goodness she was free of all the limiting restrictions by which young girls were bound. If Society thought the worse of her for standing up twice with Lord Stormaston, and engaging with him in barely respectable waltzes at that, so be it. Any man she would even consider marrying would account it of no consequence. She would *not* refine over it but enjoy the novelty of being partnered by a gazetted rake. Her pulses quickened with excitement as she prepared to meet the challenge.

The only thing was that, although she had spoken the truth when protesting that she could dance the waltz, it was not the whole truth. She knew the steps, had practised them with a dancing master in her own drawing room, but had never had occasion to use her skill in public, for the waltz had only been introduced to English ballrooms the previous year and was as yet seldom danced, except at Almack's under the strictest of supervision.

Which reminded her that she had not yet received vouchers granting her entry to those august assembly rooms. She must make herself pleasant to the patronesses, she thought, inclining her head and smiling sunnily in the direction of Lady Jersey and Lady Castlereagh, sitting together watching the dancing. Although no doubt it had been Stormaston's idea to include waltzes in the programme, the Duchess had acquiesced, risking the censure of more conservative elements in Society. But then, a duchess of Lady Downshire's standing could afford to.

And Stormaston intended to dance both waltzes with her. Why?

He must surely have recognised her. Well, he said he had, but from years ago. Something had brought about the change in his attitude.

'Thought it about time I ousted that bunch of young sapskulls and fortune hunters who have been throwin' themselves at your feet these last weeks,' he informed her as he led her out on the floor. 'Your reputation to think of, y'know.'

Lexie's pulses beat even faster. So he had noticed her, despite his keeping his distance, and had offered an explanation for his sudden attention.

'You account it a kindness to dance with me, my lord?' she demanded sweetly. 'Others might think that to partner your lordship—twice—*and* in the waltz— posed a greater threat to my reputation.'

She thought his lips twitched. She could not see his eyes, hidden as they were beneath those drooping lids. Like so many men, he possessed enviably dark, sweeping eyelashes.

'But you don't care a fig for your reputation,' he drawled as he placed a hand on her waist and with the other took hold of one of hers, much to Lexie's hidden agitation. 'Do you, Lady Amber?'

'Of course I do! Every female must!' Her breathlessness was caused entirely by indignation, Lexie knew. It was uncomfortable, just the same, since the music had begun and she had been forced to place her hand on his arm as he swung her into the fast, spinning steps of the waltz. She needed to concentrate on them but could not. He was far too near, although he held their bodies the correct foot apart.

'No lady can afford to lose her reputation!' she asserted firmly. 'That is what is so unfair! A man can do what he likes—well, almost,' she amended as his lordship lifted a sardonic brow. 'Anything short of being caught cheating, anyway—without being cold-shouldered by Society, but a lady— Well!'

'As you say. "Well!"' he mimicked, his face straight, his eyes now regarding her in just the way they had in Piccadilly. 'They would be ostracised. But only should they be *discovered* in their unconventional behaviour. Believe me, my lady,' he whispered in her ear, having bent his head forward the better to do so, 'there are many ladies present tonight whose private lives would not bear close scrutiny.'

Lexie stumbled over his feet. The import of his words, the innuendo behind them, had not been lost on her. Recovering from the shock, she struggled to take up the steps once more. He, of course, was as accomplished in the waltz as in everything else he did and thanks to his expertise and strong lead she had been managing fairly well until momentarily stupefied by what he had said.

Having recovered herself, she glanced up to find his blue eyes watching her confusion with amusement. She glimpsed again the vital, charming gentleman who had rescued and teased her in Piccadilly.

And because the memory brought a rush of pleasure, 'I have no desire to engage in scandal-mongering,' she informed him tartly. 'Your own disreputable behaviour is no secret, my lord. No doubt you are responsible for the dubious if hidden reputation of the ladies of whom you speak—'

'You flatter me, ma'am,' he murmured, whisking her round a corner and twirling and dipping to the strains of the Viennese waltz with the utmost aplomb. 'My tally of conquests is considerably exaggerated. Felix, now—' he glanced across to where his friend was dancing with Fanny again '—has made far more conquests in his shorter life than I in mine.'

'You keep tallies, my lord?' Lexie made her tone honey-sweet. 'No lady, I collect, would be flattered to discover herself upon such a list. Most would assiduously avoid the likelihood of such a fate, were it known.'

He chuckled, deep in his throat. A sound which had a strange effect upon Lexie's nerves. A challenge had been thrown down and accepted. 'We keep no tally, my lady. Our secrets are our own. But one knows one's friends—'

'And discusses one's conquests,' uttered Lexie in deepest disgust.

'Do the ladies not boast of theirs?' he enquired, all innocence.

Lexie blushed. Of course they did, but it wasn't the same thing at all! The ladies only crowed over the number of offers they had received, not...

'Ladies do not indulge in seduction!' she declared indignantly.

'No?' he purred, remembering a certain matron who had initiated him, at an early age, into the mysteries and pleasures of sexual adventures. 'You allow your inexperience to show, my dear Lady Amber.'

Lexie compressed her lips and refused to be drawn further. But she knew that a battle of wills had been joined.

He had determined to make her his mistress. He hadn't said so, but she knew it. She suspected that the languid, rakish air he wore when he was not rescuing damsels in distress was probably a mask behind which he hid a more dynamic personality. It was fashionable to appear bored. Perhaps he was. Perhaps that was why—but if so, why did he remain in Society?

Oh, it was of no use trying to decipher the Marquess of Stormaston's motives! But if she ignored his notable excesses—of which he could probably be cured if she could discover the reason for them—she had to admit that he was, in other respects, a man she could tolerate as a husband. Well born, educated, rich and—she almost blushed at the thought—exciting.

At least, in the absence of any other, he would make a stimulating target at which to aim! The Season promised to become excessively entertaining.

CHAPTER THREE

AFTER the waltz Lexie retired to the room where
Chalker waited, ready to fuss over her appearance. A
fresh dusting of powder on her nose, a quick twirl of
her curls with irons kept hot in the brazier for the
purpose, and Lexie was ready to face her partner for
the next set. She had not particularly needed Chalker's
attention but while her maid worked Lexie had time
to recover her composure and plan her next move.

He had, for some reason, decided to seduce her. She
had to admit that being pursued by Lord Stormaston
was, if nothing else, enlivening. Upon consideration,
she decided that she would not set him down. He was,
after all, a very rich, personable gentleman.

At seventeen she had not looked beyond his disreputable reputation. At four and twenty, older and wiser,
she felt able to form her own judgement. A rich,
young, apparently desirable widow, she had an alibi
for behaving with less regard for convention than the
young virgins on the marriage market.

After all, she had become slightly notorious herself
for no good reason that she could see, and so had
begun to doubt Society's verdicts. Its rules imposed a
strait-jacket no spirited young man or woman could
help but rebel against. Young gentlemen were forgiven
the sowing of a few wild oats but. . .

She surprised in herself a sudden fellow-feeling for
the Marquess. Did his additional sowing of poppies

and thistles mask a greater degree of rebellion? It would be pleasing to discover what did, even now, make him indulge in undoubtedly scandalous behaviour. And since Society accepted him, how could it possibly ostracise her simply for enjoying his companionship while in company?

When she danced with him again she would, she decided, seek to engage rather more than his passing fancy. She had to charm and intrigue him into wanting to know *her* rather than simply her body. Friendship was, after all, the best basis for marriage. And if he thought her agreeable to anything less, he had a surprise in store.

Restored in appearance and mind, Lexie returned to the ballroom to find the young Hussar waiting anxiously to lead her into the next set.

Supper was two dances away when a stir at the door announced the arrival of the Prince Regent and his party. The Duchess, the Marquess and Lady·Fanny immediately went to greet their royal guest. The honour of His Royal Highness's presence set the seal on the success on Fanny's coming-out ball.

Everyone swept bows and curtsies as, with the Marchioness of Hertford—for whom he had abandoned his morganatic wife Mrs Fitzherbert and his former mistress Lady Jersey—on his arm, the Prince Regent waddled his portly figure the length of the ballroom. Despite the grotesque figure he cut, Lexie could not, as usual, help feeling sorry for him when she remembered his spoilt life.

However much he might imagine otherwise, had he been allowed to lead his army, he would have been quite out of place on campaign, let alone on a battlefield. She simply could not envisage a man who had always so enjoyed his food and drink and who, reputedly, never rose before noon and then took hours to dress, being at home on some scorching plain or frozen hill top sharing the discomforts of his men. And, she thought, suppressing a chuckle, re-designing every uniform in sight!

Stormaston, though, the attentive host strolling by the Prince's side, would have made a fine officer. The uniform would have shown off his physique admirably and she wondered fleetingly why he had not chosen to escape the confines of English Society by purchasing a pair of colours and following the drum despite his lofty expectations.

Lord Dexter came to claim her hand for the supper dance. He was, she thought, as they executed the steps of the cotillion, rather abstracted. He scarcely attempted to flirt with her at all. But he would be bound to ask her to allow him to escort her to supper and she prayed he would not prove to be dull company tonight. He had been all attention while partnering Lady Fanny.

A sudden suspicion made her remark, 'Lady Fanny looks charming tonight, does she not?' when the steps of the dance allowed.

His brown eyes lit up, serving to confirm her notion. 'Indeed she does, Lady Alexia.'

Lexie had let it be known among those she considered her friends that she would not object to returning to the form of address which had been hers before her marriage. Lord Dexter had quickly asked permission to address her so.

'The Duchess is such a stern chaperon,' he went on, 'that I had not spoken to her before tonight.'

'Did not Lord Stormaston introduce you?'

Dexter grimaced. 'He is as jealous of his sister's reputation as any matron. I do not believe he considers me fit company for so innocent a young lady.'

'He,' said Lexie with asperity, 'should be the last to criticise or condemn! Does he not lead you and others in the paths of iniquity?'

The music stopped and Felix offered her his arm. 'Shall we proceed to supper?' She nodded and placed her hand under his elbow. As they trod through to the supper-room, he continued with the interrupted conversation. 'Indeed, he does lead his friends, and because of that he unfortunately knows all our faults and misdeeds! There is no cozening Storm! He himself will not deal with the young beauties brought to the marriage market.'

'Yet one day you will all need to wed.'

'Ah!' He looked down at her, a wry smile on his lips. He was not as attractive as the Marquess, she considered, yet his features were regular and pleasant, his eyes a warm brown, and his face held a certain strength which those of many of his contemporaries lacked. No wonder his attention had flustered Fanny. 'But even the worst of rakes may reform!'

'Ah, but persuading a prospective bride and her family of such an excellent intention may prove difficult,' teased Lexie, smiling back.

'Would you believe me, dear Lady Alexia?' he asked, and there was more than a hint of seriousness in his voice.

Lexie studied his face for a moment and then

nodded. 'I think I would. But you would have to prove it by exhibiting reformed behaviour, my lord!'

Before they had time for more, a familiar voice hailed them.

'Felix! Join our party, will you?'

The Prince Regent was circulating prior to taking his leave. He had other functions to attend that evening and had not been expected to remain long at Downshire House.

'As host I must wait upon His Royal Highness's departure,' explained the Marquess. 'I'll be back in a moment. Fetch supper for Grandmother, there's a good fellow.'

'Delighted,' murmured Felix, his eyes immediately seeking out Fanny, who, absurdly, had been escorted in by Oswald Cresswell.

How that young gentleman had managed to obtain the supper dance with the person in whose honour the ball was being held Lexie could not imagine. Except that it suddenly dawned upon her that Oswald's father, a viscount, was heir to an earldom and a vast fortune which would one day come to Oswald. Did the Duchess—even the Marquess—consider him a suitable match?

Fanny leapt upon the arrival of Lexie and Felix with obvious relief. Lexie sympathised. Oswald was not the most enlivening of companions for all his expectations.

'Lady Alexia!' she cried, blushing prettily. 'How delightful that you are able to join us! And Lord Dexter, too!'

Felix bowed to the Duchess, who twinkled at her grandson's friend over her fluttering fan.

'Fetch me a glass of wine and something substantial

to eat, Dexter. Otherwise I vow I shall swoon for lack of nourishment! I feel that I have not eaten this age, despite the banquet last evening. I declare, at my age I find two such occasions coming so close together quite exhausting.'

She sank back, fanning herself vigorously.

'At your age, ma'am?' smiled Felix. 'I vow you look not a day over thirty.'

'Away with your flummery, sir! I am over seventy and sometimes I feel it! Bring me that refreshment immediately!'

Felix grinned. He clearly knew the Duchess rather well. 'And for you too, Lady Fanny?' he enquired.

'I shall fetch Lady Fanny's supper,' insisted Oswald, not to be set aside even for Lord Dexter.

'Please, do not come to cuffs over me,' pleaded Fanny rather breathlessly. 'I require little to eat and lemonade to drink. Between you, you should be able to manage to bring enough for all of us.'

'Storm can look after himself,' declared Felix. 'But you, Lady Alexia, what may I bring for you?'

Lexie asked for an ice cream and a glass of lemonade, though in truth she would have preferred wine. But to ask for it would only serve to add more shot to the gossips' armoury and she felt they had quite enough already.

As the gentlemen disappeared, Felix heading the slighter Oswald by at least six inches, Lexie asked the Duchess if the previous evening had been a success.

'The Regent put on a magnificent show, splendid food and wine, all his gold plate on the table, thousands of candles, he himself the most affable host, but conversation was petrified. No one knew enough languages, y'see. Then afterwards, the stupid fellow insisted on introducing his mistress to the Czar.'

'Lady Hertford?' prompted Lexie.

'Aye, the ageing grandmother just departin' our door over whom the fool swoons like a love-sick youth! Alexander nodded, but refused to speak to the woman. She curtsied and withdrew in the haughtiest manner. The evenin' was doomed from that moment on.'

'How unfortunate,' murmured Lexie.

Before she could probe further into the previous evening's disasters someone else engaged the Duchess in conversation.

Fanny remarked, 'It is such a pity we did not know of the Regent's banquet until long after the date for my ball was fixed, but I do hope you are enjoying it. Do you think it a success?'

'Undoubtedly,' responded Lexie. 'What more could you wish for, having received both the Czar's and the Regent's blessings on the occasion? Not only is the ball a success but you have taken in Society, believe me. You are looking so charming tonight that it is small wonder the gentlemen are falling over themselves to serve you!'

'Do you think so?' Fanny fluttered her fan to hide her nervous agitation. 'I know I do not normally impress gentlemen, not as you do, dear Lady Alexia.'

'Only because you needed to gain in self-confidence. If you do not possess it after tonight, then I hold out no hope for you!'

Fanny laughed, as she was meant to. 'You do me so much good, Lady Alexia, I wish we had met before! I must admit I have never felt so confident in my appearance. Do you not admire my gown?'

At this point the Duchess rejoined their conversation and, having heard Fanny's question, 'I should hope she does!' she declared. 'After all the trouble Madame Aristide went to to design and make it exactly right!'

'Indeed, Your Grace, Madame Aristide has excelled herself,' confirmed Lexie. 'White was exactly the colour to throw up Lady Fanny's excellent complexion and the darkness of her hair.'

'I feel a little like a snow queen,' muttered Fanny, still not absolutely certain of the rightness of the choice, having held a preference for pink herself.

'And what is wrong with that, eh?' demanded her grandmother, nodding her plumes. 'Pity there ain't any eligible princes about to make a real queen of you one day!'

'There are the young Prussian princes,' murmured Lexie naughtily.

The Duchess snorted, her eyes twinkling, but before she could reply their refreshments arrived and in the confusion of sorting out plates and glasses and then sampling what the gentlemen had brought, the conversation died.

Before long Lord Stormaston rejoined them, apparently eating nothing but carrying a glass of claret.

The Duchess bestowed a fond smile upon her grandson.

'The Regent has departed, James?'

'He has,' Stormaston confirmed, taking the chair between Lexie and Fanny which Oswald had just vacated in order to fetch another glass of lemonade for Fanny. 'Sent his congratulations on a splendid evenin'.'

He turned his lazy smile on Lexie, who felt quite

hemmed in by gentlemen of dubious reputation and great charm but rose to the occasion by exhibiting her not inconsiderable wit and fascination, directing the latter at Lord Dexter until she caught Fanny's hurt eyes fixed upon her.

She did not imagine that Fanny's *tendre* for Felix St Clare would last, but had no desire to be accused of entering into competition for his favours, so she turned most of her attention to Stormaston instead. After all, he was the one she wanted to ensnare and he did not seem in the least averse to being enchanted.

On his return with Fanny's refreshment Oswald scowled as he seated himself between Felix and the Duchess instead of Fanny and Lexie. Lexie could tell he was considerably put out: first Stormaston had stolen both the waltzes and now he had had the gall to take his seat!

'How is your mama?' the Duchess demanded of him. 'A great pity she is indisposed and unable to come tonight, is it not Fanny?' she said, turning to the girl, who was seated on her other side.

Fanny murmured, 'Indeed it is, Grandmama.'

'And your father, of course, never appears in Society.'

Oswald flushed, an embarrassment to which he was prone. 'M-mama sent her most s-sincere r-regrets, Your Grace. She has ate somethin' disagreeable, I f-fear.'

'Pity. I would have enjoyed a coze with her. Tell her so, young man.'

'C-certainly, Your Grace.' Oswald inclined his head in acquiescence.

Poor Oswald! The Duchess's attention had reduced

him to a stuttering idiot, thought Lexie compassion-
ately, seeing the despairing look he sent across the
Duchess to Fanny, who gave the faintest of shrugs in
return.

Lexie became convinced that the Duchess did have
hopes of a match between the young people. But she
was too engaged in parrying the attentions of both
Dexter and Stormaston to give the matter much heed.
Fanny, she felt certain, would not be forced into a
match which was not to her liking. Meanwhile the
Marquess, despite his grandmother's close presence,
was passing the most audacious remarks.

'Ice cream and lemonade do not suit your tempera-
ment, my lady,' he murmured. 'They are not for one
so full of fire and spirit.'

Lexie fluttered her fan and batted her eyelashes.
Her heart had begun to thud in earnest. Would he
admit that he knew they had met before? 'But how
can you judge, my lord, after so short an
acquaintance?'

'Ah!' His smile ravished her and she felt the heat
begin to mount in her veins. If only the ice cream were
capable of quenching it! 'I can read it in your lovely
green eyes, my dear,' he murmured. Felix had leant
forward to speak to Fanny. No one could hear what
they said above the general hubbub. 'They dance and
sparkle, but in their depths I see promise—'

'Promise?' How she kept her voice cool and teasing
Lexie did not know. But she must play her part in this
charade. 'You mistake, my lord. I promise nothing.'

'Do you not, Lady Amber? I wonder.' And as he
held her chair for her to rise, the Marquess drawled,
'Until our next dance, Lady Alexia.'

The caressing tone of his voice, the wicked look in his eyes, warned her that he indeed thought her manner an indication that she was acquiescing to his seduction. She smiled back, flirting her fan as she did so.

'I cannot wait, my lord,' she murmured, adding silently to herself, 'To return home.' For at that moment she changed her mind. She would plead a headache and leave before she was forced into the Marquess's arms again. She feared that too much of such intimate contact with Lord Stormaston might test her resolution beyond its limits.

Lexie was not afraid of him, but of his strange effect upon her senses. She had never known its like. Merely sitting next to him was almost a torture. She felt so drawn to him that if she was to achieve her end at the expense of his, she must keep him at arm's length meanwhile.

She danced as spiritedly as ever during the next hour or two, a little knot of excitement gathering in the pit of her stomach as she thought of the battle to come, a mere glimpse of Stormaston across the room sending her pulses leaping. But as the time of the waltz approached she sent a footman to fetch Chalker and another to call Jethro, and made her adieus to the Duchess and Fanny. Luckily his lordship was occupied elsewhere, entertaining the Czar.

'Dear Lady Alexia, are you not feeling well?' asked Fanny. 'Or is it that you find the ball tedious after all!'

'I do not find your ball remotely tedious, Lady Fanny, it is the most famous occasion I have yet attended. But I must confess to having developed a most lowering headache,' Lexie went on, crossing her fingers behind her fluttering fan. 'The heat, I think, and the excitement. . .'

'You will call upon us,' instructed the Duchess imperiously, setting the seal on Lexie's acceptance into Society despite any scandal circulating, and even after watching her flirt with Dexter and her grandson. The words were accompanied with a gracious smile. Stormaston had inherited her eyes, recognised Lexie, and much of her aristocratic looks and manner. Fanny had most of the looks but had not yet developed the manner. Perhaps she never would.

Fanny excused herself as her next partner came to claim her hand for a dance. The Duchess watched her granddaughter's retreating back as she went on, 'We shall be at home on Monday, but no doubt we may meet you before that, in the park on Sunday. I believe all the visiting dignitaries intend to join us in our normal parade.'

'Indeed, Your Grace, I shall be there as usual. And I shall be delighted to call on Monday.'

'Good. And I will send you an invitation to my drum early in July, when I hope the Duke of Wellington will be in London and able to honour us with his presence.'

'I should be thrilled to meet the Duke, Your Grace,' murmured Lexie, curtsying respectfully. 'I should like that above everything.'

The Duchess nodded. 'This promises to be a gala summer. You'll be good for Fanny. She needs bringing out. I wish you a speedy recovery, Lady Amber.'

'Your Grace is very kind.' This was not the moment to suffer from either surprise or guilt. Lexie looked up into the eyes which reminded her so much of those others and said, 'Please convey my apologies to Lord

Stormaston. I fear that I really could not endure long enough to dance with him again. As for my other partners—'

'They will soon find others to take your place, though perhaps not ones so pleasing to them as you would be. James was to dance with 'ee again, eh? Serve the young reprobate right to be stood up for once.'

The elderly woman's eyes were twinkling again. Lexie suspected that the Duchess was not deceived by her excuse to leave yet, staggeringly, seemed not to think any the worse of her for refusing to fall in with her grandson's whim, and had actually indicated that she approved of a friendship between her and Fanny. Lexie could scarcely credit her good fortune.

As the carriage trundled the short distance back to Bruton Street she mused on that first waltz with the Marquess and found herself regretting the loss of the second. Half asleep, she was dreaming of twirling in Stormaston's arms as the footman opened the door and pulled out the step. Perhaps it was as well the dream had been interrupted, she thought wryly, as she mounted the stairs to her bedroom. Dreams had a tendency to wander into forbidden realms.

Caro would be in bed, thank goodness. By morning she would be calm enough to give her cousin a composed and edited account of the ball.

This she did over a late breakfast. Caro chuckled over her description of poor Oswald's frustrations and discomfort, poured herself another cup of chocolate and spread thick butter on a slice of fresh white bread.

'I met the Duchess once,' she remembered. 'Before

poor Mr Baldwin died.' For a moment she faltered, the ready tears springing to her eyes, but then she pulled herself together and went on, though her voice quivered rather more than usual. 'Astonishing woman. Can put the fear of the Lord into better gentlemen than Mr Cresswell if she has a mind. High in the instep, sets a person down without mercy if needs be, yet can be as charming as you like. I collect she has taken to you, Cousin.'

'Perhaps.' Lexie was at a loss to know quite why the Duchess had been so gracious to her. There were, after all, many other young matrons she could have chosen to favour on Fanny's behalf. Possibly Fanny herself had had something to do with it, having shown such a frank willingness to treat her as a friend. But however it had come about, it seemed she was destined to become intimate with the Marquess's sister. She sipped her chocolate thoughtfully.

'I think she would like Oswald and Fanny to make a match of it. But Oswald fancies himself in love with me and Fanny with Lord Dexter.'

'Young people these days!' sighed Caro. 'In my day one wed the person one's parents or guardians chose without giving anyone else a thought.'

'In my day, too,' said Lexie wryly. Though not entirely without silent mutiny.

Breakfast was scarcely finished when a footman announced the arrival of the Marquess of Stormaston, who trusted that her ladyship was at home.

Lexie swallowed, tempted to say she was still indisposed or not at home. But she had to face his lordship sooner or later.

'Show him into the morning-room. Inform his lordship that I shall join him directly.'

She had donned a small cap that morning rather than have her hair dressed in a more elaborate style, intending to spend the morning writing letters. But her blue sprigged muslin gown looked well enough and the cap quite becoming.

'Fancy Lord Stormaston calling!' exclaimed Cousin Caro breathlessly. 'Whatever can have brought him here?'

Lexie had most carefully omitted all allusion to the Marquess from her adventures on the day the Allied Sovereigns had arrived, and done no more than casually mention his name in the list of gentlemen with whom she had danced the previous evening. Displaying an insouciance she was far from feeling, she turned from the mirror.

'I cannot imagine,' she retorted. 'Come, Cousin. I am certain you will wish to meet his lordship and I would prefer not to entertain him alone. His reputation runs before him.'

'Well, if you think so...you do not usually require my presence...'

'But this morning I do. You have no objection, I trust?'

'No, none! You are showing just that discretion I have been advising.' Caro rose to her feet, tweaked her skirts into place and carefully arranged a silk scarf with a long gold fringe about her shoulders. 'But all the same, it is unlike you to require a chaperon. Did you take him in dislike when you danced with him?'

'Oh no, but I would not trust his lordship a foot

further than I could throw him. He regards widows as fair game, I collect.'

'Yet you will receive him?' cried Caro, aghast.

'Why not? Others do, and he cannot harm me while you are present. And he has most engaging manners. You will enjoy meeting him and find him quite charming, I am assured.'

Caro shot her cousin a shrewd glance, for Lexie had been unable to prevent a thread of excitement from entering her voice. He had called! To what end? She had not expected him to make his next move quite so soon.

Half a head taller than her companion, slender and exquisite, Lady Amber—Alexia—entered the morning-room slightly ahead of a much older woman of plump and flushed appearance, who tugged nervously at a length of fringed silk trailing from her shoulders rather than look him in the face.

To the Marquess, rising courteously to make his devoirs, the other woman might not have existed. He wished she did not. Did Alexia consider him a fool, to be taken in by her evasions?

He had hoped to have a private exchange with Alexia—he savoured the sound of her name in his mind—for beneath the languid air which he donned like a cloak whenever he wished—although his wild days were long over it suited him to cherish the reputation they had earned him—lay a prodigious volume of annoyance, made the more bitter because she appeared to be in the full bloom of her health this morning. And quite irresistibly desirable.

'Ladies.' He made his bow and suffered the introduction to Mrs Charles Baldwin, Lady Amber's late husband's cousin, Caroline. He wished the faintly ineffectual and disapproving Cousin Caroline to the devil. However, the knowledge that Alexia felt she needed a buffer between them gave him an odd feeling of satisfaction. He had not been wrong. Mutual desire did exist. Why else should she fear being alone with him?

And why else had she fled the ball before their second waltz? Memory of his sharp sense of loss and frustration on discovering her defection brought back the full force of his anger.

The ladies sat on a settee and he subsided back into the small, rather uncomfortable armchair from which he had risen.

'I trust you are quite recovered from your...indisposition, Lady Amber?' he enquired. 'You appear to be in splendid health this morning, what?'

Beneath the drawl Lexie detected the cutting edge in his voice and under his usual exquisitely lazy manner she sensed suppressed anger. He had disliked her leaving the ball before their waltz, then. She had, of course, known that he would.

'I am completely recovered, I thank you,' she returned, smiling, sitting quite at her ease. Caro was looking at her in an odd manner. Lexie had not told her cousin that she had left the ball pleading a headache. At the time it had seemed no more necessary than mentioning the Marquess other than in passing. But Caro, for all her *distraite* manner, was no fool. Lexie could foresee a need for uncomfortable explanations later. 'It is kind of you to trouble to enquire.'

'Not at all.' He waved aside any thought of thanks.

'I promised my grandmother and sister that I would call since they could not. They will be relieved to hear that you have made such a remarkably swift recovery.'

The anger was still there. Lexie doubted whether his explanation represented the full truth of the matter even if the Duchess and Fanny did know he intended to call. He had come because he wanted to set her down, but Caro's presence had foiled his intentions.

'It was only a headache, my lord, brought on by the heat and the stuffy atmosphere, I collect. The chandeliers give a brilliant light but the burning candles only add to the heat and their smoke combines with the presence of so many people engaged in energetic exercise to make the air thick. Once outside my headache soon evaporated.'

'Had I known, it would have given me great pleasure to escort you to the terrace for air,' purred his lordship. 'You had only to wait a few more moments for our waltz.'

'I had no wish to rob your lordship of the enjoyment of the dance,' said Lexie ingenuously, her hands folded demurely in her lap. 'You waltz so exquisitely and with such enthusiasm, while I am but an indifferent performer.'

'Did your lessons not serve, my love?' murmured Caro, glancing furtively from one to the other.

'Lady Amber has no need to fear lack of expertise, ma'am. She has the steps perfectly.'

Lexie shot Caro a repressive glance. 'But the concentration required of me quite spoils my enjoyment at present. When I left you were engaged in conversation with the Czar. I did not feel it necessary to interrupt.'

Storm inclined his head. She was clever, but she should not escape him. 'Since you appreciate fresh air, will you ride with me round the Ring in Hyde Park on Sunday afternoon? You would, perhaps, feel safer in the crush which is bound to prevail since our victorious guests are to show themselves, if you are accompanied by someone capable of defending your person.'

Wretched man! Reminding her of that other time again! Yet still not admitting that he had recognised her! One day she would find the moment to challenge him on the point. But not now.

'I regret, my lord, that I shall be unable to do so. I have already agreed to drive Cousin Caro so that she may catch a glimpse of the Sovereigns and our other important visitors,' lied Lexie.

Storm saw the startled and then agonised expression on Mrs Baldwin's face and smiled.

'If that is indeed Mrs Baldwin's wish then I shall be delighted to drive you both in my landau. The crush is bound to be considerable but I shall take every care to avoid disaster.'

Caro opened and closed her mouth but no sound came. She did, however, manage to clutch at Lexie's arm.

Lexie closed her eyes for an instant. How could she be so cruel? She knew perfectly well how much Caro feared crowds and crushes. Caro would never bring herself to set foot in a carriage destined to take part in such an outing. And Stormaston, the rogue, was playing upon Caro's undisguised fears.

'You dislike the idea of such an expedition?' he enquired solicitously. 'If so, and will entrust your charge to my care, I guarantee to return her to you perfectly safe. I am certain that Lady Amber would scorn to miss the occasion.'

'I shall accompany her, of course,' began Caro faintly, finding her voice at last and screwing up her courage only to be interrupted by a furious Lexie.

'I am not in Cousin Caro's charge,' she gritted.

'No, my love,' murmured Caro, 'but I do pray you not to venture out alone as you—'

Lexie cut her off sharply. She wanted no references to previous occasions! 'I should be perfectly safe, I assure you, but if it would calm your mind, Cousin, then I will agree to ride with Lord Stormaston.'

Storm stood up and bowed, his mission accomplished. 'We could drive should you prefer—' he began.

But Lexie was in no mood to vacillate. 'You asked me to ride, my lord, no doubt having already ascertained my preference in the matter. I am happy to accept your escort.'

'Then I shall wait upon you on Sunday, Lady Amber.'

Lexie remembered that she wished to charm the man into matrimony. She smiled her most bewitching smile.

'I shall look forward to it.'

'And will not, I trust, suffer from another indisposition?'

'I am normally extremely healthy, my lord.'

'That is what I thought.'

CHAPTER FOUR

STORMASTON took his leave. A relieved Mrs Baldwin eyed her young cousin suspiciously.

'I did not realise you were so well acquainted with his lordship, Alexia. You will take care, will you not? His reputation. . .'

'Is perfectly well known to me, Cousin. I am no foolish chit, I am entirely aware of what I am doing. Simply because I engage to ride with his lordship does not mean that I intend to succumb to his blandishments.'

'I should hope not!' cried Caro faintly. 'Alexia my dear, you cannot risk your own reputation. . .'

Lexie sprang to her feet and began to pace the turkey carpet, irritated with Caro for putting her own doubts into words. 'Why not? He is the most eligible gentleman in town.' She spread her hands. 'All the mama's would be hanging out for him for their daughters were it not for his reputation, and even so some of the less scrupulous disregard it. I, on the other hand, am free to do as I like!'

She had no wish to invite keener opposition by exposing her real intention to her cousin. Besides, Caro might gossip, and if word of her purpose were to reach Stormaston's ears, Lexie must fail. She came to a halt before the settee and addressed her cousin with great seriousness.

'But, Cousin Caro, I enjoin you not not to gossip

about my dealings with his lordship. Promise me, not a word to Mrs Seacombe or anyone else. I should not like to become an exhibition.'

'Oh, no! My lips are sealed! But others will talk, my dear. He is certainly an exceptionally fine-looking gentleman. Handsome—elegant—' Caro's flushed face became a deeper shade of pink '—and he must be most attractive to a young woman such as yourself, despite his indolent, affected manner—'

'Which I believe to be an affectation, Cousin.'

'Well, yes, it must always be, I collect. No one could be born with it except perhaps the most vacuous of creatures, which I am persuaded his lordship is not. But you are so impetuous, my love! There must be other eligible gentlemen who would make more suitable escorts.'

'None that I have so far met,' declared Lexie firmly. 'I shall not discourage his admiration, for I have found no other gentleman at present in Town able to offer such agreeable company.'

This was true, for although Lord Dexter amused her considerably, he was inclined to admire Lady Fanny, who cherished a *tendre* for her brother's disreputable friend. And Stormaston himself possessed a remarkably compelling personality he shared with no other. She already had a reputation for flouting convention in other ways so she might just as well outrage the *ton* still further by flirting with someone whose activities they loved to denounce.

Caro shook her head in helpless acknowledgement of her inability to dissuade her wayward cousin, and sighed. 'If you are determined on it I must advise you to be cautious, my dear Alexia. Some gentlemen are not always honourable in their dealings and the Marquess. . .well, you have said yourself that his reputation is of the worst kind.'

Lexie laughed. 'I believe I can handle the Marquess, Cousin Caro. Forewarned is forearmed, is it not? I shall behave with the utmost discretion. You need not fear for me on Sunday, for I intend to take a groom right into the Park with me instead of leaving him at the gate as is my normal practice. His lordship will not, perhaps, expect that, having seen me riding alone in the morning. I was used to do so all the time in Cornwall and I find the slow company of a groom tedious when I desire to gallop.'

Cousin Caro gave another faint cry of protest. 'It is so unladylike to gallop!'

Lexie chuckled. 'I know, dear Cousin! But I cannot give up every pleasure simply to please the stuffy dames who lead Society! But I do take a tiger up behind when I drive my curricle about Town.'

'You make such a spectacle of yourself, my dear Alexia! And a deal of use that lad Jeffs would be in an emergency, except to hold the horses! And to think I imagined you were learning discretion at last! But I must allow that Lord Stormaston seemed a most agreeable young man,' Caro admitted rather wistfully. 'I wonder he is not yet wed.'

Lexie chuckled. 'Because he is determined not to become leg-shackled, I dare say. He enjoys his bachelor freedom too much. Wish you were a few years younger, Cousin?'

'Well, if I were, I must confess I might be tempted. . .' Mrs Baldwin flushed and smiled rather guiltily. 'But I never had the chance to fix the interest of so fine-looking a man, even as a flirt.'

'I do consider myself fortunate,' admitted Lexie with another chuckle. 'I did not anticipate enjoying myself half as much as I believe I shall!'

Crowds already jammed the streets when Lord Stormaston presented himself in Bruton Street the next day to find Lexie waiting, dressed in a splendid leaf-green costume and with a saucy bejewelled and feathered hat perched firmly on her head. Her magnificent chestnut gelding stood at the door.

From her parlour window Lexie saw him arrive astride an expensive grey stallion, a superb figure in an exquisitely cut snuff-coloured jacket, buff pantaloons and shining hessians. Her nerves tightened in anticipation. She could scarcely have wished for a more impressive escort.

Caro, who had been watching with her, exclaimed over the perfection of his lordship's appearance and retired to her *chaise longue*, where she carefully arranged her draperies ready to receive him.

'Do take care,' she admonished after he had been shown up and made his bow. 'Such crowds! I wonder that anyone should venture forth.'

'There are thousands waiting in Piccadilly outside the Pulteney Hotel to catch a glimpse of Czar Alexander,' Stormaston agreed, offering Lexie his arm. 'We will take all care, ma'am, never fear.' To Lexie, as they descended the stairs, he remarked, 'We had best avoid passing that way.'

'I know,' said Lexie, 'they are there every day, I have seen them.'

'Of course, you must have,' he responded gravely as he offered her a lift to mount. But, meeting his eyes for a brief moment as she placed her foot in his clasped hands, Lexie became aware of amusement lurking in their depths.

Regretting her rash remark, she took refuge in settling herself in her saddle but soon, edging her horse along Mount Street to Tyburn Lane and the Grosvenor Gate into Hyde Park through the throng of carriages, carts and pedestrians, she forgot her discomfort in the excitement of the moment.

'The people have gone mad over him.' Stormaston took up the conversation again as he walked his horse at her side. 'It seems all London will gather in the Park this afternoon to watch him parade with the leaders of the other Allied countries.'

'I must confess that I myself am agog,' Lexie told him. 'I long to see Marshal Blücher and Prince Metternich.'

He smiled. 'I conceived that you might be.'

Jethro Pascoe had insisted on accompanying Lexie himself that afternoon instead of Jeffs and he rode ahead, clearing the way, making certain no pedestrian got trampled underfoot. In the Park itself chaos reigned. Storm and Lexie joined the splendid caval-cade of silk, gold lace, splendid carriages and glossy horses being ridden or driven there, only to discover that their part in the assembly was less to see than to be seen and cheered.

The Master of the Horse, wearing his garter ribbon, led the official parade, comprising the carriages carry-ing all the important visitors together with their escorts.

'All I can see,' grumbled Lexie as they trotted with other equestrians round the Ring in their wake, 'is Alexander's bodyguard, or at least their waving plumes and the flash of their cuirasses in the sun.'

'A pity, I agree,' murmured Storm, smiling down on the eager, lively face beneath the amazing thing she wore on her golden curls. 'But I would not have missed the occasion for the world.'

'Oh, nor would I! Look, everyone is following the Sovereigns towards the private gates into Kensington Gardens!'

'Then so shall we, if you wish it?'

'Why not?' said Lexie.

But she had not realised that the mass of riders, almost all men, many in uniform, would urge their mounts into a gallop, fan out to overtake the carriages and surge towards the bridge across the Serpentine. Their progress developed into a disorganised charge and, caught up in the middle of it, Lexie needed all her skill to remain in her saddle, even with Storm protecting her on one side and Pascoe on the other.

As they pounded over the narrow bridge Pascoe gave a sharp cry and Lexie turned her head anxiously to see his boot fly into the air, torn off by the impact of another rider barging into him. But he quickly recovered his stirrup and kept his place beside Lexie while Storm pressed close on her other side, their knees clashing from time to time. Lexie was too occupied in controlling her horse to do more than vaguely register a familiar tingle in her nerves.

Now they had crossed the bridge she must avoid being pushed against a tree, or, worse, crushing a pedestrian against one, as was happening to a woman screaming just ahead, as a wild-looking animal butted into her, its rider quite out of control. And surely that was the Master of the Horse scrambling to his feet after having been thrown to the ground!

'We must extricate ourselves from this,' called Storm, his voice grim. Without further ado he took hold of Lexie's bridle and edged his own mount towards the grass, pulling the chestnut with him.

Lexie's lips compressed in annoyance—did he think her incapable?—but she merely murmured 'Steady, Danny,' soothing the animal, whose staring eyes and flattened ears bore witness to its agitation. And somehow Storm manoeuvred both horses out of the throng without getting them pinned against a tree or trampling any sightseers.

Once free of the mass of riders and halted on a comparatively uncrowded stretch of grass Lexie dismounted, the better to soothe Danny. Storm swung out of his saddle and laughed a reckless, joyful laugh which set her nerves tingling afresh.

'You did not need my aid to dismount, I perceive!' he observed, taking her reins from her grasp.

'No, my lord, and neither did I need your help to escape the throng,' retorted Lexie with spirit. 'But we have lost Pascoe, and he is without one of his boots!'

'Is he, indeed! I dare swear he is not the only one to have accoutrements dragged off in that stampede! But it seems he could not escape with us. No doubt he is now before Kensington Palace with all the other sightseers! Do not concern yourself, Lady Amber, your groom is well able to take care of himself, he will come to no harm.'

'I hope you are right,' said Lexie, her anxiety for

Pascoe turning to wry amusement that, for all her care, she was now alone with Stormaston. If you could call being in the midst of a seething mass of people in Kensington Gardens alone!

Standing at the heads of their horses beneath a spreading tree they were, however, screened from most of the people still attempting to catch a glimpse of anyone of consequence who might be passing. If they themselves were the focus of a few inquisitive stares this did not seem to concern the Marquess.

'But if you will not admit to needing rescue,' he went on, 'I cannot claim a reward.'

Lexie thought she might suffocate, for the breath stopped in her throat. 'Indeed you may not, my lord!' she managed, sharply if a trifle faintly.

'A disappointment, I must confess. A kiss would have been a fitting end to our adventure.'

His tone of mock affront brought the colour flooding to Lexie's face. He knew! She had suspected as much from the first. Odious man!

'No such thing!' she exclaimed. 'And I collect that you perceived all along that it was I you rescued from the throng in Piccadilly that day! You behaved abominably, treating me as you would a servant! Why did you pretend not to recognise me?'

'You seemed to prefer to remain incognito, my dear Lady Amber. Who was I to force you to admit your identity?'

'Do not play the innocent with me, Lord Stormaston! You did it for your own amusement and have been laughing at me ever since!'

'You do me an injustice, Alexia. . .Lexie.' His pained voice yet held a thread of laughter in it but very little drawl. 'Since you were masquerading as a lady's maid I felt justified in treating you as such.'

Lexie, uncomfortably aware that she had left herself open to rough usage by her rash behaviour, took refuge in indignation. 'I have not given you permission to address me so, my lord!'

He grinned unrepentantly. 'No, you have not, my delightful child. I have taken the liberty upon myself. And I wish you would call me James. If we are to be intimate—'

Lexie suddenly relaxed. He was teasing, flirting with her. Two could play at that game. 'Are we to become intimate, Storm? Despite your thinking me a child?' she purred. She could not possibly call him James, not yet, not while she still felt so at odds with him. She hoped he would accept the compromise.

'Hmm,' he mused, 'At least that is an advance on "my lord". One day, though, I swear you will call me James. For although you may occasionally harbour childish notions, in every other respect you are a most captivating woman. We shall become intimate, you know.'

She tapped his arm with her riding crop in mock admonition. 'You presume too much, my dear Storm. However, I am not averse to your pursuit, it will enliven what might otherwise become a tedious round of pleasure—'

'Tedious, with all the pageantry we are promised, the balls, the galas, the dinners to be attended, the museums, the galleries, the theatres and the opera to be visited? You amaze me, Lexie.'

'But lacking an escort...' She allowed the sentence

to trail off, looking down in what she hoped appeared to be demure confusion.

Storm was not deceived. He scented victory and plunged headlong into the final stage of the chase. 'Then I must offer mine, my dear Lexie. I cannot have you languishing, bored, during such a joyous, triumphant summer as this!'

'Your escort, Storm?' Lexie, having achieved her purpose, lifted her eyes to his wickedly smiling face then quickly lowered her lashes, suddenly, inexplicably, shy. 'But my reputation...' she managed to murmur, achieving without difficulty just the right tone of uncertainty.

'In public I shall behave with the utmost propriety,' he promised, amusement still lurking in his voice. 'I can, you know.'

'Yes,' acknowledged Lexie. 'You reserve your most scandalous behaviour for gaming hells, mills, cockfights, curricle races and boudoirs, I am informed. You played the perfect host at your sister's come-out. Apart from your stealing of my two waltzes.'

'From that accusation I beg to be absolved,' he protested mildly. 'I stole nothing. I was perfectly at liberty to engage for any dances I chose.'

'But why?' demanded Lexie, and then, as the blue eyes swept her features and the grin spread widely over his face, wished she had not.

'Because, my dear Lexie, I desired to enjoy your delightful company and hoped to taste your delicious lips again. Had you remained for our second engagement...but you did not.'

His gaze narrowed and for an instant Lexie sensed again his anger at her defection. But almost instantly the smile was back in place and he murmured, 'Do you know, I believe we are private enough here for me to claim both vengeance and reward—'

'No!' gasped Lexie, stepping back and coming up against the trunk of the tree. 'No, Storm, indeed you must not. Look,' she cried in desperate relief. 'Here come your brother and his friends.'

Storm glanced idly over his shoulder to the carriage-way leading to Kensington Palace. The procession had long since passed on and people were beginning to straggle back. 'So they do. But do not think you have escaped, Lexie, my dear. I shall claim what I am owed, never fear.'

Hugo and his cohorts reined in. Hugo left the path to halt his horse beside them.

'I thought it was you I saw in the mêlée, brother.' He eyed Lexie speculatively and made an elaborate sweep of greeting, though without dismounting. 'When you disappeared I thought you might have come a cropper,' he added unpleasantly.

'I regret to cause you disappointment, but no such luck, brother,' drawled Storm, all his languid airs back in place. 'I merely escorted Lady Amber from what had become a dangerous game with little point to it.'

'Dashed fine run, though a deuced stupid fuss everyone is makin' over these creatures. Demmed if I can see why.'

'Mind your language, if you please, brother! Or had you forgotten the presence of a lady?'

Storm's sharp reprimand startled Hugo but he smiled, none too amiably. 'Forgive me, Lady Amber. I am not used to finding Storm alone in the company of a *lady*.'

'Were you not my brother I would call you out for that,' remarked Storm, his lazy mantle back in place. 'But perhaps not.' He shrugged dismissively. 'Such a slur from you would scarcely warrant the effort.'

Lexie, though, could see his eyes, cold blue steel, the way his jaw clenched, moving the thin line of the scar across his cheek, the whitened knuckles of the fist clenched about the reins of their horses. She thought she had never seen him look more dangerous.

Hugo's red face whitened. He wheeled his horse and rode off, his companions following after. He, too, had glimpsed the fury hidden beneath that careless exterior. And was afraid of his brother's wrath.

'You do not like him,' said Lexie without thinking.

'On the contrary,' disclaimed Storm. 'I like him well enough when he is not behavin' like an ass. But he resents bein' a penniless younger son, you know. Liked it even less when I was his guardian and still hates havin' to rely on me for an allowance.'

'Has he no money of his own?'

Storm shook his head. 'He will inherit a competence from the Duchess when she dies but not enough to live on in the expensive way he expects. He needs to marry a fortune.'

'But the mamas will not give him countenance.'

'Rather less than they give me,' agreed Storm with his wicked grin. 'But come, Lexie my love, do you wish to ride further? Or shall we return through the Park? The crowds appear to have dispersed somewhat.'

He had dropped the question of the kiss. Lexie, while noting his new and even more scandalous method of addressing her, relaxed still further and reached for Danny's reins.

'Return, I think. I shall better enjoy a ride early tomorrow morning when Hyde Park is less crowded.'

Storm relinquished the reins without demur. 'And should we meet then, I may ride with you?'

'Gladly, Storm,' agreed Lexie, allowing him to assist her into her saddle. She had mentioned riding the following morning, intending them to meet; he had not been slow to realise it.

Jethro Pascoe returned to Bruton Street limping but otherwise unhurt, greatly distressed at having failed in his duty to keep close to his mistress. Lexie, receiving her bandy-legged, apologetic coachman in the morning room, assured him that she fully sympathised with his difficulties and had been perfectly safe with Lord Stormaston.

'I am greatly pleased to hear it, my lady,' said Pascoe, his weathered face under its thatch of greying hair all smiles in his relief. 'If anything had happened to 'ee, my lady, I would never have forgiven myself.'

'None of us expected such an exhibition of misplaced enthusiasm,' said Lexie, 'and just think, if you had not been beside me, Pascoe, I would have suffered the knock you took! Soon after that the Marquess managed to extricate us from the press and escort me safely home.'

'Aye, my lady,' nodded Pascoe, 'his lordship be a mighty fine horseman. But I doubt he has a better seat or hands than you.'

'You are prejudiced, Pascoe,' laughed Lexie. 'And if what you say is true, then I have you to thank! I shall ride tomorrow morning. Tell Jeffs, will you?'

* * *

Jeffs, as usual, waited at the gate for his mistress's return. Lexie had not gone far before meeting Storm, who turned to accompany her. He made no objection to a gallop and soon they were racing along beside the Serpentine, slower riders, hearing the thunder of their hooves, moving aside to allow them to pass. Storm's stallion Brutus, with a heavier rider aboard, had difficulty in keeping up with Danny, who was exceptionally fleet of foot.

'You have a prime piece of horseflesh there,' Storm acknowledged as they paused, allowing the horses to regain their wind.

Lexie patted Danny's steaming neck. 'Pascoe chose him for me. He chooses all my horses. He is an excellent judge.'

'And a devoted servant, or I miss my guess,' smiled Storm. 'He returned safely yesterday?'

'Yes, though his slashed leg pains him and he was upset to have failed in his duty. He considers you an excellent horseman,' she added mischievously.

'I am obliged.'

Lexie chuckled. 'I thought you might be!'

'Imp!' declared Storm. 'I dare swear you are teasing me!'

He raised his hat to a middle-aged gentleman riding by, who bowed to them both but did not stop.

'Thomas Creevey,' he murmured. 'The news of our riding together will be all over town by this evening. He is an inveterate gossip.'

'It will prepare Society for our appearing together at the Countess's rout tonight.'

Storm raised his brows. 'I was about to enquire as to your intentions. You are to attend?'

Lexie nodded, the mischievous smile still on her lips. 'But not without an escort, I trust?'

He bowed from the waist. 'I shall be honoured, Lady Amber. At what time may I wait upon you?'

With the details settled they rode amicably side by side to rejoin Jeffs, who fell into place behind them as they continued on to Bruton Street.

Later in the day Lexie made her promised visit to Downshire House in Grosvenor Square. People were used to seeing her about Town alone in her curricle by now but her arrival still caused a stir of admiration for the remarkably fine horseflesh, the elegant carriage and the skill displayed by its driver.

Jeffs jumped down to hold the matched pair of black horses while Lexie gathered the skirts of her stunning violet carriage gown about her, mounted the steps and entered the hall, where the heels of her half boots clicked resoundingly upon the marble floor.

Lady Fanny ran forward to greet her when she was announced at the door of the receiving room and the Duchess welcomed her graciously. Several other ladies were already present. Mr Oswald Cresswell, the only gentleman there, looked decidedly embarrassed. He bowed elaborately over Lexie's hand and gazed devotedly into her green eyes before glancing nervously in the direction of the Duchess.

Lady Jersey, Mrs Drummond Burrell and Lady Cowper, all distinguished Patronesses of Almack's, were already sipping at dishes of tea. Lexie, persuaded to share a small settee with Fanny, accepted hers, together with a small slice of Madeira cake. Lady Jersey, as was usual, chattered away while the others nodded, smiled and made small interjections, until the lady ironically known as 'Silence' was finally interrupted by the entrance of Stormaston and Dexter.

Lexie inclined her head and then looked steadfastly into her teacup while the gentlemen made their devoirs. Fanny blushed. The Duchess, her small, aristocratic, silk-clad figure positively radiating pleasure, greeted her grandson with affection and Dexter with warmth.

Soon the talk somewhat naturally turned to the forthcoming assembly at Almack's, to be held as usual on the Wednesday evening.

'You have a voucher, of course, Lady Amber,' stated the Duchess, in such a definite tone that Lexie was almost ashamed to admit that she had not.

'I was admitted seven years ago, Your Grace, but since my return from retirement in Cornwall I have not yet been offered. . .'

'An oversight, no doubt,' drawled Stormaston. He bowed gravely in Lexie's direction. 'I shall look forward to escorting you there on Wednesday, my lady.'

There was a moment's astonished silence before Mrs Drummond Burrell smiled, murmuring, 'We shall be glad to welcome you both. To our regret you are not a frequent visitor, Lord Stormaston.'

And Lady Jersey exclaimed, 'Of course you must come!' almost at the same moment.

Lady Cowper, the most popular of the hostesses, having rummaged in her reticule, triumphantly produced a bundle of tickets. 'I have vouchers here, my lady! We do so look forward to seeing you at our assembly.'

'Thank you all,' murmured Lexie, receiving the ten-guinea vouchers conveyed to her by an outwardly solemn Storm, whose blue eyes laughed wickedly at her.

The Patronesses rose to leave and were soon followed by Oswald, who whispered that he should like to book a dance with her on Wednesday.

Lexie promised to keep him one. She could not dance with Storm all the evening; that would look far too particular and raise more eyebrows than she was inclined to tolerate. As it was she doubted whether he would be satisfied with the regulation two. The mere fact of his escorting her would set those tongues wagging which were not already engaged in the exercise.

Being even now the subject of much speculation, she had no doubt at all that the Patronesses would discuss the matter with all their vast acquaintance, wondering at Stormaston's interest, discounting, as she did herself, any honest purpose in the designs of a rake of his calibre, placing bets on whether the Dowager Countess of Amber would fall for his undoubted charm and accept a *carte blanche*.

She kept her head high as she drove home in her curricle. A reputation as the outrageously eccentric Lady Amber was not to be scorned, rather, to be encouraged if she wished to make her mark on Society, but she must show no hint of shame, no consciousness of having overstepped the mark. If one were bold enough, unconventional behaviour was often tolerated, whereas a single deviation by one who normally kept well within Society's strict set of rules could lead to ruin.

Not that she much cared if she were ruined socially.

She would, on the whole, be perfectly content leading a retired life at Merryfield once she had experienced the freedom of a London Season not overshadowed by the urgent necessity of catching a wealthy husband.

The challenge Storm presented was irresistible. A small smile played round her lips as she flicked her whip over Pitch's ear and turned her pair into Bruton Street.

An indefinable radiance surrounded her as she ran upstairs, a glow which even Caro's expression of grim foreboding could do nothing to destroy.

CHAPTER FIVE

BY WEDNESDAY, when they appeared at Almack's
together, Society buzzed with the latest *on dit*. The
Marquess of Stormaston and Alexia, Countess of
Amber, were quite openly conducting an *affaire*. How
far it had gone none could tell, but as the tongues
wagged, Lexie's reputation stood in some danger of
being besmirched.

She did not greatly care. Her conscience was clear;
she was having a splendid time, since Storm was
proving a most attentive and amusing companion, and
the old tabbies could say what they liked as long as
Lady Fanny and the Duchess continued to believe the
attachment innocent of vice. If the Duchess continued
to receive her, so would most other hostesses.

'My dear,' murmured Storm as they presented their
vouchers and were admitted, he having abandoned his
normal trousers or pantaloons to don the knee
breeches and silk stockings decreed by the Draconian
rules of the Patronesses, 'how does it feel to be
admitted to "the seventh heaven of the fashionable
world"?'

Lexie chuckled. 'I have heard it described as an
exclusive temple, though exactly what is worshipped
here I cannot tell!'

'Vanity, my love. Nothing but vanity.'

'Yet to be excluded is looked upon as the worst kind
of ill-fortune.' She shook her head in amused disbelief.

'I am amazed all over again that we plot and intrigue and use all our diplomatic arts to gain admission and are ready to pay ten guineas for the privilege of entering so uninspiring a set of rooms and partaking of such indifferent refreshment.'

'It is the exclusivity of Almack's which makes it so desirable. Only think,' said Storm, idly fingering his quizzing glass while eyeing the cream of Society wandering about the room with a cynical eye, 'three-quarters of the nobility knock at its doors in vain!' He grinned down at her. 'Do you not feel honoured to be here?'

'I must confess there is a certain sense of satisfaction!' After the briefest of pauses Lexie went on, 'Yet denial now would matter so much less than it would have done seven years ago, when to find a husband was the object of my being brought to London. Mama regarded admission here as the key to my success.'

Unconsciously, she sounded sad, almost disillusioned. Studying her vivid face, the unusually pensive green eyes in their nests of tawny lashes, the finely arched dark-golden brows, the slightly concave line of her adorable nose, the all-too-kissable lips, Storm felt the familiar stir of desire.

'As I remember it, you were a great success,' he remarked as he led her out to take their places in a set. 'Quite beyond the touch of a rake like me, of course. But that does not mean that I did not notice how delectable a morsel you were. And still are,' he added, his eyes appraising the fetching figure outlined by the folds of her delicate blue gown.

'Really, Storm, you should not address me in such a manner! Should you be overheard—'

'But I was not, and you, my dear Lexie, were pleased with the compliment, is that not so?'

'I am long past being shocked by anything even you might say,' responded Lexie, throwing him a mocking glance. But her heart had begun to beat fast. She would be obliged to use all her wit to hold this dangerous, attractive lord to a virtuous course.

When the dance was over Storm led her from the floor.

'Shall we repair to the terrace?' he asked her, with such an air of innocence that Lexie was tempted to laugh.

'I do declare!' she exclaimed without answering him. 'There are the Duchess and Lady Fanny! I must go and pay my respects.'

Storm smiled sardonically and made no demur over escorting her across to his grandparent, dressed that evening in dark blue silk, who sat stiff and upright in her seat, dominating the small party gathered about her. She immediately commanded him to fetch Lady Alexia a chair, thus drawing them both into her circle.

The moment both Lexie and Fanny had accepted partners for the next pair of dances and taken to the floor, the Duchess patted the chair beside her with an abrupt, 'Sit down, James.'

Storm obediently lowered himself beside her and arranged his long legs, watching Lexie depart with marked displeasure.

The Duchess eyed him shrewdly before she spoke.

'You cannot monopolise Lady Alexia, James,' she admonished sternly. 'It will not do. She is not one of the Cyprians or demireps with whom you are so wretchedly fond of consorting. I am quite sure that even you would not wish to shred her reputation beyond repair.'

'You amaze me, as ever, with your command of low language, Grandmama,' teased Storm, reluctantly removing his eyes from Lexie to meet his grand-mother's critical gaze. 'But no, of course I do not. However, since she is of age and willing to accept my escort—'

The Duchess snorted, tossing her head, making the jewels in her turban flash. 'What young woman would not be dazzled by your attentions after years of mar-riage to an old man, years spent buried in the depths of Cornwall! Lady Alexia is a high-spirited filly but virtuous. I doubt she is willing to be seduced by you or anyone else, and I should think it a great pity should you see fit to attempt—'

'Grandmama,' interrupted the Marquess with rather more firmness than he usually used with his grand-parent, at the same time laying a restraining hand upon her arm.

'You will allow, I trust, that I am not irredeemably lost to all sense of propriety, that I have never yet caused damage to any lady whose reputation had not already been sullied past redemption and that I am of an age when I may do as I please. I have always done my utmost to abide by Your Grace's wishes. But, much as I love you and hold you in respect, in the matter of my private life I must protest my right to conduct it as I please.'

The Duchess reached up to touch the scar on his cheek with a knotted finger, her faded old eyes tender. 'I know, my dear. You have always had a keen, if sometimes misguided, sense of honour.'

Storm gently took her small, veined hand in his. He smiled cynically. 'I was young and idealistic then. I have since learned the true value of women of her sort.'

'But do not think all women unworthy of your regard.' The Duchess recovered her hand and tapped him on the shoulder with her folded fan. 'As for obliging me by following my wishes, I know how much it cost you to give up your ambition to purchase a pair of colours, my dear boy, and that much of your rackety behaviour since has stemmed from your obedience to my wish. But you are Downshire's heir and the thought of Hugo's inheriting almost gave your grandfather a stroke.'

She nodded solemnly at Storm, who had given a rueful half-laugh followed by a sigh. 'You have responsibilities, James, most of which I know you shoulder with determination and great skill. But you have not yet provided yourself with an heir—certainly not a legitimate one. Have you fathered many bastards?'

The question came out in the Duchess's best *grande dame* manner accompanied by another sharp tap with her fan and for an instant even Storm looked slightly taken aback by her outspokenness. But he quickly recovered himself.

'Two, to my certain knowledge,' he drawled. 'Both are well provided for.'

'They should be legitimate and gracing your nursery! You are depriving us of the joy of watching our great-grandchildren grow up! You must wed, James, and Alexia Hamilton would make you a fine wife.'

Storm crossed his legs and eyed the toe of one brilliantly polished pump.

'If I wanted a wife,' he agreed, lazily flicking a speck of dust from the black sleeve of his coat. 'But I do not, at present. It may surprise you to discover, ma'am, that I have every intention of avoiding marriage until I am certain that it will contain at least a measure of felicity. I have seen too many men in my position ensnared by some scheming chit for their title and wealth, only to serve long years of domestic warfare and unhappiness. I have no wish to be caught in that matrimonial trap.'

'God love you, my dear, I should not wish it for you—' began the Duchess, but at that moment the dance ended and their tête-à-tête with it.

Storm was not sorry. He was exceedingly fond of his grandmother and did not relish her strictures. But he only bent to her will when his conscience told him he must, as over the question of joining the army.

His own much-loved estates, attached to the marquessate of Stormaston, required considerable attention, and the extensive lands and fortune pertaining to the honour of Downshire would demand an efficient and conscientious hand to guide them on the demise of the present Duke.

Hugo would not do. Even at the age of eighteen, when Hugo had been a mere lad of twelve, Storm, like his grandparents, had been able to see the weakness and wildness, the envy in his younger brother, and to anticipate the probable dissipation of the family fortune were he ever to inherit.

At one and twenty, when Storm became entirely his own master and could have done as he pleased in defiance of his grandparents' wishes, Hugo's fifteen-year-old character had appeared even less promising.

And so Storm had heeded his grandmother's pleas, shouldered his duty and forsworn the army as a career. But his high spirit of adventure had demanded other outlets and thus his reputation as a rake had been born.

He stood silently behind Lexie's chair, admiring the golden swathes of hair so ingeniously intertwined with pearls and ribbons, longing to touch, to kiss the tender spot exposed on the nape of her neck, and wryly admitted to himself that any hint of real wildness now was entirely for the sake of appearances.

Of course, like any other gentleman, he had kept a succession of mistresses. And soon, perhaps very soon, he would dismiss Hermione from his flat. Lexie filled his thoughts; he had no inclination to bed his mistress now. She would find no difficulty in securing another protector, of that he was assured.

He had won her generous favours in the face of stiff opposition and Storm, who was perfectly aware of his own ability to attract but did not suffer from any great degree of self-consequence, believed she had chosen him solely because he had the most money to lavish upon her. So she, like others before her, would suffer few pangs at being deprived of his favour. For all his faults and reputation, he had never been promiscuous, had been particular in his choice of *chère amies*, and had never indulged in more than one lover at a time, demanding fidelity in return.

Lexie, he brooded, was proving a provoking creature to ensnare. Of course the Duchess was right; he could not risk damaging her reputation beyond repair. Unsubstantiated gossip was one thing, certain knowledge of indiscretion quite another. He would have to conduct this affair with the utmost discretion. He was quite prepared for that.

After another dance with the object of his desire he danced with Fanny, while Lexie danced with Felix, who had joined their party. After that the girls were claimed by a succession of partners, though Storm had insisted Lexie keep the waltzes for him.

The Czar, who loved dancing, arrived with his entourage and accompanied by his sister, the Grand Duchess, a fair-haired, vivacious widow whom Storm abhorred, for it was she who had turned the Czar against the Regent, whom she had taken in intense dislike. For some little while Storm found himself cornered by the Grand Duchess and it took all his resolution to maintain his languid, charming mask.

Extracting himself from the reach of her caustic and critical tongue, he returned to claim the hand of another fair-haired and vivacious widow, in whose company he would gladly spend the remainder of the evening if only convention would allow.

Mr Cresswell had turned up with his mama, the Viscountess, and dutifully asked Fanny to stand up with him, after which he requested the honour of standing up with Lady Amber.

'Mama is gettin' most insistent,' Oswald grumbled as they came together in the dance. 'Orders me to seek permission to pay my addresses. But Lady Fanny don't want to marry me any more than I want to marry her.'

'So you have said before,' murmured Lexie. The steps of the dance gave her a few moments to think before they met again. 'Why don't you approach Lord Stormaston?' she suggested. 'He is Fanny's guardian, you know. I fancy he might solve your problem for you by refusing permission.'

'You mean he don't like me, don't think me good enough,' muttered Oswald gloomily.

Lexie shook her head. Poor Oswald, he had little self-confidence. He was probably right, though. But if the Duchess pushed the match Storm would no doubt agree in the end.

'I did not say that, Mr Cresswell,' she told him firmly. 'But I doubt he thinks you would suit. And if he did give permission, Fanny has only to refuse, you know. He would not force her to wed against her will.'

Oswald brightened visibly at this. 'I sit at your feet in admiration, Lady Amber,' he declared as they made their bows at the end of the dance. 'You are divinely beautiful and extraordinary clever, too. You would not marry me yourself, I collect?'

Lexie smiled, a certain compassion in her gaze. He really was the nicest of young men, but not to her taste and too immature altogether. 'You do me great honour, Mr Cresswell, but no, I would not. We should not suit, either, I am far too rackety for you. Your mama would never agree.'

'I'll be out of leading strings in a couple of months, you know,' Oswald informed her. 'Mama won't be able to tell me what to do once I'm one and twenty.'

But she would still try, and Oswald, bless him, would not have the strength to resist. Lexie could see it all. However, all she said was, 'If you wish to please her, Mr Cresswell, do as I suggest. Once you have been refused she must give up.'

'She'll only pick on some other female I ain't interested in,' he prophesied dismally.

The next dance being a waltz, Lexie found herself taking the floor with Stormaston and afterwards, breathless from a number of causes, allowed him to lead her to the refreshment room.

He handed her a glass of lemonade. 'We should drink it outside,' he murmured. 'It would be cooler there.'

And darker, more private, thought Lexie, a thrill of excitement sending a shiver down her spine. But she could not risk such an expedition yet. She trusted the Marquess not one inch and herself little more, knowing the strange, dizzying effect his nearness had upon her. So she must hold him at arm's length for as long as it took to bring him to the declaration she desired.

'I would rather sit here,' she said, choosing a chair. 'Tongues are wagging quite enough already. Were I to disappear into the darkness outside with you, I tremble to think what would be said. And,' she added quickly, before he could challenge her on the point, 'although I do not object to being spoken of as unconventional or even as a flirt, I would dislike intensely being thought to play the whore.'

For an instant Storm frowned, as though he found her reasoning distasteful. But then he dropped into the seat beside hers, draping one arm across its back as he faced her with a lazy smile. 'You disappoint me, Lexie, my love. I thought you had more courage.'

'And I thought you a gentleman, my lord, despite your reputation! Never tell me I was wrong!'

He suddenly put his head back and laughed. '*Touché*, my love! Despite all appearances, I would not have your reputation sullied. I see I must bide my time and find a more suitable opportunity for dalliance.'

Lexie smiled. 'But I have never promised to dally with you, Storm. Merely to accept your escort to certain events and occasions. Do not read more into my offer of friendship than is there.'

'But you still owe me a kiss.'

This time Lexie, prepared, was able to meet his words with equanimity. 'You may consider it so, but I do not.'

He smiled that lazy, devastating, knowing smile.

'We shall see.'

Over the next weeks they appeared everywhere together. In the end the gossip waned for lack of further fuel. The couple behaved with the utmost propriety apart from dancing together rather more than was acceptable and spending more time sitting together when in company than did most married couples. Lexie enjoyed it all hugely.

Storm was a charming, amusing and knowledgable companion. They talked about everything under the sun. He was certainly not the idle fop he appeared. He spoke with enthusiasm about his country house in Wiltshire, Stormaston Park, his extensive estates and the modern farming methods with which he was experimenting.

'You would like Stormaston, Lexie,' he told her as they chatted quietly waiting for a concert to begin. Caro, who had accompanied them since she was fond of music, had found a place near the front, sitting with the chaperons. 'You must visit there with me when the Season ends.'

'I planned on going to Brighton for July,' said Lexie, hiding her jubilation at the invitation although she would not go, of course, unless it was to join a house party. 'And then back to Merryfield. My estate needs my personal attention if I am to introduce all the reforms you suggest. Although I have an excellent steward, he is set in the old ways and will need persuading to change.'

'Perhaps we should exchange visits,' murmured his lordship. 'I should be happy to assist you in any way within my power.'

'You are kind, Storm. Perhaps we should. But I promise nothing.'

Storm, who found his companion more enchanting by the day, hid his frustration in some lazy rejoinder. The minx was teasing him to distraction, giving freely of her company yet granting him no chance to deepen their relationship except upon the most austerely friendly terms. Even in his own coach, with Lexie chaperoned by her maid or by her cousin, who, on occasion, could be tempted out by a visit to the theatre or to hear a musical concert, he must sit properly in his corner.

Despite her fluttery ways he liked Mrs Baldwin, who amused him by regarding him with rather suspicious awe. Beneath her ineffectual manner she was, he had discovered, perfectly capable of ordering Lexie's household and helping to organise an entertainment to which most of the *haut ton* had been invited.

It was to take place on the thirteenth of July and the Duke of Wellington, who would be in London by then, had promised to attend. The Sovereigns had departed on the twenty third day of June and London was enjoying a slightly less frenetic few days before the Duke's arrival. Because of this they had met only twice in the last week and Storm found he missed seeing Lexie more than he was quite ready to admit.

Hermione had been dismissed and his discreet flat lay empty. Perhaps, he thought vaguely, his opportunity would come when they joined a party to visit Vauxhall. That was not for two weeks yet, a couple of days after Lexie's soirée. But they would all wear masks and the possibilities of luring a female into dark, lonely paths was one of the main attractions of the place. He cared little for the amusements laid on or the firework displays either, but such things pleased the ladies.

'The arrangements for your soirée are going well?' he enquired out of politeness. He did not expect to enjoy an occasion where Lexie would be a busy hostess while he languished on the sidelines. He would, he decided, make for the card room and spend the evening there.

'Excellently, I thank you. Cousin Caro is a wonder.' Suddenly Lexie smiled. 'You and she are alike, you know. You hide your true self behind a lamentably foppish mask while Caro's efficiency is concealed behind a vague, fluttery manner. I do not believe her deception is deliberate. But yours is.'

'A protection, merely,' drawled Storm.

'Oh dear,' muttered Lexie. 'Here comes Hugo.'

'Young puppy.'

Lazy amusement filled Storm's tone, yet Lexie knew he was not pleased. Hugo had been pursuing her for the last couple of weeks, and despite all her efforts to dissuade him he persisted in asking her to stand up with him, which she could not refuse to do without appearing to lack conduct.

Under normal circumstances he would not be seen dead at a musical evening. He was quite deliberately attempting to oust his brother in her affections; the very idea that he thought himself able made her want to laugh.

Hugo greeted them with one of his extravagant bows and demanded to know whether there was any way in which he might serve Lady Amber.

'Should Lady Amber require anythin' I am, despite my great age, quite able to render the service,' pointed out Storm agreeably.

'I lack for nothing, I thank you,' put in Lexie quickly, 'and I am certain you would find entertainment more to your liking in the card room, Lord Hugo.'

'Oh, I shall retire there once the music begins,' said Hugo. 'In fact, I may as well wander along now,' he added, seeing the musicians about to take their places. 'I shall look forward to seein' you again at supper, Lady Amber.'

'Does he annoy you?' asked Storm, watching the departure of his brother with narrowed eyes.

'Not really.' Lexie had no wish to stir up more animosity between the brothers. She sensed that there was quite enough already. 'But I do wish he could take a hint!'

'Hugo,' stated Storm grimly, 'never could.'

Hugo did not appear for supper after all. 'Deep in a game, no doubt,' observed Storm when Lexie remarked on his welcome absence.

Later, returning from a visit to the cloakroom, she heard Storm's unmistakable voice as she approached an open door on her way back to the salon. She was quite alone in the corridor and his words rose easily above a distant hum of conversation and the faint strains of instruments being tuned in the background.

She halted, not wishing to intrude, and realised he was speaking in a tone she had never heard him use before, authoritative and implacable, as he declined to meet Hugo's vast gaming losses.

'You'll not allow the name of Graham to be sunk in iniquity!' declared Hugo.'

'You think not?' came back the biting retort.

'I had thought better of even you, brother!'

'You repose too much faith in my determination to defend the honour of our name,' came Storm's cold response. 'I have bought you out of enough sad scrapes in the past, I will do so no more. If your allowance will not cover your expenses and losses, then I suggest you do not incur them. I have no intention of allowing you to squander any more of the Graham fortune. You will live within your generous allowance or find some honest way of supplementing it. Gaming is not the way, as you must by now be fully aware.'

'I was attemptin' to recover my fortunes at the tables tonight. But Lady Luck was against me.' Hugo sounded childish in his whining truculence.

'The war with France is over at last. You could do worse than join the army. Your life would no longer be at great risk. I doubt you would be posted to America to prosecute the war there, which in any case is likely to be over shortly.'

'You forget, I would have to purchase a commission. I cannot pay my debts so I could not do that, either.'

There was a moment's silence. 'Would you like to follow the colours, Hugo?' Storm sounded surprised.

Lexie could hear the shrug in Hugo's petulant voice. 'There is little to entertain me here if I cannot afford to gamble. To be a half-pay officer would suit me well, and there will be plenty of those commissions for sale now Napoleon is defeated.'

'I will buy you a commission—but only provided it carries a posting.'

A stunned silence followed. Then, 'Not in a line regiment,' came Hugo's slow answer.

'Very well. And, Hugo, once you are commissioned and posted, I will pay your current debts and gaming losses. Let me have a list tomorrow. But mark me well, this is the last time I shall come to your rescue. Officers are cashiered for accumulating debts they cannot meet, and often end up in prison.'

'You'd like that, wouldn't you?' ground out Hugo viciously. 'Sittin' on a fortune, refusin' to help, black-mailin' me into going into the army and takin' up what will probably be a dashed uncomfortable posting in some foetid hole—'

'No fortune is inexhaustible, my dear Hugo. I am responsible for husbanding that of our family for future generations. My own extravagances, whatever you may think, are not now excessive, whatever they may have been in the past. The Graham fortune is in truth greater now that when I inherited it. Not even you, my dear brother, will be allowed to undo all the work I have put in over the last few years to achieve that end.'

'Unless I inherit.'

'I do not intend to quit my lease just yet, even to please you, Hugo. And I expect one day to set up a nursery of my own. You are not Marquess of Stormaston yet.'

'I shall return to Grosvenor Square and prepare my statement. You shall have it in the morning,' said Hugo stiffly.

Lexie had been standing mesmerised by what she was hearing, seeing Storm for the first time as a man of power, of stature, of principles. She had glimpsed this man before, but not in such convincing guise.

She came to herself with a shock, realised the interview was at an end and wondered what to do. She could not retreat. There was only one thing for it: to pretend to be hurrying back to the salon. Picking up the train of her skirt she went swiftly forward, feigning complete surprise when she bumped into the retreating Hugo.

'Why, Lord Hugo! You must excuse me for being such a gawk,' she cried, 'but I was hurrying back and never expected to meet with anyone—'

Hugo had his hands on her arms as he sought to help her recover her balance while retaining his own. They were hot and trembling.

'Lady Amber! My deepest regrets...my fault entirely...please allow me—'

'I will attend Lady Amber.'

Storm stepped from the room and Lexie turned. 'Lord Stormaston! I had thought to rejoin you in the salon!'

'Indeed, I should have been there except that Hugo and I had some business to discuss.' He nodded at Hugo. 'I will expect you in the morning, brother.'

'My duty, Lady Amber,' muttered Hugo with a sketchy bow, and hurried away.

Lexie stared after him and then looked up at Storm's grim face. 'A family rift?'

His face softened as he smiled at her. 'Nothin' to worry your head about, m'dear. A little business matter to be taken care of. Hugo has decided to follow the drum. He requires me to purchase him a commission.'

Lexie could not help her frown. 'Will the life suit him?'

'I doubt it, but it may do him a service. Forget Hugo.' He muttered something she could not quite catch. It sounded suspiciously like 'Lucky young dog,' but she could not be certain. And then he was drawling, 'Let us go and enjoy the remainder of this entertainin' concert.'

But Lexie was seeing her companion with new eyes and found it extremely difficult to concentrate on the music.

The days sped by. The Duke of Wellington arrived in London to be greeted by ecstatic crowds. The dinners, the balls, the parades began all over again. This was the man who had commanded the British army to victory in the Peninsula, who had chased the French out of Spain and back into France and taken Toulouse on the tenth of April, at great cost of dead and wounded, not knowing that Napoleon had abdicated over a week earlier.

And then, despite the peace, the Governor of Bayonne decided to fight on, causing the slaughter of several hundred troops on both sides in a useless sortie from the besieged town.

But Wellington was not to blame for that. He had

restored British pride in her army and returned a hero. His arrival at Lexie's soirée caused such a stir that everything came to a halt; men left the card tables to come to greet him, the musical trio ceased to play, the ladies to chatter.

He came dressed in the field-marshal's uniform designed for him by the Regent, the scarlet coat embroidered on collar, cuffs, down the front and at the seams. A flock of aides-de-camp followed at his heels and he had soon collected a bevy of lovely, adoring women around him.

As the evening resumed its course Lexie smiled indulgently to where the Duke, an indifferent conversationalist, nodded, smiled modestly and murmured 'Yes, yes,' to whatever was said to him and paid laboured compliments to the ladies.

Lexie, aware with every fibre of her being of Stormaston's approach, was not surprised to hear his voice in her ear.

'You find the Field Marshal attractive?'

His voice held a tone she could not quite interpret. It seemed to hold an undercurrent of anger laced with jealousy, yet somewhere regret lay hidden. Looking up, she could see the mixed emotions reflected in his face as he studied the Duke through his quizzing glass, an affectation he seldom used.

Lexie placed her hand on his arm, feeling the muscles tense as she did so. She suddenly felt extremely hot, but she kept her tone light as she said, 'Not at all, although he does exude a certain aura of power, which I suppose some women find engaging. But I do believe his authority to be more contrived, a product of his calling, than natural. On the whole, I find him agreeable, but he has not brought his wife to London to share in his triumph.'

The muscles under her hand relaxed and Storm dropped his glass, allowing it to hang upon its ribbon. 'Nevertheless, I would have counted it a privilege to serve under him.'

That answered another question she had been nursing in her mind. He envied Hugo. He had wanted to join the army. 'Then why did you not?' she asked gently.

'As Downshire's heir...' he shrugged, letting the gesture speak for him.

'I see. Well, I am glad you did not volunteer, for had you been killed I should have lacked an escort this Season.'

'Soon,' he rejoined, his blue eyes brilliant, 'I intend to be more than merely your escort.'

CHAPTER SIX

VAUXHALL Gardens blazed with the light of innumerable lamps as darkness fell. They had arrived to enjoy their big adventure as the midsummer sun dipped below the horizon: Lexie, Storm, Fanny, Felix, Oswald and several other young people of their acquaintance, accompanied by Oswald's mother, Lady Wighton, as chaperon.

To Lexie, Lord Stormaston was immediately recognisable despite his black cloak and mask. He had, of course, called for her in his carriage, so the chance to mistake him for another was nil, but in any case she would have picked him out from any throng. He possessed such an air. And she could never have mistaken his blue eyes, dancing at her through the slits of his mask.

In truth, she had little difficulty in recognising Lady Fanny, Lord Dexter or Mr Cresswell, despite the last's devilishly pointed creation encrusted with gold embroidery, though the identities of some of the others, with whom she was less well acquainted, did tease her at first. Once safe in the pavilion reserved for their use, they discarded their disguises amidst much laughter and teasing before partaking of the refreshment provided.

The young people were eager to explore. Lady Wighton, a plump woman of some five and forty years, had an aversion to exerting herself. She lacked the breath to walk far and, although she took her duties as chaperon seriously, she was not persuaded of the necessity to accompany the young people on a stroll of exploration.

'Lady Amber, I entrust the office of chaperon to you!' she declared with an arch smile, forcefully poking her son into offering Lady Fanny his arm. 'Do not forget to wear your masks! And do not wander far,' she enjoined their departing backs. 'I shall look for you to return within the hour!'

'Very well, Mama,' muttered Oswald from beneath the weight of his gold thread.

Lexie, wearing a light green spotted muslin gown and close-fitting head dress, masked like all the rest in a matching creation which suited her admirably— Vauxhall was not the place for any members of the *haut ton* to be seen officially—took Storm's arm.

'I believe Lady Wighton has instructed Oswald to further his suit with Lady Fanny,' she murmured, watching the pair strolling in front of them.

'I have already refused him my permission to address her,' declared Storm, stating a fact of which Oswald had already apprised Lexie. 'Fanny begged me not to allow it.'

Lexie squeezed his arm without thinking. 'I am so glad you did!' she exclaimed. 'I was certain you would! Neither of them want it, you know.'

Storm tried to steady the hammering in his veins occasioned by her intimate gesture and to control his body's response. 'I collect you enjoy Mr Cresswell's confidence and that it was you who inspired him to approach me?' he asked.

'I hope you did not mind!' Lexie had become aware

of the consequences of her intimate gesture, not only upon herself but upon the Marquess as well. She would have to control her spontaneity in future if she were to avoid provoking him into thinking her a tease. She therefore took care to keep her hand featherlight upon his arm as she went on, 'It seemed the easiest way to dissuade Lady Wighton from her purpose, but her ladyship is not easily deterred.'

Oswald, still with Fanny, turned into one of the many byways, already becoming shadowed where the coloured lamps did not reach. Felix followed, a young woman on either arm. Others of the party hesitated at the junction.

'Lord Dexter,' murmured Lexie, 'is scarcely qualified to act the chaperon. I think perhaps we should follow. The Viscountess did say. . .'

'But without meaning it,' said Storm firmly. 'We shall leave them all to their own devices. Little harm can come of it. I have other things in mind for us.'

Lexie's conscience smote her but her heart leapt. When she had accepted the invitation to join the party, she had guessed Storm would take advantage of the surroundings, the occasion, to claim a kiss. And she had encouraged him by her unthinking, grateful squeeze of his arm!

Vauxhall was known to be the place for forbidden assignations, for the carrying out of plots to waylay and abduct the unwary. Lexie feared being alone with him, not because she anticipated Storm to have any devilish designs on her but because she did not trust her own responses where he was concerned. But the others had all disappeared from view and Storm was leading her behind a booth containing a bearded lady into the dark, labyrinthine byways behind.

'Storm!' she protested, trying to tug him back to the main path and virtue.

'You do not fear me, Lexie, surely?' he asked softly.

'No, of course not, but I think—'

He placed a reassuring hand over the one now clutching desperately at his arm. 'Then do not. Let us enjoy these moments of seclusion. The rules which decide that a man and woman may not be alone together without causing scandal are stupid and archaic, except, perhaps, for the very young.'

'Reason tells me so, but—'

'But dire warnings have been instilled into your mind since childhood! I know, my dear, but I mean you no mischief and what harm can there possibly be in our spending a few moments apart from others in a public garden where you would have but to scream and the world would come to your rescue in an instant?'

'None at all,' agreed Lexie, who had only been protesting because she wanted to be with him so much it must be wrong. How she longed for his kiss! But to what might it lead? She knew it would be prudent to insist upon joining the others or returning to Lady Wighton immediately, but prudence lost out to anticipation as Storm drew her into a tiny glade just off the path and took her into his arms.

Music, shouts, laughter, all faded into the background as she felt the urgency of his hold, the hammering of his heart, his breath fanning her face as his mouth hovered over hers while he removed first his own and then her mask, dropping them to the ground.

Her own heart beat hard and fast, her limbs turned to warm, sweet, viscous wine as she dropped her reticule and flung her arms about his neck, abandoning all modesty as the need to be close to him swept over her. Ridiculous as it seemed, this was, she suddenly knew, where she belonged. In Lord Stormaston's arms.

'Lexie!' he murmured deeply before his mouth claimed hers.

Lexie had never known such sweeping desire as possessed her in the next few moments. His kiss, deep and penetrating, tasting her and giving her a taste of him, lasted until it dragged a groan from her throat. Had her arms not been clasped tightly about his neck she would have fallen, so limp had her muscles become. Her body did not belong to her and neither did her mind, which whirled kaleidoscopically from sensation to sensation, drowning fear, responsibility, time itself.

His lips moved from her mouth to her eyes, the tilted tip of her nose, the fluttering pulse in her throat, and all the time he murmured words of endearment. Lexie's fingers tangled in his hair, quite destroying the careful arrangement his man had achieved.

He shifted his hold to turn her slightly so that his hand could cup one of her breasts, his thumb finding its peak through the thin muslin of her gown and chemise. Lexie gasped as new sensation lanced through her body.

'I want you, Lexie,' he said strongly; although his heart beat like a hammer, his breathing came harsh, his voice trembled slightly and she could feel the urgency of his desire, he was in complete control of his actions. He went on, 'I know you want me, too. My love, I own a flat where we could meet discreetly. You need have no fear for your reputation, I shall guard it well. Will you come to me there?'

Abruptly, the rosy euphoria deserted Lexie. Disappointment surged through her. Sounds, harsh, jangling sounds, bestial, drunken laughter filled her ears. But she had known he wanted her for his mistress, not his wife. She should not feel so mortified.

She struggled to escape his hold. 'Are you offering me a *carte blanche*?' she demanded, her voice quivering uncontrollably.

At her tone he lifted surprised eyebrows. 'Naturally, my little tease. What else did you think I had in mind?'

She could not possibly mention marriage. She had known he did not intend that and apparently all her wiles had not changed his mind. She drew a breath.

'Friendship. Flirtation, maybe even dalliance. As tonight. But no more. You must have known that I could never accept such an offer, my lord. I may flout certain conventions, but I consider myself a respectable widow. You would have me become a whore.'

'I would have you become my lover, Lexie. There is the world of difference—'

'Not to me!' she raged, to cover her distress. 'How dare you. . .?' Words failed her as tears of frustration and anger filled her eyes. She dashed them away and pushed past him to regain the path. 'I would be much obliged if you would escort me back to our pavilion,' she managed on a choking sob.

Storm bent down to retrieve her reticule and their masks. He did not argue further, knowing it to be fruitless in the face of her real distress. Painful frustration expressed itself in his grim expression. His eyes, warm, holding fire a moment ago, became chips of blue ice. All his patience had been worthless. He had thought her merely playing hard to get, been confident that in the end she would capitulate as had so many others in the past.

But she had not. He deliberately encouraged wrath to replace rejection. He had seldom—never!—had his well-rehearsed advances refused before. Lady Amber, an amusing, stimulating companion, had encouraged his friendship. She was far from indifferent to him and should have fallen into his arms with cries of joy. She was, he decided, exactly what he had jokingly called her, a tease. There was nothing he hated more than a tease. She deserved a sharp lesson. A very sharp lesson indeed.

Lexie, glancing up to thank him for returning her mask and reticule, saw the harshness in his face, saw the white line of his scar shift as he clenched his jaw, and a tremor of fear added desperation to her already disturbed emotions. She had led him on, but in her mind towards marriage, a respectable union. But surely he was gentleman enough not to seek revenge?

Storm allowed nothing of his thoughts to show in his face or manner as he delivered her back to the chaperonage of the Viscountess, behaving as though nothing untoward had happened. Lexie, he noted, was trying to do the same and succeeding to all intents. Only he would notice the strain in her eyes, the slightly higher pitch to her voice, the tendency to distraction in her manner.

While Lexie, acting a part as she had never acted before, noted the disappearance of that dangerous expression and began to relax again.

At more or less the same moment as they had approached the pavilion Fanny had appeared at some distance walking between Mr Cresswell and Lord Dexter, with a group of their friends following on behind. By unspoken consent they had waited for the others and met up amidst great exclamations and enthusiasm over the pleasures of the gardens.

Despite the fact that he knew Fanny had been perfectly safe with Mr Cresswell, Storm felt uneasy. The Viscountess had proved a most dilatory chaperon. Could it be that she had planned to trick him into being compelled to allow a match between the two young people? He had not regarded that possibility earlier and had neglected his duty to Fanny while pursuing his own dalliance.

But it seemed that all was well. Despite all her arch questions to the young people, no hint of impropriety on Fanny's part emerged. Fanny and Oswald had kept with the others and his own laxity had been of no consequence.

Fanny, looking flushed and pretty, had arrived back at the pavilion as she had left it, on Oswald's arm. But behind her mask her shining eyes kept straying to the elegant form of Lord Dexter. Lexie wondered what had given the child such an air of hidden exaltation, but under the circumstances nothing untoward could have occurred. It was, after all, Fanny's first experience of Vauxhall and its wonders and no doubt this accounted for her excitement.

As the fireworks began to light up the sky with red, blue, silver and golden stars, Lexie dismissed a vague uneasiness in favour of living again those delicious, stolen moments spent in Stormaston's arms. If only he could be brought to propose marriage! She would be the happiest of creatures. But the evening had proved him proof against all her lures.

Having arrived in Stormaston's crested coach, Lexie had little choice but to return in it and that evening, for various reasons, neither Caro nor Chalker had accompanied her. Acutely aware of his presence inches away, Lexie pressed herself against the side of the carriage and gazed steadfastly from the window as they traversed the streets back to Mayfair.

Despite the hour they met plenty of traffic. After the fresh airiness of Vauxhall Gardens the coach seemed stuffy but the narrow, odoriferous streets rendered opening a window unwise. The weather really was too hot to remain much longer in Town. She would have retired to the country except that she would miss too many of the extraordinary entertainments planned for that summer.

She did not want to miss the centenary of the Hanoverian succession on the first day of August, when the Regent's grand jubilee celebrations would take place and all the royal parks be thrown open to the people.

Clinging to such thoughts in an effort to take her mind from the awful possibility that Storm would use their isolation to attempt another attack on her determination to resist him, Lexie did not speak. Storm, immobile beside her, travelled in equal silence and the tension flowed between them like a web of silken thread, strong, elastic, not easily broken. He had been confounded and angered by her refusal to accept his *carte blanche*. What would he do now?

She had grown used to his company. Without it,

events to which she had been looking forward with pleasure would no longer appeal. She did not like to admit how much she had come to rely on his presence beside her. For one thing, it kept a host of unwanted, importunate suitors at bay.

A small sigh escaped her. Her soliciting of his escort for her own ends had rebounded with a vengeance. She should have seen long ago that an attempt to lure a gentleman possessed of the Marquess's rakish reputation into matrimony was doomed to failure. And in the failing she had lost even his friendship.

Her cogitations brought no comfort, simply gloom to add to her mortification. For if *he* would not wed her, she would remain a widow. She would consider no one else as a husband after the joy she had found in his arms that evening. She need not be lonely. She could buy companionship. Only weeks ago she had viewed such a prospect with equanimity, if not pleasure. But that had been before. . .

Such was her despondency that, when they arrived in Bruton Street and the Marquess saw her to her door, bowed and asked at what time he should wait upon her the following evening, Lexie was taken aback.

She quickly gathered her wits and named an hour. He bent formally over her hand in farewell and departed, watched by an astounded Lexie. Instead of quickly mounting the stairs to her bedroom, she stood rooted to the spot, watching his cloak swirl about his tall, commanding figure as the door closed behind him.

Slowly, it dawned upon her that he had not given up his pursuit. He anticipated that in the end he would emerge victorious.

So she would not accept defeat, either! Her hold on him was tenuous, but it did exist, for her attempts to bring him to a declaration had in truth succeeded. Because he still shied at the idea of committing himself to marriage, he had offered her the status he accorded all his women.

But she was not just one of his women! One day he would accept the inevitable. Dear Lord! he must, for in truth she doubted she could live without him as her mate, however unsatisfactory he might turn out to be as a husband. Of the alternatives, to become his mistress was impossible for her and to lose him from her life inconceivable.

She must think of something.

And so the next morning when, not at all to her surprise, Storm met her in the Park as usual, she behaved as charmingly as she knew how, totally ignoring the contretemps of the previous evening. It must be within her power to fascinate Lord Stormaston into a proposal—of marriage. He must now realise that, if he wanted to enjoy intimate relations with her, he had no other choice. And her life would be blighted for ever if she did not succeed.

Storm, chagrined by the rejection of the previous evening, had become more determined than ever to lure Alexia Hamilton to his bed. Of one thing he was now certain beyond all doubt. Her lightly flirtatious ways, her air of intrinsic innocence, hid a passionate nature which he had begun to stir into life. He doubted whether she knew the depth of the well of passion within her and he took secret satisfaction at the prospect of plumbing its depths.

For losing one battle did not mean that he had lost the war. The challenge of Alexia Hamilton excited him. There would be another day, another occasion. She *must* succumb! No woman's virtue was inviolable, he had proved that many times, and a few amorous encounters with him could do her no possible harm. On past experience, once he had possessed her his urgent need would die.

Not that he had ever felt quite the same compulsion to possess any other woman, but his desire could only be a matter of degree. It might take him a little longer to slake his thirst with her but. . . But first he had to achieve the seduction.

He therefore rode out the next morning determined to use every ounce of the charm he knew so exactly how to wield. And did not know whether to laugh or fume when he discovered her to be employing a similar weapon. What did the little tease expect to achieve? Did she think to render him so addle-witted that he would propose marriage? She would soon learn that he had no intention of being enticed into parson's mousetrap just yet!

If he begot an heir at around the age of forty, he should still live long enough to train the child and to see him achieve his majority. And a young girl, absorbed in her duties as wife and mother, would not interfere with his pursuit of his own life. Lexie, he knew, was bright enough and interested enough to want to share his interests: she would demand more from him than he was willing to give.

His grandmother's voice echoed in his ears but he refused to listen. Lexie wanted marriage, but had given him no reason to suppose that she held him in anything but critical regard. She did not, at bottom, approve of his manners or behaviour. Why should she? Like everyone else she believed him a rake, beyond redemption. Why should she even attempt to look behind the façade he chose to present?

He did not want her to. Or anyone else for that matter, apart from his grandmother who knew him too well. But why, then, did Lexie wish to become Marchioness of Stormaston? For the same reasons as all the other hopefuls he had discarded over the years, in order to become a Duchess one day and to become wife to one of the richest men in the country. Had she shown any sign of affection or tenderness he might, just, have heeded the Duchess's words. But she had not.

He smiled at her, a devilish smile that let her know he had guessed her purpose. She really was looking remarkably attractive, flushed and eager, full of life and vigour, up to anything.

Except allowing him to have his way with her. The smile spread even as desire made him shift in his saddle. His resolve deepened. In a young girl such reticence was only to be expected. A widow should not be so stiff-necked in her attitude to an *affaire* outside marriage. She probably wouldn't be, he thought grimly, if it weren't for his title and his money.

Lexie, seeing the dangerous glint in his eye, almost panicked, but her inherent courage quickly reasserted itself. Whatever he liked to pretend, the Marquess was not an evil man. He would do her no true harm. Although, of course, he would not consider discreet seduction to be in any way grievous.

And she had to admit that, shocking as she found

his offer of a *carte blanche*, all she would lose in the event would be her own integrity. A private pain that would not otherwise affect her life in any essential way. So she had no great reason to fear the worst Stormaston could contrive, although his intention remained unchanged. He would not, she was certain, force himself upon her. But he might easily seduce her were she not constantly on guard.

In this spirit of armed truce they continued their association much as before. Lexie took even greater care to have someone else in the carriage with them and never to be beguiled out to dark terraces or into empty rooms. Not that Storm tried excessively hard— he was behaving with the utmost propriety. He appeared to be biding his time.

Meanwhile, their discussions covered all manner of subjects of which Lexie knew a great deal, having devoured the contents of the Amber library during her exile at Porthewan and she eagerly absorbed any information he had to offer. Storm teased her over what he termed her magpie mind, which picked up snippets of information to store for future airing.

They enjoyed visiting exhibitions, the theatre, the opera and musical evenings together and discussed their merits afterwards. Despite the tension running beneath the surface of their relationship, Lexie had never been happier. And by the way Storm sometimes smiled at her she thought him to be enjoying himself, too. Even his grandmother remarked.

'I do declare,' she said one evening while she and Lexie were alone. 'James has lost much of his air of boredom recently. Your company is proving good for him, my dear Lady Alexia. And he has dismissed that actress creature from his flat, I hear. I never could approve his choice of *chère amies*—flighty, dimwitted chits I have always considered them.'

Lexie blushed, but laughed at the Duchess's outspoken words. 'I am certain you are not supposed to know of their existence, dear ma'am!'

'When the entire *ton* knows of his *affaires*, it would be difficult to keep the information from me, don't you think? Don't approve of the boy's behaviour, never did, but he was not allowed to join the army, so he had to find another outlet for his high spirits.'

'They have to sow their wild oats,' murmured Lexie with a wry grimace, remembering the conversation she had overheard between Storm and Hugo. Storm had lost no time in purchasing one of the many commissions now up for sale and Hugo was preparing to join his regiment, stationed somewhere in the north. 'Men are fortunate to be allowed such licence.'

'Women are allowed a certain amount, too, after the heir is born. That's what all this charade is about, y'know. Young girls put on show to catch a prize but sheltered and chaperoned so that there can be no doubt as to the paternity of the heir. Blood lines are important, d'y'see.'

Her gaze settled on Fanny, swinging down the centre of a set with a youthful partner. 'I'd like to see my granddaughter settled,' went on the Duchess with a sigh. 'Pity she don't like young Cresswell. Shan't force her, of course.'

'Unwise to do so, ma'am. It could lead to great unhappiness on both sides. He has no wish to form an alliance with your granddaughter. He is merely following his mother's orders.'

'Fancies himself in love with you, don't he?'

Lexie laughed. 'Fancies is the word. He is poetically in love with love and I am a safe object of adoration. He has no wish to shackle himself in marriage.'

'No more do most young men, more's the pity. James patronisin' the card tables tonight?' demanded the Duchess with a sharp glance from her old eyes.

'I believe so.'

'Devilish lucky at cards. There are those who will be sorry to see him there. Pleased to see him dancin' attendance on you these last weeks. They say you're his mistress, but I don't believe 'em. Hasn't he declared himself yet?'

Now Lexie's face positively flamed. 'He has made it most plain that he has no thought of marriage,' she informed his grandmother tartly. 'We remain friends, nothing more.'

'Humph,' said the Duchess, snapping shut her fan. 'D'y'think I'm blind, young woman? He's after you and you're holding him off, although I'd wager you're not indifferent. Holdin' out for marriage, though. Aren't I right?'

Lexie drew a deep breath. 'He does not intend marriage,' she informed Storm's grandmother with rather more bitterness in her tone than she realised.

'Don't he, now?' muttered the old lady. 'Young fool.'

But she said no more. She had discovered all she wished to know, thought Lexie resentfully, and much good might it do her.

* * *

Some days later, following a habit equally as reprehensible as riding alone in Hyde Park, Lexie took her usual afternoon stroll round Berkeley Square. She found the solitary walk relaxing after a morning spent calling, receiving or shopping, and spent the hour before changing for dinner taking the air. The open, leafy Square, inhabited by friends and acquaintances, was an oasis of comparative calm amidst the crowded streets and mews surrounding it.

She felt quite safe walking beneath the trees and saw no reason to ask Chalker or a footman to accompany her, however correct such company would be. After the freedom Amber had allowed her in Cornwall, she resented the necessity to have someone shadow her all the time. The servants had more useful things to do than to walk behind a woman quite able to take care of herself.

It had been raining earlier and everything sparkled, fresh and clean, in the sunlight as Lexie left the shade of the trees to return to her house. Caro had gone to visit her friend and Lexie had no evening engagement that day so she had dismissed Chalker, telling her maid to take the evening off, and informed cook that she would send down for a tray as and when she became hungry. So there was no hurry and she had loitered rather longer than usual.

Someone was throwing a dinner party at an establishment at one end of the Square and carriages were rumbling up to the door as Lexie strolled back towards Bruton Street. When a coach clattered to a halt beside her, she barely looked up until a voice hailed her.

'Lady Amber? His lordship is asking for you, my lady. Pray come at once!'

Lexie looked at the coach, expensive but plain, no crest on the door to identify the owner.

'His lordship?' she demanded of the man—a servant, evidently—who had accosted her.

The man bowed with perfect deference. 'The Marquess of Stormaston, my lady. I am Marlow, his lordship's valet. He sent me with a most urgent request—'

'Is he ill?' demanded Lexie, sudden anxiety in her voice. She did not know what to make of this sudden, most unusual and rather improper request. A lady did not visit a gentleman's rooms unaccompanied, for whatever reason.

'He was most insistent in his orders to me, my lady,' urged Marlow without directly answering her question. 'He instructed me to bring you to him without delay. He has been in low spirits recently, ma'am,' went on Marlow less formally. 'I quite despair of bringing him about without your help.'

Storm in low spirits indeed! He had seemed abstracted and subdued at the theatre last evening, but she had thought his mood due to the indifference of the acting. Even if this duel between them was affecting him as much as it was her, she could see no purpose in rushing to his succour. Only one thing would cure him of his megrim, and she had no intention of supplying it.

Undecided, Lexie eyed the valet. She saw a man of medium height and middle age, impeccably attired and very correct in his manner. Storm often mentioned his man, Marlow. And, when she looked more closely, she recognised the Marquess's coachman mounted on the box. The man acknowledged her by smiling and touching his hat with his whip.

They would probably do whatever the Marquess told them. But the coachman's presence was reassuring. 'Very well,' she told Marlow. 'I will return to inform my staff of my absence and find a footman to accompany me.'

She turned towards Bruton Street, but Marlow's voice stopped her. He placed a strong but deferential hand on her arm. 'There is no need, my lady. You will not be away long and his lordship was most particular that I take every care of you. Will you not allow me to help you into the coach?'

The thoughts raced round in Lexie's head. She knew this must be the Marquess's coach, however incognito, for these were indubitably his servants, though the horses harnessed to it were a lesser team that she did not recognise. He would not send his four famous matched bays if he did not wish to advertise the ownership of the coach—they were too well known. Why he should send for her she could not fathom, but he would not wish to put her reputation at risk by sending for her openly.

Her curiosity was aroused. He might truly need her presence for some reason but if it were some hoax he was perpetrating upon her, then she would simply enjoy the joke, walk out and take a hackney back to Bruton Street. St James's Street was not far away. Real uneasiness had left her with the realisation that these men really were Storm's servants. She still believed that he meant her no harm. She would be, in all essentials, perfectly safe with him. Besides, she wanted to know what he was at.

Coming to her decision, Lexie stepped towards the coach, wondering at the same time what Marlow would do if she refused. Would he force her inside? She did not feel disposed to put that question to the test. 'If his lordship truly needs my presence, for whatever mysterious reason, then I will come with you,' she told him, mounting the step.

Marlow shut the door, raised the step and joined the coachman on the box. The carriage, a comfortably sprung, beautifully upholstered vehicle, moved off. Lexie sank back into a corner, tense, nervous, excited and strangely exultant. Perhaps the weeks of tension and waiting were over at last. Storm was making his move.

What a tease he was! She could not believe he was ill. Marlow had not said so. This was part of his campaign to seduce her, of that she was becoming more certain every moment. And the moments were passing. They should have arrived by now.

Suddenly anxious, Lexie sat up and looked out of the window. The coach was moving fast, threading its way through the traffic with speed and expertise, for the coachman was excellent at his job. But they were not headed for St James's Street. She did not recognise the area at all at first and when she did, she did so with dismay. Covent Garden. Not far from Drury Lane. Where was she being taken?

She tried banging on the roof of the coach, but her urgent rapping brought no results. Perhaps they hadn't heard, she had only her knuckles and the roof was padded on the inside. But she doubted they would have stopped even if they had heard.

Not until they reached a respectable back street did

the coach pull up, stopping outside a freshly painted door, which opened from the inside at their approach. Marlow jumped down, let down the step and opened the door for her.

'I will take you to his lordship, my lady. He is inside,' he informed her, his face completely inscrutable.

Lexie, trying to look as though she had known all along where they were bringing her, nodded and stepped with dignity towards the open door.

'Thank you, Marlow,' she said as she entered what could only be the flat where the Marquess kept his mistresses.

CHAPTER SEVEN

WHOEVER had opened the door had disappeared by
the time Lexie entered. Marlow led her up a narrow
staircase to a flat which must be over the draper's shop
beside the front door. A small vestibule led through to
a large, well appointed room containing an upholstered
settee, several chairs of varying design, a *chaise-longue*,
a collection of small tables holding various objects, a
glass-fronted cupboard displaying pieces of ornamental
china, a whatnot, and a writing table upon which sat a
dainty pen and inkstand filled with quills and ink.
Expensive rugs covered the floor and striped drapes
dressed the windows.

Altogether a charming, feminine apartment, thought
Lexie, cosy in winter when the fire was lit, but quite
lacking in any trace of masculine occupation. Storm
could not spend much time here. He must simply make
brief visits to an available woman.

Gall rose in her throat. How dared he bring her to
this place? For there could be no doubt that this was
the flat so recently occupied by that Hermione woman,
the actress he had been keeping as his mistress.

And where was he? She turned to ask Marlow, but
he had withdrawn. She was about to investigate further
when, beneath the window, she heard the rattle of
carriage wheels, the clatter of horses' hooves on the
cobbles. She looked out and drew a quite audible

breath of distress, for she saw the carriage which had brought her disappearing round the nearest corner.

She heard a deep chuckle behind her. 'So you came. I thought you would be unable to resist the challenge, my dear,' came the familiar drawling voice.

Lexie spun round.

'The carriage!' was all she could gasp as she looked into devilish blue eyes sparkling with mischief and something more, which seemed to wrap her in heat.

'Do not disturb yourself, my love.' His voice came soothing, gentle. 'Grimshaw will return to convey you home when called.'

Lexie met the flare in those eyes, the eyes of the rake she knew him to be, and called upon all her strength to resist him.

'Why did you send for me? Why bring me here?' she demanded fiercely—for anger was her only defence—before noticing that his lordship's bare legs could be glimpsed beneath a long dressing robe of maroon satin with black lapels and girdle. Despite her resolution, her voice faltered as doubt crept into her mind. 'Are you unwell, as Marlow implied? Have you been confined to bed?'

'By no means,' said Storm with a predatory smile.

Lexie swallowed. They might well have been back in Vauxhall except that here she felt completely vulnerable. If only the correct, teasing yet perfect gentleman who had squired her to so many functions recently would reappear! This devilish male creature she did not trust an inch.

'He said you needed me,' she said faintly. He was coming nearer, his intention more plain with every step he took. She backed away, exclaiming, 'I suspected the summons was a ruse! How dared you send for me in that underhand way, sir!'

'Yet you came!' His grin was wolfish. 'And I do need you, my lady,' he returned plaintively. 'I have needed you in my bed this age. And you, and I mistake not,' he went on seductively, 'entertain a desire to be there.'

Lexie, his heat suffusing her body, longing to throw herself into his arms, clenched her fingers into fists. She must resist him! 'You are impertinent, sir!'

His dark brows lifted above those all-seeing, flaring blue eyes. 'Is it now impertinent to speak the truth? Lexie, my love, stop prevaricating. You are no green girl but an experienced woman. We want each other. What is to stop us indulging our desire?'

'I am not your love!' gulped Lexie.

'Through no fault of mine,' he pointed out reasonably.

Lexie ploughed on, ignoring his words. 'A matter of right and wrong must stop us, sir! I possess morals, even if you do not!' She began to tremble as he reached out to pull her towards him. 'We are not wed! Any union between us would be a sin!'

His voice caressed her as his fingers kneaded her shoulders in a soothing rhythm. 'You believe it would take a few words intoned over us by a parson to make expressing the feelings between us legal?'

'The Church and Society—' began Lexie desperately.

'May pronounce disapproval, but cannot make the deed wrong. Any more than they can, in my opinion, make the compelled union of two completely incompatible persons right. What of a bride forced to endure the attentions of a man she loathes? Do the parson's words make that morally right?'

'They have been married before God,' uttered Lexie faintly, resting her hands, partly in protest, partly in surrender, against his broad chest, for at last he held her close and was busy removing her bonnet. 'A husband has rights his wife cannot deny.'

Storm smothered an expletive. 'There lies your sin! No woman should be coerced into a marriage where such a possibility exists,' he opined forcefully. 'Married before God or not, the joining of a man and a woman should be a matter of desire between them.'

In her heart, Lexie knew he was right. She should never have had to endure the attentions of Amber, kind and considerate as he had been. It had been like going to bed with her grandfather. She shuddered at the memory and felt Storm's arms tighten about her. Yet she could not have refused her husband, he had had the legal right to use her body as he willed. And, in fairness, she had, however reluctantly, chosen to wed him. No one had thrashed or starved her into submission.

'What is it, my dear?'

The gentle concern in his voice told her he had not mistaken her shudder for either desire or revulsion. He was experienced enough to recognise desire and of one thing at least he could be certain: he did not repulse her!

'Nothing,' she lied. 'But, Storm, I cannot agree to what you wish.'

'Can you not?' he murmured in teasing tones as he swept her into his arms.

His movements had loosened the girdle about his

waist and the silk of his robe slipped apart. Lexie's breath caught at sight of the muscles revealed, the dusting of dark hair giving him an appearance of virility Amber had lacked. His sparse hair had been grey. She had had no desire to explore his old body but he had taught her where he liked to be touched and, to please him, she had complied.

Of its own volition her hand reached out to feel the roughness of Storm's body hair; her finger sought the nipple it only partly concealed.

At her touch, Storm sucked in his breath as he carried her through to the bedchamber. She heard the heart beneath her ear begin to hammer and snatched her hand away. This would would never do!

As he set her on her feet again, she vaguely took in a vast bed hung with creamy silken drapes, a large kidney-shaped dressing table with triple mirrors and matching hangings, frilly curtains and a full-length cheval mirror. Then Storm's fingers began to remove her gown with the expertise of someone quite used to undressing a woman.

She should stop him but her will had fled with the strength in her limbs. Dear God, why did his touch have such a devastating effect upon her? He hadn't even kissed her yet and she was like clay in his hands!

Her gown dropped to the floor and Storm flung off his robe to reveal the full glory of his strong, beautiful, roused body. After that she had eyes for nothing else but him as he followed her down on the bed and began to loosen the ties of her chemise.

When he was like this, tender, teasing, yet betraying controlled passion, she could deny him nothing! Her body opened, rose instinctively to meet his. But even as he lifted himself above her she caught a breath of unfamiliar perfume still lingering in the drapes of the bed.

That woman's!

What was she thinking of! She could not, simply could not make love with Storm in this bed, in the flat where he had entertained his other women!

'No!' she gasped, pushing at his chest, struggling to release herself from beneath him. 'No, Storm! I am not one of your lightskirts, to be taken in your love-nest like some cheap actress! Do not force me!'

For an instant Storm did not move, held still while he controlled his breathing. Then he lifted himself from her and, back turned, flung on his discarded robe.

'I have never yet had need to force a woman, madam,' he informed her icily, frustration clipping his words in a totally unfamiliar way. 'I am persuaded that I shall survive well enough without the gift of your valuable favours.'

In her distress Lexie fumbled to fasten her chemise, bent to rescue her gown, tried to find the opening, the sleeves, to pull it over her head. It was so long since she had dressed herself! His words brought her efforts to a trembling halt.

She had lost him now! 'Oh,' she cried. 'Are you so without feeling that you cannot understand, Storm? Or are your desires the only things that matter to you? Your morals the only ones you can comprehend?'

The tears began to stream down her face unheeded as she at last managed to insert her arms into her gown and attempted to reach the fastenings down the back.

'I certainly cannot—'

'You have no finer feelings at all! To mortify me so

by bringing me here, to this place where you have kept your cheap women!'

Storm frowned and, for the first time, looked slightly less than self-assured. 'Most were far from cheap,' he muttered wryly, then added, 'My dear Lexie, I merely sought to preserve your reputation. Here, you are unlikely to be recognised. I considered it a safe place for our tryst.'

'Tryst!' almost screamed Lexie, scrubbing at the tears she had previously ignored. How could she be so weak as to let him see how much he had hurt her! 'This was no tryst! Abduction would be a better description of the means you used to lure me here! I had not agreed to meet you! But Marlow was persuasive, I thought he was escorting me to St James's—'

'Had he done so your reputation would have been in shreds!' pointed out Storm coldly. 'No lady walks or drives down that street with impunity! Did you think me so shabby as to lay you open to abuse by every gabble-grinder in London?'

'I did not think,' admitted Lexie more calmly. 'But that does not excuse you for bringing me here and attempting to seduce me when I have rejected your *carte blanche*! And now, if you please, call Grimshaw to return me to my home!'

Storm had pulled on pantaloons beneath his gown. Now he removed it to don a shirt, which he tucked in at the waist but left unfastened. No doubt Marlow would dress him properly before he departed. Lexie only hoped that she looked respectable enough not to cause undue comment when she reached Bruton Street. She still had not fastened her bodice, and her hair must look a terrible mess.

Unexpectedly, Storm smiled, and led the way through to the sitting-room. Lexie, glad to escape the close proximity of that bed, quickly followed. Storm handed her her bonnet.

'Since I was so remiss as to remove your gown, allow me to fasten it for you, madam.'

His nimble fingers at her back shook Lexie to the core. Oh, why could he not woo her respectably?

Storm noted her quick breathing, the fluttering pulse in her neck, the feverish light in her eyes, and cursed her scruples. He could not resist the gentle kiss he placed in the sweet curve of her neck but regretted his impulse the moment he felt her whole body stiffen.

Secretly he honoured her for her principles. Society was loose in its morality, few members of the *ton* being quite the whited sepulchres they pretended. From the Prince Regent down, men and women indulged in numerous *affaires*; few behaved in private with the decorum they enjoined in public. Those noted Patronesses of Almack's, Lady Jersey and Lady Cowper, both had lovers. But then, like so many others, they had been married to men they did not love for dynastic and financial reasons.

He had, following his own code, always avoided such a marriage. He would demand faithfulness in a wife. Whether he would be able to return the compliment he rather doubted. He could not imagine the woman able to satisfy him for the remainder of his life.

He finished his task, lifted Lexie's chin with gentle fingers and brushed her lips with his own. And then startled both himself and her by saying, 'I apologise for my treatment of you, Lexie, my dear. I should have realised how sincerely you meant your refusal at

Vauxhall. But please do not run away so soon. Marlow is an excellent cook and is preparing our repast. Will you not remain and enjoy it?'

Seeing her shaken, almost fearful look, hand on heart he added hastily and sincerely, 'I promise to behave!' And smiled his most wicked, teasing smile.

An apology and an olive branch. Lexie's heart melted. He could be both wicked and generous. That must be how he managed to seduce so many women to his bidding. Instinctively, she had known he would never truly harm her, never force her against her will. Otherwise she would not have entered his coach.

Surely she could be as generous, accept his apology and forgive his treatment of her? Apart from her own inclination to fall into his arms and forget scruples, the world, and every responsibility, she would be safe. And she was quite capable of resisting her own emotions. She had already proved that.

So, 'Very well,' she accepted. 'I must confess to being sharp set and whatever it is that Marlow is preparing smells delicious. Thank you, Storm. I will stay a while, although I could never feel truly comfortable here in this place. But I must be back before Caro and Chalker return, so that I am not missed.'

He nodded and moved to pour her a glass of sherry. As he handed it to her he said, 'I intended to return you in good time.'

Lexie accepted the glass while giving him a fleeting, suspicious glance before hurriedly averting her eyes. She did not trust herself to look too long on the magnificent physique displayed beneath that open shirt without weakening. His garb was quite indecent but so alluring. She suppressed a smile. Rakish, in fact. 'You knew they would both be absent this evening?'

'And that you had no engagement. That you often walked in Berkeley Square before dressing for dinner, I already knew. Cousin Caro informed me of hers and your maid's plans while I was waiting for you yesterday. The opportunity to lure you here seemed too good to miss. I fell into temptation,' he confessed with a wry smile, a lift of one dark brow, and overdone contrition.

Lexie thought the best thing to do was to laugh. 'You almost made me fall, too, my lord!' She drank some of the wine, which seemed to loosen her tongue. 'I would not have come had I not trusted you, in the end, to behave as a gentleman should.'

'I am flattered. You do not, then, entirely believe in my reputation as a rakehell?'

Lexie smiled. 'I believe that in public you hide behind a mask, my lord. In private, I have often glimpsed the essential gentleman concealed beneath. Besides, your grandmother would not be so fond of you were you as bad as you are sometimes painted.'

He regarded her quizzically. 'And that is why you consented to my escort, despite the gossip our constant appearances in public together has generated?' She nodded and he went on, 'Were my intentions known to be honourable, we would already be as good as betrothed. Since they are extremely suspect, you must, in their opinion, undoubtedly be my mistress.'

'I know, but gossip without foundation has little sting. Were it to be known that I had been here, even though nothing dishonourable has actually happened, I would be branded a harlot.' She met his eyes boldly.

'My chances of contracting a felicitous marriage to an honourable gentleman would be quite gone.'

'Do you wish for marriage again?' asked Storm interestedly.

Lexie drank the last of her sherry and then studied the glass in her hand with a slight frown. 'Yes,' she answered honestly. 'But only wed to a man who can be lover, companion and friend. I should like,' she added wistfully, 'to fall in love. If I do not find such a creature, then I shall be content to remain a widow. I have my freedom and sufficient means. I will not surrender those precious things merely in order to satisfy my longing for a family.'

She had, she realised too late, opened her heart to him. And he had made no reply. She risked a quick glance and saw that his brow was now marred by a slight frown. His lazy lids covered his eyes and his studied air of casual, indolent ease had been replaced by one of concentration. She wondered what he could be thinking.

He was wondering, in truth, why he did not propose matrimony there and then. And knew it was because he could not risk hurting such a jewel as Alexia Hamilton by the transgressions he would undoubtedly perpetrate at some later date. She would expect, nay, demand, fidelity, which he could not offer. So he would offer nothing.

He was saved the trouble of answering her by the timely entry of Marlow to announce that dinner was ready to be served.

'Bring it in!' ordered Storm, relaxing again. 'Lady Alexia, will you sit here?'

As Lexie took her place at the small, intimate table

laid for two, she thought how wonderful it would be if only they could live like this, without ceremony, sharing the intimacy of companionship, friendship—and love.

But Storm had not reacted to her indiscretion save by that slight frown of concentration. And as the meal progressed and the atmosphere became easy she forgot everything else in the joy of sharing the company of so entertaining, considerate a companion.

With Storm on his very best behaviour—apart from the occasional glance from desirous eyes—she even managed to forget the real reason for her being there and the past history of the cosy flat. Only when, the platters empty, Storm called Marlow to summon the carriage, was the true nature of her presence brought home to her again.

Then she could not leave fast enough. But, it seemed, he was still escorting her to the theatre the following evening.

'We must not feed the gabble-grinders more grist to their mill,' he remarked calmly. 'I shall continue to escort you to those functions you choose to attend.'

Nothing had changed. Except that everything had changed.

She was hopelessly in love and did not know how she was to bear his constant attendance on her without giving herself away.

Lexie thought and thought. Somehow, the deadlock between them must be broken. It was, after all, mostly convention that coloured her morality and prevented her from casting prudence to the winds and agreeing to his offered *carte blanche*. That and an instinctive desire to know the man she loved would be hers for life. A mistress could be cast off at any moment. A wife could not so easily be set aside.

She saw rather less of Storm over the next week, since she chose to accept fewer invitations. When he did escort her he behaved with punctilious correctness, his languid manner and drawling speech never more in evidence. He had withdrawn behind his mask. Lexie ached to penetrate it again.

But Prinny's festivities were a must and Storm was taking her in his curricle, with his tiger up behind to act as chaperon. Caro, frightened of crowds, refused to be cajoled into accompanying them.

'It is high time his lordship declared himself,' she grumbled, fluttering her fan, for the weather was sultry. 'You have allowed him to make a spectacle of you all the Season, Alexia,' she went on querulously, 'and soon, no doubt he will retire to his estates and forget all about you! You have not made the most of your chances, my dear.' Caro, who had been quite won over by the Marquess's charm, added, with a languishing sigh, 'I always mistrusted the wisdom of your association with that rake.'

Lexie spread her hands, mischief lighting her features despite her broken heart. 'Confess, you have always wished you were in my shoes, Caro! He is not so very bad a rake, after all. He is too much of a gentleman.'

'But he has compromised you without being honourable enough to offer for you, it seems! Despite his reputation, he would make you a fine husband, Alexia. Can you do nothing to bring him to the point?'

Assiduously studying a slightly ragged nail, 'It seems

not, Cousin,' said Lexie. 'Always assuming I have tried.'

'You are no more than a foolish chit if you have not! Your reputation is almost in shreds. . .'

Caro's indignant censure amused rather than offended Lexie. She looked up and grinned. 'Do not concern yourself over me. We are still received in the most austere of drawing-rooms!'

'But if his lordship casts you off—'

'Stop prating, Cousin! I am used to being the object of the latest *on dits*. We shall be retiring to Merryfield next week and people will soon forget the scandals of the Season. My present aberrations will be history by next year.'

'Unless you return to London and continue with your rackety ways. Then the gossip will start all over again,' wailed Caro.

'It scarcely affects you, Cousin, so do not refine over it,' said Lexie tartly. Caro's lamentations were chafing her raw nerves. 'Think of Merryfield and how much we shall enjoy the fresh country air!'

Thinking of Merryfield, an idea entered her head, so bold and outrageous that for a moment it stopped her breath. She had been recalling the pleasure of driving Pitch and Tar around the estate roads, racing them as she had been used to do in Cornwall. And an audacious plan formed in her mind.

'The Duke of Wellington is leaving Town soon, to take up his post as Ambassador in Paris. Once he has gone, London will empty. We will hold a house party of our own,' she declared with sudden decision. 'In fact, Caro, it would be most beneficial if you were to go on ahead to consult with Mrs Panning, open up the house and prepare it for the guests. Mrs Walker and Mr Dymock will accompany me down, and as many of the staff as you think necessary.'

The plan had an added advantage. She could well do without Cousin Caro's fussing and refining over her while she remained in Town herself.

'How many guests did you have in mind?' asked Caro, her eyes beginning to gleam, all cares forgotten in anticipation of this new enterprise. She would be in her element at Merryfield planning a house party.

'I don't know,' admitted Lexie slowly. 'I must make a list of those I wish to invite and then send out the invitations. As soon as possible, I should think, so that our guests may travel straight down.'

'Will they not have already planned to go to Brighton or Eastbourne for sea bathing or to Bath to take the waters?' objected Caro anxiously.

'Not those I would wish to invite, I think,' said Lexie thoughtfully. She had heard no mention of the Duchess doing anything other than returning straight to her husband and the Downshire estates in Kent, taking Fanny with her.

Storm, she knew, would make speedy tracks for Stormaston House, his favourite residence, which he spoke of with real affection but which she had yet to see. An invitation for her to go there would give her so much delight... But he would never be so foolish as to invite her to his home unless...

She cut her daydreams short as a waste of time and emotional energy. Her own plans had to be laid.

For propriety's sake, she would have to include a few others, of course, the Duke for one, whom she had never met, though she doubted he would be persuaded to come. Storm's friend, Felix St Clare, who had become her own dear friend must be asked, for Fanny's sake, if for no other, for Lexie was quite certain they were fond of each other.

Oswald Cresswell, too, whom she rather liked and felt sorry for. His boyish devotion acted as an antidote to Storm's aggressive, sexual pursuit. She could bask in the young man's adoration without fear of any untoward consequences. But what about his mother?

She did not, for Fanny's sake, want the Viscountess there to bully her son into pursuing a lost cause. Lady Wighton might allow her son to come alone. She would try to arrange it, for his sake. He needed to escape his mother's leading strings.

There was a girl, one of those who had been at Vauxhall, what was her name? Melissa Daventry, that was it. Miss Daventry cherished a *tendre* for Oswald and would gladly come if she knew he was to be there. She would bring her duenna, of course. They would all bring servants. Merryfield would be full of life and laughter for the first time since she had inherited it.

Excitement surged through Lexie. She would make her list but she would not issue the invitations until after the Centenary celebrations. For it was during those that she intended to make her bid to engage the Marquess of Stormaston, that acknowledged gamester, who would bet on the most ridiculous of things if challenged, in a wager that would settle the matter of her future status in his life.

She could not allow things to go on as they were. She would end up a diminished wreck. Her gowns were already hanging loosely upon her. She must settle matters once and for all and then set about living contentedly, whatever the result.

She dressed carefully for the great day, choosing a becoming outfit in the latest fashion comprising a sky blue petticoat with braces, worn over a white spencer—ideal for walking in the summer heat. A large bonnet with matching ribbons tied under her chin covered most of her golden curls. Half-boots completed her toilet, for the ground was bound to be somewhat damp and she anticipated leaving the curricle to enjoy the promised spectacles.

'You look a perfect picture!' exclaimed Caro as Lexie presented herself for inspection, flourishing a matching parasol. 'But isn't the waist of your gown a little low?'

'Waistlines have been dropping for several years, Cousin. You,' teased Lexie, eyeing her companion's sprigged muslin and accompanying drapes affectionately, 'are old fashioned!'

'I am too old to change my style now,' fluttered Caro anxiously. 'Do you think I should?'

'Not at all,' assured Lexie. 'You have no one but yourself to please.'

'Thank goodness the morning rain has stopped. Do have a nice time, dear,' said Caro. 'I am so glad you have the protection of a gentleman. You will need it amongst all those crowds.'

Lexie, remembering a previous time when she had ventured alone into the crowds and been rescued by Storm, could do nothing but agree. It was so infinitely reassuring to be able to rely upon his strength. But today, win or lose, her dice must be thrown. He would agree to her proposition or he would not. If he did, Caro could be despatched to Merryfield on the morrow and there, she herself would have one final chance to fulfil her dearest wish, to win him as her husband.

He knew now that she would not respond to any illicit advances on his part and so she felt secure in accepting only his tiger, Bill Trappin, as chaperon. Of course, the tiger's presence would be a mere gesture toward the proprieties, but that no longer concerned her. They were to join friends by the Serpentine and her entire day would be coloured by finding the right opportunity to lay down her wager.

Storm was dressed as though for riding, in buff pantaloons and shining hessians topped by a snuff-coloured jacket. A large, reassuring umbrella reposed behind the seat of the curricle with the basket of food she had anticipated, for they did not intend to return before darkness fell.

'In case the rain returns,' explained Storm with a grin.

'I do hope it does not! Just think of all these crowds getting soaked!' said Lexie, eyeing the orderly throng spreading over the grass of Hyde Park as they entered the gates, having avoided the congestion in Piccadilly and elsewhere.

Storm was forced to drive slowly and carefully, threading his way through the crowds of pedestrians as well as other carriages and the many equestrians. People milled everywhere: eating their food, climbing trees, patronising the many gaming, drinking and other entertainment booths erected on the grass.

Lexie eyed his matched, almost pure white greys with a critical eye. She could not fault them. Mettlesome, reputedly prime goers, Storm had won a number of curricle races with them put to. But Pitch and Tar were equally fine cattle. She knew how fast they could travel, knew her own ability to drive them to an inch. Yes, win or lose, it would be worth the risk.

Before long they had to abandon the curricle.

'I fear we must walk from here,' apologised Storm, swinging himself to the ground. Trappin ran to the horses' heads and Storm assisted Lexie to descend. His hands on her waist were firm and warm. She shivered. 'Trappin,' went on Storm, 'I trust you to return my cattle safely to their stables. After that, you may take the rest of the day off.'

'But your hamper, my lord!' cried Trappin, scandalised at the idea of his master demeaning himself by carrying it himself.

'I'm sure this boy will be only too pleased to carry it and the umbrella down to the Serpentine,' said Storm, picking up his silver-mounted stick and beckoning the child towards him. 'Will you not, my lad?'

'Do anyfink fer a tanner, yer lordship!' grinned the cheeky youngster.

'A tanner it shall be.'

Lexie saw the boy's grin, a response to Storm's easy manner. Most of the nobility assumed a lofty air when dealing with inferiors. But not Storm.

When they finally reached the water's edge and found their friends, Storm paid off the lad, leaving the impedimenta with the others' servants.

While he was engaged in making these arrangements, Lexie, having greeted the other members of their party, stared wide-eyed at the display on the water. The Serpentine had become an ocean on which sailed a fleet of miniature ships of the line, from three-deckers with up to seventy guns protruding from their ports, to lightly armed, graceful, fast-sailing frigates, all fully rigged.

'Just one of the Regent's grand flights of fancy. A representation of the battle of the Nile. An awesome sight were they real and not ships' barges dressed up!' came Storm's comment from her side.

'I saw such a fleet once, off Cornwall. Distant, of course, sailing for Plymouth or Portsmouth, I suppose. But at the time it appeared a reassuring sight.'

'Returning from blockade duty off Brest, I dare say,' said Storm, offering his sleeve. 'Shall we stroll along the bank?'

'Oh, yes, do let us!' cried Fanny, overhearing. 'Come, Lord Dexter, Mr Cresswell! Do join us!'

Unable to evade the unwelcome company, Storm accepted the situation with grace.

'Miss Daventry!' called Lexie. 'Will you not walk with us?'

Melissa Daventry accepted with confused alacrity.

Lexie found herself walking with Felix while Storm, swinging his stick, escorted Melissa, leaving Fanny and Oswald to accompany each other. But conversation was general and partners quickly changed, more than once. Lexie had no opportunity for private converse with Storm.

The afternoon progressed. They ate their refreshments sitting on horse blankets on the damp ground before walking through to St James's Park, hung even by day with coloured lanterns, to find a band playing so that the populace could dance. A huge Chinese bridge and a pagoda, seven storeys high, lit by gas, caused astonished interest and admiration.

After a while, 'You are, I collect, able to walk back?' asked Storm of the company in general. He had, with natural authority, assumed command of the expedition. 'The sun has already almost set. We should make our way through to Green Park if we want to see the climax to the day's events. It is there that the Regent has really excelled himself.'

The rather large party had, before its arrival before Buckingham House, split into several smaller groups, each attended by chaperons and servants. Storm and his immediate party arrived in time to see a hot-air balloon ascend from the platform especially built for it. The Regent and his guests were watching from the Royal Pavilion erected for the purpose but, 'We can see better from here!' cried Lexie.

Up the balloon majestically soared, dropping coloured parachutes, weighted at the bottom, which floated down amongst the happy, cheering throng. The balloon drifted off and was presently lost to sight.

'It will land safely, won't it?' asked Fanny anxiously.

'One can only hope so,' said Felix, giving her arm a reassuring squeeze, which brought a blush to Fanny's cheeks.

'But look!' cried Lexie. 'Just look at that castle!'

'I am told it is one hundred and thirty feet high,' said Storm dryly. 'It is symbolic, you know, a Castle of Discord and a Temple of Peace. The Prince designed most of it himself.'

'I am quite looking forward to the staging of the storming of Badajoz!'

'You sound quite bloodthirsty for a poet,' Lexie

teased Oswald. His mother had not come. This seemed to be one of those rare occasions when the young people were allowed to play without much attempt to chaperon them. Fanny's maid and Melissa's duenna had accompanied them, ready to intervene but otherwise keeping well in the background.

'Poems have been written about it!' protested Oswald, affronted.

'I wonder what His Grace the Duke of Wellington will think,' ventured Melissa shyly. 'I can see him sitting in the pavilion with the Prince.'

'He will consider the whole show to be in bad taste, I should imagine,' remarked Storm.

'Why?' demanded Lexie. 'The representation is put on in his honour!'

'But so many of the ordinary men who were the real heroes, those who survived, are now reduced to begging in the streets. Just like the veterans of the Nile. We do not treat our soldiers and sailors well once the need for their services is over.'

A momentary silence descended on the party. Not one of them had escaped the sight of poor, maimed wretches with their begging bowls. Even those discharged fit were often reduced to begging or crime to keep body and soul together. And Chelsea was full of still others waiting demobilisation, lounging about the streets reeling with drink or squatting on the steps of the public houses.

'Nelson tried to do something and Wellington will, too,' said Felix seriously. 'But remember, most of the ordinary soldiers and seamen were recruited from the gutter. It will be no change for them to return to it.'

'But after serving their country—' began Lexie, frowning, only to be cut off short by Fanny.

'Today is a day of rejoicing! Do not let us refine over problems we can do nothing about!'

'Well said, little sister,' drawled Storm. 'Leave such problems to those who have the power.'

Yet Lexie could detect an undercurrent of anger in his languid voice. She looked at him quickly and saw the emotion reflected in his eyes. 'You have a seat in the House of Lords,' she reminded him softly.

'But no wish to engage in national politics,' he returned, equally quietly. 'Running my estates efficiently and seeing to the welfare of my people is more than enough to keep me occupied.'

'They are starting!' cried Fanny excitedly.

A battery of Congreve's rockets fired into the air, lighting the sky before descending in sheets of fire. Maroons went off, mines exploded. Redcoats, their faces blackened, crept through the fast descending darkness with bayonets glinting. Men dressed as Frenchmen stood waving their arms on the battlements of the Castle of Discord. Over in Hyde Park four of the Nile ships burnt with vivid flame and black smoke, while the swans screeched in protest.

The show went on for an age and the party wondered what more the Regent could possibly offer, but the entertainment was designed to go on until midnight. As the hour arrived, a deafening explosion made everyone jump.

The canvas walls of the Castle of Discord lifted to reveal the Temple of Peace, with its mock columns, rainbows, vestal virgins and pictures painted on transparent silk depicting the Golden Age Restored.

Coloured lamps lit the scene, water flowed from the mouths of mock lions while fireworks shot skywards and guardsmen held aloft the Royal Standard where, earlier, the mock French soldiers had been seen. Peace had triumphed over war and destruction.

'A worthy sentiment,' murmured Storm.

'Oh, look! cried Melissa. 'Whatever can be causing that great blaze?'

Despite the distance, it was clear to see that something other than the ships on the Serpentine had caught fire. A sort of rumble rippled over the crowd, bringing the news that the Chinese Pagoda had gone up in flames. Most people seemed to think it was all part of the Regent's planned spectacular but Storm shook his head.

'I doubt it. I imagine the gas lamps have set it ablaze. But come, it is time we all returned home. Mr Cresswell, you will no doubt see that Lady Fanny, her maid and the Duchess's servants reach Downshire House safely. Felix, I leave the escorting of Miss Daventry and her chaperon to you.'

Murmurs of assent followed, though both Fanny and Melissa looked disappointed.

'I'm glad the Regent put on such a splendid show!' said Lexie stoutly as she and Storm detached themselves from the others in order to thread their way through the streets back to her residence. 'London has never known such a celebration! The crowds have enjoyed every minute of the day!'

'You have, I collect,' murmured Storm with an indulgent grin.

'Yes,' admitted Lexie. She had, in the end, quite

forgotten her need for a private word with Storm. 'Did you not enjoy it, too?'

'This kind of entertainment is not normal fare for rakes like Felix and me,' explained Storm.

'Then why did you agree to come?'

'Ah, now that is an excellent question. I came to offer you my escort. It is, after all, what I have been doing these past weeks. Felix, I believe, came to lend me his support. Normally, wild horses would not have dragged us to an extravaganza of this sort.'

'I do not believe you!' protested Lexie, seeing the twitch of his mobile mouth. 'You are bamming me! No one wished to miss the occasion!'

'Ah, but most of Society saw fit to watch from the comfort of a pavilion. To think,' he added self-right-eously, 'that I could have been enjoying the sights from the Royal Pavilion but for my promise to you!'

'Would you have gone?'

Storm shook his head, grinning ruefully. 'No. I have little liking for being confined on such an occasion.'

'You were strolling the streets when the Allied Sovereigns arrived,' remembered Lexie.

'So I was. At least we have that much in common. A sense of wishing to escape the confines of our milieu once in a while.'

'We have more than that in common,' said Lexie slowly. Now, surely, was her moment. She stopped, drawing him to a halt beside her. They had reached Piccadilly and one of the new gas lamps lit her earnest features as she gazed up into Storm's face. 'We both enjoy a challenge. I have a wager to offer you.'

CHAPTER EIGHT

'A WAGER?'

Storm's brows rose in surprise, as well they might, thought Lexie, almost losing her courage.

'Yes.'

Carriages rattled along the road, people swarmed past on foot, homeward bound. Hardly an appropriate place to hold the discussion yet, essentially, they were alone for the first time that day. Noises, odour, the presence of others, faded into the background as Lexie waited apprehensively for Storm's response.

'And what would the subject of this wager be?' Storm's tone was as languid as she had ever heard it and her heart sank still further in the direction of her half-boots.

'A curricle race.' Lexie dropped her hand from his arm. Why was she having so much difficulty in saying what she had to say, she wondered despairingly. What had seemed such a good idea in theory had become the least clever notion ever to enter her head.

'Between whom, may I ask?'

Lexie swallowed. 'Us.'

She watched a slow smile spread itself across Storm's face and inwardly cringed.

'You are challenging me to race my curricle against yours? Driven by yourself?'

Lexie's voice failed her. She nodded.

Storm leant negligently upon his stick. 'Indeed.' The

smile became a grin. 'You little hoyden. Do you seriously believe that you could beat me?'

'I would not suggest the wager if I did not,' protested Lexie hoarsely.

'Hmm. My accepting your challenge depends largely upon the stake. What did you have in mind?'

She was forced to clear her throat before she spoke. Her hands were damp with sweat. 'If you win, you win my outfit. My blacks and the curricle.'

'And if you should beat me?' He regarded her musingly. 'Since you have not mentioned them, I collect that you have no use for my match pair?'

'No.' Another swallow. 'No particular use.'

'Then what is it that I am to put at risk?'

Storm's bored tone did not match the intent expression in his eyes. Some emotions his mask was unable to hide. He was deeply interested in her reply.

'If I win, you agree to marry me.'

There, it was out. Lexie waited for him to burst into ribald laughter.

He did not. But the intentness in his gaze gave way to pained affront.

'You lose your horses and carriage or I lose my freedom, is that it?' At Lexie's timorous nod, he pursed his lips, stood up straight and swung his cane. 'That scarcely seems a fair wager to me. I have no more need of your horses than you have of mine.'

'Then I will stake their worth,' said Lexie desperately.

He shrugged a negligent shoulder. 'But I have no particular need of money, either.'

'Oh.' Lexie drooped. Her voice dripped disappointment. 'Then you do not accept the bet?'

'I have not yet decided.' Storm shifted his stance and waited for a crowd of merrymakers to pass. 'Tell me more. Where, for instance, is this proposed race to be run?'

'Around the estate paths at Merryfield.'

'Ah! You allow yourself an advantage, I collect.' *His* voice dripped cynicism.

Lexie fiddled nervously with the strings of her reticule. 'You could arrive several days before the race and familiarise yourself with the route.'

'What?' Storm swung his stick, leant against the lamp standard and infused his voice with shock. His eyes, however, held sheer, devilish hilarity. 'Reside with you at Merryfield? What would people say?'

Although Lexie knew he was only bamming her, she felt obliged to answer. 'There would be others there. Invited particularly to watch the race.'

'And to be privy to the nature of the wager?' enquired Storm interestedly.

'Well, no. They would think us racing for cash stakes.'

'You seem determined to have me leg-shackled, my dear.' He straightened up, reached out and flicked her chin with one long finger. 'I wonder why?'

Lexie clutched her reticule and parasol tightly with her sticky, gloved hands. He must not see them shaking. Or guess what was now the truth, that she loved him and longed for him to make love to her. So she admitted only her original reason for wishing to wed him. 'I should like a family and you need an heir. We deal well together. The match would be suitable.'

At this he took on a haughty demeanour. 'And you would become a Duchess in due course. And find yourself wed to a man of considerable wealth and influence. From your point of view I can well see the advantages, my love,' he asserted arrogantly. 'But for myself, they appear, forgive me for saying so, rather less obvious.'

'You say you want me,' uttered Lexie almost inaudibly, blushing a furious red which she hoped would not be noticed in the glare of the lamp. 'And I cannot come to you outside wedlock.'

But the gaslight which she hoped would conceal her blush sparked devilish fires in Storm's eyes.

'Rakes,' he informed her, still arrogant, 'do not *wed* the ladies they desire. They have no need. They wed a suitable young dimwit to bear them an heir.'

He sounded as though he found the idea distasteful. Lexie smiled grimly. 'And endure a lifetime of boredom.'

He settled himself back against the lamp standard, long legs crossed, a thoughtful expression replacing his former hauteur. 'Not necessarily. He need not endure much of her company. But you give me an idea,' he declared lazily. 'I offer you an alternative wager. If you should beat me, I will marry you.'

Lexie gasped, scarcely able to believe he had accepted such a stake until he went on, softly, mockingly, 'But should I win—an outcome which, I should warn you, I confidently expect—then you overcome your scruples and consent to become my mistress.'

Dead silence greeted his words. The bottom seemed to have fallen out of Lexie's stomach. Why, oh why, had she embarked upon this nonsensical plan? She might have guessed the Marquess would turn it to his own advantage! Now it had come down to his liberty against her virtue.

And she had no guarantee of winning, although she did know a thing or two about the tracks at Merryfield which he did not. She had driven along them at reckless speed during her lengthy sojourn there while waiting out her period of mourning and Pitch and Tar knew every rise, dip and turn.

But he was a noted whip, a nonpareil. She must have been mad to think she stood any chance against him! It had not mattered so desperately when all she stood to lose was her precious pair of blacks. But pride would not allow her to back out now.

'Very well,' she said, as firmly as she could make herself.

Storm grinned, reached into his pocket and brought forth a slim notebook and pencil.

'I always record my wagers and the stakes,' he announced, Lexie thought insultingly smugly, as he wrote down the terms. 'Time and route to be agreed later,' he murmured, signing with a flourish. 'Now if you will append your mark, Lady Amber. . .'

'My mark!' muttered Lexie scathingly as she accepted the book. She scrutinised what he had written and signed her name, deliberately and clearly, despite trembling fingers and a renewed sense of doom.

Storm inspected her signature, grinned wickedly as he observed, 'You write an excellent hand, my dear,' tucked the book away and courteously offered his arm. 'Shall we walk on? People will begin to notice us if we remain idling here too long.'

Lexie put her fingers on his sleeve, glad of the support offered. But the deed was done. All that remained now was to sort out the details. And run the race. And pay the price if she lost.

But that was something she preferred not to contemplate. It stirred too many mixed emotions. How deep did her convictions really run?

The rain and unprecedented traffic had conspired to mire Piccadilly's carriageway with a noxious sludge. They waited while a ragged lad swept a clear path for them to cross. Storm tossed him a penny and they proceeded towards Bruton Street.

'Did you have a date in mind for this event? he enquired. 'I cannot delay my return to Stormaston Park much longer. There is much to be done there.'

'I thought the house party should be gathered as soon as possible, so that people who accept may travel straight to Hertfordshire before returning to their own estates.'

Storm nodded. 'An excellent notion. And who, exactly, did you have it in mind to invite?'

'Your grandmother and sister and the Duke, too, if he will come. Lord Dexter, Mr Cresswell, and Miss Melissa Daventry will form the core. More or less our set. Merryfield is not a large house. I could not accommodate many more.'

'They should prove witnesses enough to the fairness of the race. Were I you I should not invite others, even if I had room to spare. Few ladies of breeding have in the past dared to embark upon such a scandalous enterprise as you contemplate. Curricle racing is the dangerous preserve of gentlemen. If knowledge of the wager becomes widely spread, your reputation will suffer another blow. It would be best not to invite any who would be likely to censure the endeavour.'

'The Duchess might, I suppose,' said Lexie uncertainly. 'But I do so want her to come.'

'Why?' demanded that lady's grandson with interest.

'Because she has been kind to me and I value her opinion,' explained Lexie, leaving out the fact that the Duchess's presence tended to moderate the Marquess's more extravagant behaviour and that she enjoyed observing the affection in which they obviously held each other.

'I would not like her to think I was behaving in a havey-cavey manner, hiding my intention from her. And the Duke must receive an invitation out of courtesy. I have never met him, you know.'

'Grandmama,' said Storm with a chuckle, 'will be much diverted at the prospect of such a race. Wild horses will not stop her from accepting your invitation.'

'You think so? Then I shall send it tomorrow!'

'But I doubt those same wild horses would drag my grandfather from the Downshire estates,' added the Marquess crushingly.

'I shall still invite him. Or would you rather he were not present to watch your defeat?' speculated Lexie mischievously.

'Outrageous wench!' uttered Storm, unable to suppress a chuckle at her audacity.

'The party will be invited to gather a week today, the eighth,' went on Lexie, unperturbed. 'And the race can be run on the tenth. The social calendar is fairly empty now that the victory celebrations and the centenary jubilee are in the past.'

The discussion had brought them to Bruton Street, where Storm escorted her up the steps of her town house. Luckily there were few about in this comparative backwater to observe the indecorum of Lady Amber arriving home at two in the morning, on foot, and quite alone apart from the dubious escort of the Marquess of Stormaston. Or to witness the speaking kiss he planted on her willing lips before he lifted the knocker and the door swung open.

As she lay sleepless in bed later that night Lexie again wondered why she had ever imagined Storm would accept such a one-sided wager.

She came to the conclusion that she had suppressed any doubts in her eagerness to find a way to bring him to an honourable declaration.

But if he won, he would surely not keep her to her side of the bargain. No gentleman would.

But Storm relished his role as a self-declared rake. If he did not forgive her her debt, she would have to overcome her scruples and honour it.

She dropped off to sleep with a smile curving the soft line of the lips he had so recently kissed.

The arrangements went smoothly. Caro was dispatched in the curricle with Pascoe, who received the news of the race with his usual dispassion.

'If you want the cattle in racing trim, my lady, I'll see that they have never been in better fettle. A week is not long to prepare them, but they are already fit and the journey into Hertfordshire will help with their endurance.'

'I stand to lose a substantial stake if I do not win, Jethro. If I fail because of my own lack of skill I shall not complain but to be let down by out-of-condition horses would appear inexcusable. Providing they can be brought up to prime condition in time, my pair should be able to hold their own against his lordship's, I think you'll agree?'

'His lordship's greys are fast, larger animals and heavier, but Pitch and Tar are fine little beasts, nimble and quick, sound in wind and limb. Round the estate tracks at Merryfield they should prove the most manageable.'

'And they are familiar with the terrain. Yes, Jethro, a win must be possible,' said Lexie, trying to convince herself as much as Jethro.

'I shall do my best to ensure it, my lady, you may rely on that.'

Lexie smiled affectionately. 'I know it, Jethro.' She often called her chief groom and coachman Jethro when they were alone, just as she called her maid Florence. 'And if I do win it will be thanks to your teaching me to drive, as well as your skill in training the horses. There will be a bonus for you, win or lose.'

Pascoe touched his forehead. 'Thank you, my lady. I hope the weather holds, for Mrs Baldwin will not like to get wet in the curricle.'

'If it rains she will have to ride in the old chaise, surrounded by her portmanteaux and bandboxes!'

'Travel in the curricle!' exclaimed Caro, upon learning her fate. 'I do declare, I never heard of such a thing!'

'On a fine day there can be no better way of travelling such a short distance! But if you wish, you may ride in the old coach with your luggage. . .'

Lexie left the threat of an uncomfortable, unsprung journey hanging, amused by Cousin Caro's horror at travelling in an open carriage. She herself much preferred it. She considered Caro privileged to be driven by Pascoe behind the blacks.

She would herself travel down to Merryfield at the weekend in her travelling chaise, her only carriage remaining in Town, which was why she could not spare it to transport Caro. Storm would be driving himself down in his curricle on the Sunday in order to have three clear days in which to familiarise himself with the route. Felix St Clare intended to accompany him on horseback. She must be there to receive them.

The acceptances arrived by messenger the following day. Only one snag arose concerning the arrangements. The Viscountess proved intransigent over allowing poor Oswald out of her sight for more than a few hours. She therefore had to be invited to join the party.

Lexie had only one evening engagement that week, a visit to the theatre with Storm, who had been asked by friends to share their box. She had been included in the party because of her known association with him, she supposed, for she did not know her hosts well.

The ladies sat in the front of the box with the gentlemen behind. Storm maintained an unusual silence throughout. In the intervals he appeared abstracted rather than languid. The play was not particularly enlivening and Lexie wondered why her hosts had chosen to patronise that particular theatre. The explanation came right at the end.

The leading lady, a dark beauty with flashing eyes whose appearance had been the only alleviation of an otherwise drab production, stepped forward, stared up into their box, sought out the figure of the Marquess sitting behind Lexie, gave him an elaborate curtsy and blew a kiss in his direction.

The lady next to Lexie began to titter.

'Your former doxy does not forget you, Stormaston!' chuckled their host.

'His women never do,' murmured another of the party.

Lexie sat frozen. Dignity and self-respect demanded that she give no sign of discomfort. She pinned a smile on her lips and stared down on the still bowing and curtsying figure.

So this was the woman who had been Storm's mistress! She possessed a faultless figure, an entrancing face and a captivating manner that Lexie knew she could never hope to equal. Yet Storm had dismissed the actress apparently without regret while he concentrated on his pursuit of her, Lexie.

He must tire of his women easily. He was a hunter. The chase was all. He would become bored with her once he had secured her as his prey.

'She would do well to behave with more dignity,' observed Storm lazily, adding, 'How could she have known that I was here?'

No one bothered to speculate. Lexie could feel the anger vibrating through Storm's body and her own growing suspicion was confirmed. They had been lured into a trap. She was supposed to create a scene. Storm was supposed to lose his self-possession. The summer would end on a highly entertaining note of scandal.

She turned to her hostess as the final curtain fell and the torches and candles blazed.

'Thank you for a pleasant evening, my lady,' she said, smiling thinly. 'Despite the poor production, I managed to enjoy the performance. I thank you for inviting me to join your party, but I fear I shall not be able to remain for supper. I have developed such a headache. Perhaps due to the putrid acting. Lord Stormaston, may we please leave now?'

Cries of shock and concern greeted her words although no one was taken in by her excuse. She gave Storm her most brilliant smile as she prepared to take his arm.

Storm made his formal devoirs, every inch the cool aristocrat. He expressed no thanks to his supposed friends for their hospitality, merely remarked that the evening had proved extraordinarily interesting.

Now that the die had been cast, the race arranged and the outcome, one way or the other, decided, they had managed to relax in each other's company again. In the privacy—for their final engagement in Town Lexie had dispensed with the services of a chaperon— and darkness of the coach his voice came to her.

'My most humble apologies, my lady. My mortification is such that I dare scarcely ask your forgiveness for exposing you to such an unpleasant episode. Even when I recognised Hermione Green on stage I did not imagine. . . The thing was arranged, of course, for the titillation of those I had considered my friends. Hermione had been bribed, I have no doubt. Left to herself she would not have thought. . . She needed no revenge. She left me possessed of a substantial settlement.'

This quietly desperate, abject gentleman was not the Storm she knew! Impulsively, Lexie turned to him and laid a hand on his sleeve.

'It was not your fault, my dear. How could you have supposed anyone would stoop—?'

Despite his humiliation, Storm's heart leapt at the

endearment. She had not taken offence. There must be a chance to win her willing surrender, whatever the outcome of that damned race. He hurried to interrupt. 'I should know the *ton* by now. God knows, I have had enough experience. I should have checked the playbill before accepting the invitation. Had I known Hermione Green was in the play I would not have accepted.'

'Storm—'

'You were perfect in your dignified behaviour, my dear.' He had taken both her hands into his own and drawn her closer. 'You gave them no cause to gossip over the affair. Anything they may say will be quickly forgotten.'

'Storm—'

In his agitation he cut her off again. 'For myself, I do not care. But that they could treat you so shabbily—'

'Perhaps, by indulging in rash behaviour I asked for such treatment,' said Lexie honestly. 'My dear Storm, we are both used to being the subject of gossip. There is nothing for me to forgive.'

He drew a shuddering breath and pulled her to him. In an instant she was in his arms, his mouth had found hers and she lost all sense of time. The sound of the coachman's voice addressing the horses, the screech of the brake, the jerk as the carriage came to rest, brought them both back to reality.

'Now I have something else to apologise for,' muttered Storm.

Lexie withdrew from his arms reluctantly. 'Apologise? You, my dear?' She laughed, albeit a little shakily. 'No rake apologises for kissing a woman, given the opportunity.'

Footmen carrying flambeaux hurried down the steps to open the door. Lexie saw the wry smile which accompanied his response. 'Neither does he, my dear. God's blessings until Sunday, at Merryfield.'

'Until Sunday,' echoed Lexie as she left the coach. She did not question the cause of his not accompanying her indoors. After that kiss, any further exchange between them could only prove an anticlimax.

Merryfield Manor nestled in the Hertfordshire countryside, the colour of its slate roof and mellow brick walls ever changing as the clouds scudded overhead. The original manor house had been built in Tudor times and beams still laced the brickwork in the oldest parts. The wings, added on over several later ages, reflected the times in which they had been built yet managed to tie in together to present a harmonious whole.

Lexie loved it. This was home as she had never known it before, her domain to order as she willed, to enjoy at leisure. Residence in her town house in Bruton Street could not give her the same contented pleasure.

One of Merryfield's attractions for her, having so long been buried first in Ireland and then in Cornwall, was its proximity to London, which could be reached easily within a day, the estate lying not far from the turnpike to St Albans.

Arriving on the Saturday, to be greeted by a flustered, bustling Caro with a buxom and smiling Mrs Panning bobbing behind her, Lexie sighed inwardly.

At that moment, after the traumas of the past week and a long day's travel, she would have appreciated Merryfield's normal serenity; but the cause of the upset was all her own, so she could scarcely complain at the furious activity taking place all around her.

'We are almost ready to receive the guests,' reported Caro breathlessly. 'Mr and Mrs Panning have kept the house and grounds in excellent condition during your absence.'

Lexie gave the middle-aged caretaker, neat and comfortable-looking in her grey gown and snowy apron, an approving smile. 'So I notice.'

Mrs Panning bobbed again. 'I hopes as how you'll be pleased, my lady.'

'I'm sure that if Mrs Baldwin is satisfied, I shall be, too.'

'The Marquess's rooms are prepared, and we have put Lord Dexter in the adjoining suite, with Mr Cresswell beyond him. The ladies will occupy rooms in the other wing, the Duke and Duchess of Downshire occupying the main guest suite. I trust that meets with your approval, Alexia?'

'Splendid, Cousin.' To her surprise, the Duke had been prevailed upon to travel to Merryfield, from where he would be able to escort his wife back to their estates without setting foot in his detested London. 'That means that we—' she grinned '—will occupy the middle ground between. I'll go straight up and change.'

Chalker had already gone upstairs and footmen were humping her luggage in. Lexie mounted the stairs to her suite on the upper floor, which looked out over the sweep of the gravel drive to a fine view over the countryside, much of which she owned. She looked out of the window, glanced up at the sky and smiled.

'Thank you for all this and so much more, dear Amber,' she murmured. 'I know you would approve of this race. You loved to watch me drive. And you would not object to Lord Stormaston taking your place. I believe you would like and trust him.'

'You were saying something, my lady?' asked Chalker, hurrying into the bedroom from the adjoining dressing room. 'Your boxes have been brought up. I was just unpacking them.'

'I was talking to myself, Florence. A bad habit. Just help me out of my travelling gown and into something cooler, nothing formal. We have no guests for dinner tonight.'

'A good night's sleep is just what you need, my lady,' said Chalker. 'You've had too many late nights over the past months, in my opinion.'

'Which I do not remember asking for! But I have kept you out late, too, on many an occasion, for which I apologise, Florence. Once this race is run, we can settle down to a quiet sojourn in the country.'

'It's not London I object to, my lady, it's my home. But you've been overdoing things. Mrs Baldwin has been most concerned...'

'Quite unnecessarily,' said Lexie, irritated by what was fast becoming Chalker's familiarity. But she knew that it was born of genuine regard and so did not berate her loyal maid.

The Marquess of Stormaston and Viscount Dexter arrived in time for dinner. Lexie smiled when she saw his groom leading Brutus, for it meant that his lordship intended to ride horseback as well as drive while he was at Merryfield. All her horses had been brought from London and so she anticipated being able to ride out in the morning on Danny, accompanied by both gentlemen.

Dinner proved a cheerful occasion, everyone in splendid spirits. Lexie's excitement was mounting hourly. Both Stormaston and Dexter, while maintaining their natural air of breeding and conduct, nevertheless shed much of their Town bronze now they were in the country and appeared perfectly at home.

They did not linger over their port and brandy but quickly joined the ladies. It did not take Storm long to suggest that they should take a walk in the grounds, since the evening was both warm and bright.

The old building glowed in the declining sun. Storm turned to study it.

'You possess a fine dowry, my lady,' he said approvingly. 'Some gentleman will surely be happy to wed you to obtain control of the estate.'

'That,' said Lexie with a sidelong glance, 'is my one regret whenever I contemplate marriage. I wonder whether it is me or Merryfield which is the object of my suitor's desire. Besides, I know I shall lose control of it if I accept.' She gave a heartfelt sigh. 'Sometimes I am tempted never to wed again.'

Storm's eyes mocked her. 'Really? That is not the impression I had gained.'

'Yet you must know that I have rejected several gentlemen over the last months,' Lexie returned.

'You would have to trust the man you married to administer it well,' put in Felix, looking with interest and barely concealed amusement from one to the other.

He was not privy to the exact terms of the wager but it would have taken a complete dimwit not to sense some undercurrent of hidden meaning lying beneath the surface of their banter. Lexie smiled at him.

'Indeed, administration of the estate has been much in my thoughts recently.'

'The fields we passed through—I imagine they belonged to the estate—looked productive enough,' mused Storm, 'but from what you have told me, Lady Alexia, I believe their yield could be improved. You have not, I conclude, had a chance to consult with your steward yet?'

'I arrived only yesterday, but I shall put your suggestions to him, my lord. Perhaps you would consent to be present at the interview? I am certain your word would carry more weight than mine in such matters, and you would explain in terms he could understand and pass on to the tenants.'

Storm, his face inscrutable, bowed. 'I shall be delighted to be of service in any way I am able, my lady, once this plaguey wager is behind us.'

Lexie caught his *double entendre* and fought down her blush. '"Plaguey", is it, my lord? Yet you seemed willing enough to accept my challenge when it was made!'

She knew he was teasing her. Just as she was teasing him. Merryfield would make an excellent addition to the Stormaston estates just as he would make an excellent master. If she won the race.

If not. . .

Lord Dexter, unable to properly interpret the

hidden meanings behind their words, remarked, 'I, for one, am anticipating your contest with keen anticipation. The Duchess and Lady Fanny arrive tomorrow, I collect?'

'Indeed, as do the remainder of the party. I do hope Lady Wighton does not irritate everyone to distraction!'

'I believe,' said Felix quietly, 'that both her son and Lady Fanny are clever enough to pull the wool over her eyes and keep her temper sweet.'

'You do, do you?' murmured Storm with a sideways look. 'Just as long as they do not engage in some deceit which puts my sister in a compromising situation. Since she is so against the match, I should dislike having to play the heavy-handed guardian and insist upon a marriage neither party wishes.'

'I am convinced they will make every endeavour to avoid that possibility.'

'So I should hope!' exclaimed Lexie, wondering that Storm did not seem to have noticed his friend's interest in Lady Fanny. Though perhaps he had, and approved the budding romance.

But that seemed unlikely. Fanny was young and innocent, Felix older and a confirmed rake, like Storm himself. Were Felix ready to reform, however, she for one would thoroughly approve the match.

She thought the strong-minded woman, so speedily emerging from the chrysalis of the uncertain young Fanny who had arrived in Town six months ago, might well tame Felix. The regard in which they held each other appeared to be mutual. But Felix would have to tread warily. Storm, so disreputable himself, would require respectability in the man he allowed Fanny to wed. If Felix persisted in his discreet pursuit of Fanny, Lexie could see a rough passage ahead.

Storm, she thought ruefully, was unlikely to be tamed by anyone. But should he choose to mend his ways, for whatever reason, he would make the most satisfactory of husbands. But—her nerves tensed—if she won the race he would wed her under duress. Such a forced match would be unlikely to inspire him to reform. It might have quite the opposite effect.

Something else she had not foreseen when she conceived her stupid idea, she thought miserably. Did she really want to win, when the felicity of her reward was so uncertain?

Yes! For a wife must necessarily exert more influence than a mistress—how she hated that term! And feared the consequences of being forced into becoming Storm's! But she would never give up hope of winning not only his hand, but his love as well.

'How long is the course we are to run?' asked the object of her thoughts, bringing her back to the realities of the situation.

'Pascoe says it is about three miles. I will ride out with you tomorrow morning and take you round the route.'

'My thanks.' Storm's smile had a certain cynicism about it. 'I shall spend the remainder of my time familiarising myself and my team with the terrain. That, I conceive, is only fair.'

'Perfectly fair, my lord. But the evening grows chilly and Cousin Caro will be anxious. Shall we return to the house?'

*　*　*

They had both ridden round the route, which grounds-men, under Pascoe's direction, had marked out with whitewash.

'I hope it does not rain!' had said Storm.

'If it does, they will do it again,' had returned Lexie.

This had left Lexie with little time the following day to watch Storm taking his team gingerly around the twisting tracks, making the sharp turns required both in the woods and out in the fields, and negotiating the narrow, humped bridge across a stream which me-andered through the estate or to traverse it herself.

She took Pitch and Tar around the route once, an hour or so after breakfast, Storm following at a respectable distance. Naturally, she did not drive as fast as she usually did, for she had no intention of showing off her prowess to her adversary.

But Storm kept the same distance behind her all the way, apparently finding little difficulty in negotiating the difficult corners. He had only driven round it once before. He and his team learnt fast. But the ease with which he was mastering the course only confirmed her in what she already knew: Storm was a formidable opponent. But... Well, she would simply have to use all her skill and knowledge and leave the outcome to Fate. And accept the result.

Storm, with Felix riding with him as advisor, continued to study the route until dinner, which was taken early in the country, driving his team around for a third time after consuming a light nuncheon. Lexie noted that he was careful not to overtire his cattle. He had all the next day to continue his preparations, as did she. Tomorrow, her other guests would be settled in and able to amuse themselves while she took her blacks round the course.

The Duke of Downshire arrived just before dinner in a chaise driven by postilions who trumpeted his arrival, escorted by outriders and with a coach following behind with his servant and luggage. The Duchess and Fanny had earlier travelled in similar style. That they had condescended to visit so small an estate as Merryfield still caused Lexie some surprise.

As Lexie greeted the Duke and made her curtsy, she studied his face, seeing the resemblance Storm bore to his grandfather. He had his grandmother's eyes and something of her looks but his grandfather's nose and chin.

'Well, m'dear,' he greeted his wife, 'here I am.'

'Did you have a good journey?' enquired Lexie courteously.

'Damned uncomfortable.' The old face suddenly creased into a mischievous smile so like his grandson's that Lexie almost gasped. 'But worth it to make your acquaintance, Lady Amber. Where's that scapegrace grandson of mine?'

'Still out with his team,' Lexie told him rather breathlessly. That the Duchess had persuaded her husband to accept her invitation she did not doubt. And he had come especially to meet her.

As Fanny greeted her grandparent and he was introduced to those he did not already know, Lexie considered. Could the Duchess possibly suspect. . .?

More to the point, was it possible that she was trying to promote a match between her and her grandson?

Lexie gave her head a tiny shake. Such a notion must surely come purely from her own desire.

CHAPTER NINE

RAIN on Tuesday afternoon sent all those guests who had been out watching the practice runs scurrying for the house.

'Some of the going will be heavy after this,' observed Pascoe quietly when Lexie returned her team to the stables as it began.

'I suppose so,' muttered Lexie, wondering whether the conditions would favour a heavier or a lighter outfit. 'Pitch and Tar are used to the conditions here so I hope it will be an advantage. I shall need every assistance I can find. Do not forget to have the groundsmen mark the course again in the morning.'

'No, my lady.'

Pascoe's dry tone made Lexie realise she had succumbed to unnecessary fussing in her anxiety. As though Jethro was likely to forget!

That evening, although she joined in the general conversation, listened to Lady Fanny's rendering of 'Greensleeves' with apparent appreciation, watched the glances exchanged between Fanny and Felix with some misgiving and noted Miss Daventry's attempts to monopolise the attention of Mr Cresswell, despite Lady Wighton's forbidding frown, her mind refused to focus on any of these things.

While Storm, apparently completely relaxed and unconcerned, played a hand of piquet with his grandmother, she could feel her own nerves tightening in anticipation of the morrow.

Of one thing she could be certain, Storm would no more injure his cattle than would she. Neither would risk foundering their animals: they were far too valuable to be ruined, quite apart from any question of sentiment. So she would go only as fast as seemed safe. On certain paths, where overtaking was impossible, the one in front would set the pace. On more open, wider stretches the other would then try to overtake.

They must make the main circuit twice, but at the end would race up the drive to the finish, a line drawn across the sweep outside the main entrance to the house. There would be room along the drive for them to race neck and neck if necessary and, the ground being drained and level, they could risk going all out.

If she could keep in touch until that point her sprightly, game pair could surely overtake Storm's greys. Better still, if she could manage to be in front, then Storm would never manage to overtake her, for the course should take more out of the greys.

But what use speculating? Storm would have his plan worked out. He would not easily be beaten. Nor, she imagined, would he take defeat kindly. Although normally, as a sporting gentleman, he took his losses philosophically, this was no ordinary wager.

To be beaten by a woman and to lose his precious freedom—it would be too much. Whatever the outcome, Lexie knew that by dinner tomorrow her life would have become fraught with difficulty. She could see little chance of happiness in either outcome.

The temptation to withdraw was almost overwhelming. She could feign an illness. . .but that would only put off the moment. Storm would expect her to renew the challenge the instant she recovered. Even if he believed her truly indisposed.

Pride came to her rescue again. What she had started, she would finish.

Thanks to a posset administered by Chalker, Lexie slept better than she had anticipated. She woke with a slight headache which disappeared as soon as she had drunk her morning chocolate.

She went out to the stables to inspect her team long before breakfast, to find Storm already there.

'You slept well?' he enquired after greeting her with a formal bow.

'Perfectly well, I thank you,' returned Lexie, noting the excellence of his green coat, the fit of his buckskin breeches, the perfection of his shining boots. 'Your greys are on form?'

'So Coltby and Trappin inform me. And your team?'

'I am just about to find out. Excuse me.'

She swept across the yard, the skirts of her blue velvet carriage dress lifted to escape the mire. She really could not stand exchanging pleasantries with him, she was far too nervous.

Jethro Pascoe greeted her with a wide grin. 'They've had their feed and enough water, but not too much,' he reported. 'Couldn't be in better condition, my lady. They'll take a bit of handling to start with, mind. Eager and lively as young colts!'

'They'll behave for me. Won't you, my loves?' she asked the horses as she allowed them to nuzzle her hands and find the lumps of sugar held in her palms. Although she trusted Storm to be honest, she wondered about Trappin. But she could not ask Pascoe to guard her pair against the supposedly kindly act of offering them a bucket of water just before the start. So, 'Look after them,' was all she said as she prepared to return for her own breakfast.

'I'll do that, my lady, never you fear,' answered Pascoe. 'No one but me or Jeffs shall enter their stable, that I promise you. Nor will any of us be allowed near his lordship's cattle. 'Tis best that way.'

Reassured, Lexie returned to partake of several cups of coffee but little else, pecking at a freshly baked roll spread with butter from her own dairy. His lordship, of course, ate a substantial breakfast of eggs, kidneys and ham, together with several rolls.

Most of her other guests drifted in to eat while she was there. Felix entered, dressed ready for walking in the country, for he, Marlow, Coltby and Trappin were to join Pascoe, Jeffs, the caretaker Panning, and several other grooms and groundsmen in lining the route at intervals in order to be on hand should there be an accident and, at the same time, to ensure that neither outfit deviated from the route.

'I trust both contestants are fit and ready?' he drawled as he took his place at the table by his friend. 'The day looks set fair. We should all avoid a soaking.'

'We shall walk over to the copse,' said Fanny, indicating Oswald and Melissa. 'It is the nearest point on the circuit to the house and once you have both passed there for the second time we shall come back here for the finish.'

'A convenient point from which to watch, as you discovered yesterday morning,' grinned Storm. 'Do not exert yourselves too much, ladies, or catch cold.

The temperature is much lower after the rain. You will need extra clothing if you are to stand about in the open.'

The race was due to start at midday. Lexie returned to the stables to oversee the harnessing of her team, unable to relax enough to let Pascoe deal with it on his own. He seemed to understand and put up with her restless interventions stoically until Pitch and Tar began to sidle and sweat.

'You are upsetting your horses, my lady,' he pointed out. 'May I suggest that you take a short walk while I finish preparing the outfit?'

'I'm sorry. You are quite right. If I do not relax, neither will the horses.'

Chastened, Lexie walked from the yard towards the designated start, some hundred yards distant. She heard a tread behind her and turned to see Storm striding out to catch up with her.

He swept her a lavish bow. 'You are determined on this?' he asked, eyeing her flushed face critically.

'Of course!' Lexie, setting the pin in her driving hat to fix it more firmly on her head—for she had felt it shift as she inclined her head in greeting—met his gaze defiantly. 'I will not pretend not to be nervous. Unlike your lordship, I have never engaged in such an enterprise before. But that does not mean that I shall drive any less well!'

'Good girl!' He smiled suddenly, an admiring, encouraging smile that did more to make her nervous—in a different way—than any anticipation had so far achieved. But it was an agitation which, surprisingly, settled her nerves as far as the race was concerned. For she knew that, whatever the outcome,

Storm would accept the result in good spirit. Both their futures would be settled by a combination of skill and chance.

Her hands stopped trembling as she lowered them from her hat. The stable clock chimed the hour and the grooms led the outfits from the yard as the group of spectators came into view, led by Lady Fanny.

'Too late to back out now,' grinned Storm, holding out his strong, lean hand.

Lexie looked at it in astonishment. He was treating her as an equal. With a quick smile she took it and shook it, her own small fist quite engulfed by his, in a friendly gesture before the serious competition began.

'Good luck,' she said.

'And to you, my lady. You'll need it,' he warned.

They parted to mount their respective curricles. Lexie paused to fondle the muzzles of Pitch and Tar as she passed, glad to see that Pascoe had managed to settle them down again, though, their spirits being high, the groom was having a job to hold them.

Storm's greys were restive, too, full of running. He slapped their necks in passing and was up in his seat first. Lexie gathered her ribbons, flicked her whip and walked her pair to the start line. Storm brought his carriage alongside and grooms held both teams to steady them.

'Ready?' cried, Oswald, hat held high.

He had agreed to be the official starter. He had opened a book and had his money on Stormaston. The ladies had backed Lady Alexia. The staff all had money on one or the other or both of them. How each one had bet was Oswald's secret. Lexie felt the pressure of wanting to win so as not to let her supporters down more than that of winning for herself. Her own fate she had come to view largely as a matter of providence. Resignation had taken the place of apprehension.

Both contestants nodded.

'Then *go*!' shouted Oswald, dropping his hat with a flourish.

The grooms jumped back. Lexie gave her pair the office and set them to a modest canter. The first stretch, like the last, was comparatively straight and wide. She hoped that Storm would take the lead. Her plan was to overtake him here the second time around and make use of her better knowledge of the twists and turns of the route to get far enough ahead for him not to be able to pass her on the straight before the finish.

But Storm did not oblige. Doggedly, he remained almost abreast, his greys' heads level with her horses' withers. Either he would shoot ahead before the track narrowed or would fall behind and follow her lead through the looming wood. To force him ahead, she would have to pull her horses, make them lose their stride and rhythm.

She waited until the last moment. As the greys' heads began to slip backwards, Lexie reined the blacks in hard, making them snort and shake their heads in protest, but dropped to a trot so abruptly that Storm was past before he could do anything but take the lead.

As his outfit plunged into the comparative darkness beneath the trees he gave a great whoop of laughter and waved his whip in acknowledgement of the success of Lexie's tactic.

Lexie, loving the feel of the ribbons in her small,

capable hands and the responsiveness of her horses to her slightest command, urging them to pick up speed again as quickly as possible, laughed herself, exhilarated not only by her triumph but by the mere fact of driving in competition with so worthy an opponent. She had lacked such a challenge before. However well and fast she had driven, she had had nothing to tell her whether she was as skilled as Amber and Pascoe assured her she was.

Storm negotiated the remainder of the first circuit with care but fast, giving the path his undivided concentration, avoiding roots and potholes, mired patches and puddles with uncanny skill, taking the narrow bridge at a brisk pace, his wheel hubs always a safe inch from the stone parapets.

His curricle swayed dangerously only once, when a wheel found a root on a sharp bend. Groans from Felix and a groundsman greeted this potential disaster and scattered cheers followed their progress, especially when they came to the copse, but neither driver spared a thought for their audience.

Lexie had no difficulty in keeping close behind. In fact she knew she could have driven her horses faster. Her hopes began to mount. Pitch and Tar, straining at their bits, could surely pass their opponents on the straight!

She kept her place along most of its length, giving Storm no indication that she intended to pass him. Then, with room for manoeuvre running out, she flicked her whip and gave her pair their heads.

Storm did nothing to prevent her passing him. In fact he gave her a cheery wave as she sped by. He thought she had played into his hands, did he? Lexie smiled grimly as she set herself to show him just how speedily she was capable of setting her horses to cover the difficult ground.

They were, naturally, not as fresh as they had been on the first circuit, but she knew they still had a good turn of speed in their legs. She must reserve that for the chase along the drive. The track, too, had suffered from their first passage. Hooves and wheels had churned the surface, hiding many of the hazards.

Should she become stuck with Storm trapped behind her, she would have to allow him past as soon as the groundsmen and grooms had extricated her from the mire. So although she negotiated bends, bridges and rough ground at a faster pace than Storm had done, and the high-sprung vehicle swayed alarmingly once or twice, she drove within her limits. And tried to conserve her horses' energy for the final sprint.

Storm disappointed her by keeping up, too close behind for her comfort. She had expected to gain a hundred yards or more over the second circuit but she gained only a length. As both curricles burst out on to the drive his horses were snorting at her heels.

But the drive was smooth, well gravelled, safe. She leant forward to urge Pitch and Tar to give of their utmost. Gallantly, the small blacks took up the challenge of the larger greys thundering along behind. Lexie glanced over her shoulder. Inch by inch, Storm was gaining on her. But did he have time to overtake?

Looking forward again she simply concentrated on getting the utmost speed from her horses, ignoring as far as possible the threatening drumming and rattling which told her Storm was gaining even more ground, coming up fast. She could have used blocking tactics, but it did not even occur to her. This was a race, personal between her and Storm.

While tricks had seemed allowable in its first stages, now it had come down to who could cover the last straight in the least time. The greys' heads appeared at her shoulder. Another hundred yards to go! Grimly she hung on but, with a tremendous surge of power, the greys shot forward at the last moment and their heads were well ahead as both curricles crossed the finishing line to the sound of enthusiastic cheers.

Quite a crowd had gathered to watch the finish. Most of the ground staff and all the others scattered about the course had raced back to view the outcome. A few returning from steward's duties at the further reaches were still straggling in, the result being shouted at them as they panted up.

Storm, triumphant, appeared magnanimous in victory.

'My dear Lady Alexia, I confess myself surprised! I have never driven against a more worthy opponent,' he declared, springing down from his seat and stretching out a hand to assist Lexie to dismount.

The sheerly wicked look in those blue eyes, the devilish curve to his lips as she looked down into his lean face and saw the livid scar standing out from his tanned skin, increased the weight of the lump of undigested suet pudding which seemed to have settled in Lexie's stomach.

His hands closed about her waist as he lifted her down. His touch had never seemed more intimate. Colour flamed in Lexie's cheeks. She felt light-headed.

'Thank you, my lord,' she managed to say. 'Congratulations on a splendid race. Your greys are nonpareil.'

He grinned again. 'I did warn you.'

Lexie turned to their audience. Her stomach might be churning, she might feel exhausted by the sheer mental and physical effort of controlling her horses and bringing her outfit safely home, but she managed to maintain a cheerful if rather wry countenance.

'I can only apologise to those who have lost money on my performance. I did my best but lost to a better team—which includes the driver!'

A chorus of disclaimers greeted this, all the ladies protesting that it did not matter in the least, but nevertheless their disappointment showed.

'No, our disquiet is not in that we lost money on you, Lady Alexia,' Fanny hastened to inform her, 'but that you could not win against my arrogant brother! He has too high an opinion of himself and it would have been so satisfactory to see him beaten for once!'

'Wretch!' chided Storm.

'No more than you deserve, James!' declared his grandmother, leaning heavily on the stick she used when her joints stiffened and became painful. The overnight rain had quickly had its effect.

The Duke joined in the congratulations being showered on Storm's head. 'Well done, Stormaston!' He chuckled. 'I trust your winnings are handsome?'

'Handsome indeed, sir,' acknowledged Storm, not looking at Lexie, for which she silently thanked him.

'And you, young lady, I take it you can afford your losses?'

'I would not have staked something I was unable to deliver.'

The Duke chuckled and offered her his arm. 'Allow

me to escort such a gallant loser back to the house. I am certain my grandson can find his own way.'

Lexie took the offered arm and had her mind taken off the future consequences of her loss in answering the questions put to her by the old man, knowledgeable about land management as only the owner of vast estates could be, who wanted to know all about the house and gardens, for which he professed a great admiration.

He was nice, Lexie decided, glad he had been able to come. She would not enjoy deceiving him or the Duchess, but she would do it to protect her name and keep their regard. The Duchess appeared to ignore the rumours circulating about her and Storm. Maybe the Duke had not yet been regaled with them. She liked them both far to much to want to cause them any hurt.

Back at the house, Oswald set about paying out the winnings. Any profit was to be divided amongst the servants.

'I will settle my debt to his lordship later,' murmured Lexie, preparing to escape to her room to change.

'Make sure she doesn't renege, Storm,' grinned Felix.

'You may be sure of that,' murmured Storm, bowing over her hand with perfect elegance. 'But I do not anticipate any such possibility. Lady Alexia is above all things an honourable lady.'

Only Lexie could see the questioning, challenging look in those blue eyes.

'I always pay my debts,' she retorted tartly, 'however reluctantly.'

'So I should hope!' cried Oswald's mother, the only guest not to venture out to watch the race.

Cousin Caro, following inclination and her duty as surrogate hostess, had remained indoors with Lady Wighton but had watched the finish from a window. She sprang to her young cousin's defence.

'Of course she will! Alexia is the most principled of creatures! How can you doubt it?'

'I cannot feel able to rely upon Lady Amber's doing anything any lady of sense and breeding would think proper,' retorted Lady Wighton spitefully. 'To think of her racing her curricle against a gentleman! I have never heard of such an outrageous thing!'

'Really, Mama—'

Oswald's brave protest was lost in a chorus of indignant dissent. Only the Duchess's voice could be distinguished above the rest.

'I believe you owe Lady Amber an apology, Lady Wighton! To so insult a fellow peeress in her own house!'

Lady Wighton bridled. Before she could respond Storm intervened.

'I, personally, shall count it a grave disservice if I ever hear any hint of disapproval of Lady Amber circulating. If I discover you to be the source, madam, then I should most certainly be forced to terminate our acquaintance.'

A murmur of assent greeted his words. Such a refusal to acknowledge her would amount to social disaster. Lady Wighton smiled, if thinly.

'My dear Stormaston, I shall, as always, keep my opinions to myself. As long as you are satisfied that the debt will be met I have no more to say.'

'I should think not!' muttered Oswald furiously.

For Lexie the remainder of the day passed in a kind

of limbo. She performed all her duties as hostess, entertained her guests, laughed with them, chatted on inconsequential matters. But her mind had run on to the night ahead. Would the Marquess claim his winnings straight away? Here, at Merryfield?

He could do so with a certain amount of security. Chalker slept in a room some distance from her suite and Caro's rooms, although leading from the same landing, were entirely separate. Were he to leave his room to visit her no one would be any the wiser.

When the time came she dismissed Chalker, telling her to leave a branch of candles burning, for she wished to read.

'Sleep well, then, my lady,' said Chalker as she left the room. 'You must be worn out after that race this morning.'

'I hope you did not lose too much money on me, Florence,' said Lexie ruefully. 'I did my best to win.'

'I knew you would my lady and I placed some money on you.' The maid coloured as she stood with her hand on the door to the dressing room, where she would tidy up before going to her own bed. 'But his lordship has a formidable reputation. I put money on him, as well. So I didn't lose anything in the end.'

'Well, I'm glad of that,' said Lexie, wondering how she could have been so naïve as to think anyone would have backed her to win without hedging their bet.

'By the way, Florence, after this house party you may take a holiday,' she promised. She could not be sure of the Marquess's intentions but having her as his mistress seemed to imply more than a single night spent in her bed and she wanted to be free to please herself—and him.

Not that she did not trust Chalker's discretion, but to Lexie, keeping the affair secret was all-important. If the liaison could be kept entirely hidden from others, she would not feel quite so bad about it.

'I can manage without you for at least a week. Say two. Make what arrangements you like.'

Chalker's face lit up. 'You mean it, my lady? Then I'll send a message to my mother. She'll be glad to see me. She hasn't been too grand lately, by all accounts. I can travel by stage from the posting inn in St Albans.'

Lexie nodded. 'And you may sort out a couple of my old gowns to take with you. Do it tomorrow and let me know which ones you would like.'

'Very well, my lady. And thank you.'

With Chalker's departure nervousness started the butterflies fluttering in Lexie's stomach. Storm had said nothing, but the expression in his eyes as he had bidden her good night led her to expect him. The memory of the fire in his gaze sent frissons of anticipation down her spine. She shivered, despite the warmth of the night, and pulled her dressing wrap close about her.

She could not bring herself to get into bed to wait for him—that would be too embarrassing—so she sat in her chair with a book open on her lap, listening to the sounds in the house gradually die away. If he was coming, it would be soon.

The candles guttered and she sprang up to take a taper to light others to replace them. The activity took away some of her nervousness and she was so concentrating on her task that at first she failed to hear the soft sound of her door opening.

When Storm came in, she was standing with a

freshly-lighted branch of candles in her hand. The glow from their flames fell upon her luxuriant hair, cascading like molten gold from beneath her lacy cap. Colour flooded her face and then fled, leaving her skin alabaster white apart from the freckles sprinkled across her nose. Her hand began to shake, the flames to waver.

Storm turned the key in the lock before striding forward to take the candelabra from her grasp.

'You'll drop it,' he chided, putting it down in place of the others, which he carried over to a distant table where he proceeded, quite calmly, to extinguish the flames.

'I did not know whether to expect you or not,' gulped Lexie.

'Did you think I would not claim my winnings?' His eyebrows lifted quizzically as he came back to her.

'A gentleman would not,' uttered Lexie.

'No?' The eyebrows approached his hairline. 'But then, you knew I was no gentleman when you accepted the wager.' His hand came out and his fingers lifted her chin so that their eyes met. Wide, anxious green met teasing blue in which the fires of passion burnt, but well banked down. 'Would you have let me off, had you won, my lady?'

Lexie gulped. 'I might have done. Had you appeared too greatly displeased at the idea of marrying me.'

'If I had threatened, by my behaviour, to make your future life a misery?' He laughed, none too pleasantly. 'But had I accepted my debt in good spirit, then you would have claimed your reward. Is that not so?'

Dumb, Lexie nodded.

'And are you, by your behaviour, going to make me wish that I had not won today?' he demanded softly.

Lexie shook her head.

'I thought not.' His fingers stroked the line of her cheekbone, ran down to her firm chin. His thumb lifted to smooth across her full lips and Lexie's limbs melted. 'We both want this too much. But, my dear, if I thought lying with me would harm you in any way, then I should withdraw. But I believe the opposite. And I cannot conceive that, to one as unconventional as yourself, indulging in an *affaire* with me will cause undue distress.'

'Provided no one knows,' managed Lexie hoarsely. 'My conscience is bad enough as it is. If I thought people—the servants, for example—were sniggering behind my back I should not be able to hold my head up.'

'No one will know. No one saw me come.'

'The sheets. . .'

He pursed his lips, his head on one side. The candles lit his dark hair, painted his face with shadows. 'You could come with me to my room. The servants would think nothing of finding soiled sheets on my bed.'

He was not serious. His eyes were dancing. But he should not laugh at her scruples.

'You are a beast!' she accused, pushing him away.

'Not at all.' He refused to retreat and was, suddenly, in deadly earnest. 'If the problem troubles you, then I suggest spreading a towel, which I undertake to smuggle into the linen basket for you. Will that serve?'

'You think me a fool,' muttered Lexie. 'But I could not bear for the servants to gossip.'

'No, I do not, dearest Lexie. I think you absolutely adorable but a little naïve. They will already be gossiping. What harm can their speculations do you?'

'Speculation, none. But the stating of a proven fact. . .that would be different.'

'I suppose it would. So now, if you will point me towards a convenient towel. . .'

'The washstand is in the dressing room.' Lexie indicated the door.

Without further ado Storm went through to return with the necessary item, carefully locking that door after him, too.

'Now we cannot be disturbed,' he announced, turning back the bedclothes and spreading his trophy over the sheet. 'Come, my lady. Allow me to relieve you of your wrap.'

CHAPTER TEN

HE REMOVED her garments, each operation a caress, lifted her up and laid her on the bed. Lexie, her senses heightened to an almost unbearable pitch, watched as the gown concealing his nakedness followed her night-gown to the floor. She remembered the first time she had seen him unclothed, when she had come to her senses just in time and, for an instant, panic almost overcame her.

What was she doing, waiting for a man who was not her husband to join her in her bed? But the dismay had no time to bite, for his weight shifted the mattress beneath her and she felt the warm, entrancing silkiness of his skin against hers as he pulled the light covers up. Then she was in his embrace. After that, nothing mattered except that she was where she belonged, cradled in his arms. This was truly coming home.

As she relaxed against him, she realised with aston-ishment that he was trembling. Somehow, that gave Lexie the courage to touch the scar on his cheek, to whisper, 'I am glad you gave me no choice, Storm. My conscience has been such a trouble to me.'

'To you!' He pulled her closer. 'I have never known such a stubborn woman!'

'Then perhaps the experience has taught you a lesson, my lord,' she teased, poking admonishingly at his chin. 'Some females do value their virtue. You cannot assume all of us will fall into your arms as easily as you might expect!'

'I have only previously come across the other sort. You, my dear, provided a new experience.' He chuckled, kissing her curving nose. His tone deepened. 'Oh, Lexie, my adorable one, how I have burned for you!'

'And I for you,' she confessed shyly.

'Have you truly? Then the strength of your will is greater than I had supposed.' He shifted, leaning his weight on one elbow as he leant over her, smoothing the golden mass of hair spread over the pillow. 'But let us not waste time on post-mortems when all joy lies ahead. Come, my dear, allow me to worship your body.'

Oh! the exquisite sensations he roused as his hands and lips travelled from her hair to her toes. Bed with Amber had never been like this! Then, having exhausted new places to explore, Storm's caresses returned to her breasts, moulding them to his touch, taking each peak in turn into his warm, moist mouth, teasing, suckling, sending exquisite pain to the depths of Lexie's being. Eventually, as her hips moved instinctively, seeking release from the almost unbearable ecstasy, his fingers probed the source of her demand.

'How long. . .?'

He had no need to finish his murmured question. 'Five years,' muttered Lexie, ashamed to have to admit it.

'Then I will be careful, my love.'

My love! Did he mean it? Or did he use the endearment to all his mistresses? Lexie did not, at that moment, care.

'Please, James! Hurry!'

In her passion, Lexie did not notice that she had called him by his name for the first time. But Storm did. His already thundering heart gave a great leap as he moved to cover her awakening body. That one word coming from her lips was worth more than a thousand other endearments! He had, at last, truly broken through the barrier of her resistance.

Despite the urgency this knowledge added to his own need, he managed to control his entry, to test her readiness before plunging deeper into her velvety depths.

Once there he paused to regain control. Lexie moaned and he groaned as he began to move. Her arms clasped his shoulders, her hips thrust upwards in perfect rhythm with his, her beautiful legs—having kissed and caressed them he could envisage every strong, perfect inch of them—tangled with his. He stopped again, fighting against the consummation of his own passion.

Lexie clasped him anxiously to her, strained upwards to take him deeper inside her, shifted her legs to embrace his hips. Why had he stopped? Amber had simply gone on and on, wearing away at her patience as she waited for it to end. But with James she did not want it to end.

'James?' she whispered.

His voice came, ragged, breathless. 'One moment, my love. Otherwise I shall come too soon and I want to make this last.'

'Oh.' Her hands wandered over the muscles of his back. 'But I want. . . Please?'

A sort of gasping laugh greeted her plea. 'How can I refuse?'

And then he was moving again, raising the tempo, filling her senses until she lost them completely in a wave of such purely breathtaking sensation that she seemed to come out of her skin to hover over her own limp, exhausted body.

For long moments she was unaware of anything but sheer joy. Then she discovered Storm collapsed on top of her, shuddering his own abandoned pleasure. She lay still, waiting for him to recover, moving only to kiss his neck, his shoulder, in awestruck gratitude.

Eventually he lifted himself up on his elbows and looked down into her flushed, drowning face. Unable to resist, he kissed the passionate mouth which had been sending messages to his groin even as he recovered.

He gave a rueful, triumphant laugh. 'Truly a diamond of the first water,' he murmured, kissing her again, giving new meaning to a hackneyed expression. 'Even without recent practice,' he added wickedly. 'I cannot imagine what your response will be like after a little more application.'

'You have had plenty of experience,' retorted Lexie pertly. 'Such expertise! But oh, James, it was wonderful! Thank you!'

'You are calling me James,' he murmured. 'Do you remember my asking you to?' She nodded. 'And you said it sounded too familiar. Can I presume that no longer applies?'

'Not in private. But in public I must continue to address you as I have always done.'

He sighed. 'I suppose so. To do otherwise now would certainly cause speculation.'

Lexie was slowly coming down to earth. She landed with a bump.

'As would your absence from your bed were it to be discovered!'

'Marlow is the only one even remotely likely to venture into my room, and he has no reason. And in any case I would trust him not to mention the matter, even to me!'

'But you must go!' urged Lexie, wishing with all her heart that he had the right to remain. 'Supposing we fall asleep and the maid comes in with my morning chocolate only to find us together!'

Through an exaggerated yawn, 'I feel more like repeating our experiment than sleeping,' Storm informed her.

'Again? Is that possible?' Amber had only ever performed once at a time. It had taken him a day to recover.

'Give me a few more minutes and I will show you. Meanwhile, there are certain areas of your delectable body I have yet to explore.'

He proceeded to do so and Lexie found her hands wandering over his hard form, discovering the splendid muscles hidden beneath the smooth surface of his skin.

'No fat,' she murmured, pinching his ribs playfully.

He sucked in his breath as the ticklish shock shook him. 'Riding, boxing, fencing, all keep me in as fine a fettle as my cattle,' he gasped. 'Lexie, stop it! You'll have me helpless. . .'

'That will never do,' she murmured provocatively. 'Can you not manage just a little—?'

He gasped as she pinched him again. 'Witch! It seems I can excel even my own past performances with you! Come here!'

She was under him again, experiencing the same sublime sensations, finding her own exquisite release even as Storm subsided in his.

She could, thought Lexie contentedly, become addicted to the attentions of James Graham, Marquess of Stormaston.

He left shortly afterwards, taking the towel with him. But Lexie could still detect his scent, that indefinable odour which was James Graham, in the bed. It was something, but not enough. She wanted him there, sleeping beside her. Until death did them part.

Anyone looking perceptively at Lexie the next day might have guessed that something monumental had happened to her during the night. And anyone that perceptive would have been in no doubt as to the cause of her inner glow. Or the identity of the person responsible.

Lexie, cocooned in her euphoric dreams of the past night and of those to come, for she had little doubt that Storm would be back, bubbled with new energy and happiness, keeping all her guests occupied and entertained like the able hostess she was.

Whenever she thought of what she had done she almost blushed. She still felt like a scarlet woman, but was too happy to care. She wanted to ride out with the men, to be with Storm, but dutifully remained behind with the ladies, picking up some needlepoint she had started during the winter and taking the frame and her silks out into the garden where the others were enjoying the shade of an arbour built at the end of the formal gardens.

'Why gentlemen must always be taking exercise I do not know,' lamented Miranda, for Oswald, taking his example from Storm and Felix, had decided that an excursion on horseback would not come amiss.

'I have never liked horseback riding,' Fanny remarked.

'I used to be a great horsewoman in my youth,' said the Duchess. 'Could have given you a run for your money, Lady Alexia!'

'Indeed, ma'am, so your grandson has informed me.'

'Used to ride all over our estates with me,' said the Duke with a fond smile. 'Until she started breeding, of course.'

'That do put a restriction on a female's activities,' agreed his wife. 'But once I stopped breedin' I took it up again. Nothing like it.'

'Oswald has never shown any inclination to like horses until now,' lamented his mother, throwing Lexie a louring glance.

Oswald, enjoying the close company of two extremely experienced gentlemen, had begun to develop his own brand of independence. He tended to disregard his mother's wishes rather more than that lady liked.

Lexie wondered that no one else seemed aware of the undercurrents flowing between the young people. Perhaps, being in love herself had made her more sensitive to atmosphere, for to outward appearances Felix divided his attention equally between the two young ladies who were his fellow guests.

Oswald did likewise, although he did also contrive

to attend Lexie as often as he could. Unfortunately, his *tendre* for her had not yet died. Lexie felt sorry for Melissa but there was no more she could do to help her cause.

The servants plied them with refreshing drinks and the afternoon passed pleasantly enough. But Lexie's eyes kept straying in the direction of the stables. The men must return soon! Her steward and home farm manager, John Lyme, had ridden out with them as guide. She wanted to know what he and the Marquess had discussed.

Storm spoke so confidently of the advantages of the new ways of farming. She hoped Mr Lyme would be receptive to his ideas, for only he could persuade her tenants. She must fix a time for the meeting they had discussed.

The men returned. The Marquess and John Lyme appeared to be on the best of terms and the steward presented himself before her to request an interview to discuss the estate's affairs. Lexie, at a nod of approval from Storm, fixed the meeting for noon the following day.

When she went up to her room to change for dinner, Lexie discovered an unpalatable fact. Her monthly indisposition was upon her. She would be unable to receive Storm for several days. Certainly not before the planned end of the house party on Monday. Perhaps—devastating thought—last night would be the only night of love she was ever to know.

'Devil take it,' she muttered to herself as she applied bandages. Disappointment sent her spirits plunging. And what would Storm think? Although he must be familiar with women's fertility cycles, she thought cynically.

She tried to warn him of her indisposition during the evening but the opportunity never presented itself. She gave him a speaking look and a tiny shake of her head as she said good night, but he simply raised his brows in interrogation, not understanding the message she was trying to impart.

So his arrival was not unexpected. Again, she was not in bed but sitting in her chair. She had thought it best to greet him in a less suggestive pose. His ardour would need dampening, not inflaming.

Nevertheless, at his stealthy entry, her heart leapt and rosy colour flooded her cheeks. He did want her again! He could not have found bedding her too disappointing.

That fact was evident in the way he looked at her as he advanced, carrying a towel over his arm like a waiter, and with two glasses filled with blood-red wine balanced in one hand.

He handed her one of the glasses with a flourish and bent to kiss her lips.

'You seemed a little doubtful as to whether you wished to receive me earlier,' he murmured. 'I therefore thought it prudent to bring a little stimulant to our enjoyment. Let us toast each other.' He raised his goblet. 'To us, my dear Lady Amber.'

All colour fled from Lexie's face. She sat down on the chair abruptly, shaking her head. Storm eyed her ashen cheeks and his own expectant expression chilled.

'Do you intend to reject me?' he drawled.

Lexie shook her head as she struggled for words.

'No, believe me, James, but it is the wrong time of the month for me. I am indisposed.'

He relaxed, quite visibly. 'Is that all, my love? Then drink up! We can still have a night of loving ahead, for there is no reason why we should not cuddle each other, is there? Here's to us, and confound our critics!' He watched her as he drank.

Her face returned to its normal colour and a look of radiant delight took the place of apprehension. 'To us,' she whispered, lifted the wine to her lips and gulped down a large mouthful.

He took the glass from her and raised her to her feet. 'We shall be fully together again, never fear. But tonight,' he murmured, 'I shall give you pleasure and teach you how to release me from my frustration. Unless you already know?'

'I have an idea,' she admitted. 'Amber—'

'Do not let us speak of him! I have no wish to be reminded of any man who had you before me. I—' he laughed ruefully '—who have never yet despoiled a virgin and have therefore always followed others in tasting the delights of feminine charms, discover that I am capable of sexual jealousy! An emotion new to me. I find this difficult to explain, even to myself.'

As she slipped out of her garments and took her place in the bed, Lexie's spirits lifted. If he felt like that then perhaps she could hope that he might come to love her as she loved him. The likelihood appeared remote but it was a hope she must cling to. Nothing else could keep at bay the chilling prospect of rejection when he tired of her. As he had tired of all his women before her.

At least, she consoled herself, he found her a new

experience. Her pride would have suffered sorely had he simply classed her with all the rest. She could not have borne to be simply one of his women, no different in his eyes to all the others.

Once the house party broke up he planned to take her to stay with his old nurse, in whose eyes, apparently, Master James could do no wrong, who would have no objection to their sharing a bedroom, and whom he could trust never to mention their visit to a soul.

'She wished to retire to the sea,' he had explained before leaving her, 'and I set her up in a house in a tiny resort on the Essex coast called Frinton. Neither of us is known there, although I have visited Nanny Dean once or twice—on my own,' he hastened to reassure her.

'We may stay with her completely incognito. Marlow can put up at the local inn. I shall need him with me to fetch and carry and generally make himself useful to us both. I would trust my life to his discretion. What do you say, my love?'

'Yes,' responded Lexie, after only the slightest hesitation. Desperate as she was to spend time with Storm, she could not rid herself of the idea that to do so was a sin. But her conscience had caused her to hesitate for too long already. She would take what happiness he offered and suffer the consequences later, if she must.

Which reminded her of another unpalatable fact she had ignored until now. Clearly, their single act of union had not resulted in any unwanted child. Unwanted only because she was unwed, of course. Wanted most desperately, if only she were Storm's wife. But facts were facts and faced with them she could not contemplate giving birth to a bastard.

On past performance Storm would not care, though he would take care of the child financially—but what of her? If she did not suffer her confinement in secret and abandon the child immediately afterwards, but brought it up herself, which she would most certainly wish to do, she would be branded a harlot and ostracised from Society. More to the point, the child would bear the brand of bastardy all its life.

She could decide to wed another suitor in haste to obtain a name for the infant, but that would not be honest or to her taste. Storm might offer marriage—but he had never felt under any obligation to do so in the past, so why should he now? And she would never ask him to marry her again. So it would be best to avoid any such complication.

In Cornwall Lexie had visited the local wise woman several times in her capacity as the lady of the manor. Desperate over not conceiving Amber's heir, she had sought her advice.

''Ee can try this potion, my dear, but 'e be too gone in years, to my way of thinking,' old Demelza had told her. 'Find yersel' a young man and 'ee'll start breeding soon enough. Then, like as not, 'ee'll want to know as how to stop being brought to childbed too often.'

Lexie, from curiosity, had asked her how this could be achieved and been regaled with details of many devices to prevent conception and some proven ways to abort an unwanted baby. She could not remember them all, and would never get rid of a baby once conceived, but she did remember something of what the old woman had said. And decided to acquire a sponge and a supply of vinegar before leaving for Essex.

Foresight had already dealt with the question of Chalker. Her only remaining problem would be getting to the Saracen's Head at Chelmsford, where she was to meet Storm. But even that was solved by the end of the house party. On Storm's suggestion she announced her intention to make a very private visit to an old—fictitious—school friend she had discovered to be living in St Albans.

In her own unorthodox way, Lexie would insist on riding there without escort, stable Danny in the city, and from there make her way to Chelmsford. An adventure! She had a choice, she could go by post chaise, but preferred to take the stage coach, a new experience which she did not expect to be pleasant, but if Chalker could do it, so could she.

On his way back to his room one night, Storm almost bumped into Felix. Both men looked put out until the comedy of the situation shook them both with laughter. Felix, Storm thought, looked decidedly sheepish and he wondered into whose bed his friend had strayed.

Felix might well guess where he had been, but Storm could rely absolutely on his discretion. As Felix could rely on his. That two confirmed rakes should meet in a dark corridor after each had visited an obliging female caused neither of them undue surprise.

'Go and get some sleep, my dear fellow,' chuckled Storm.

'You too, my friend. It would not do for either of us to appear exhausted tomorrow.'

'What would my grandmother say?' agreed Storm lightly. He had refused to allow her presence to inhibit his actions. Lexie, he suspected, might have invited his grandparents with that hope in mind.

'Or our delightful hostess. I wish you a good night— what is left of it!'

Felix did guess, thought Storm ruefully. For himself he did not mind, but he hoped Lexie need never discover that Felix had guessed their secret.

Lexie would take only what would fit into a couple of saddlebags and a pack strapped behind her saddle. Chalker, due to leave for London at any moment, had insisted on helping her mistress, murmuring all the while, 'However will you manage, my lady, with only these few things?'

When Cousin Caro joined in Chalker's lament, Lexie lost her temper.

'Excellently well, I believe. Now, stop your lamentations, if you please! I am quite capable of looking after myself for a week or so, and if I find I lack for anything I can always visit a shop! Really, Caro,' she went on, when Chalker had been persuaded to go down to the gig waiting to take her into St Albans. 'Such a fuss! You know how I dislike being trammelled by convention! I am taking an opportunity to escape! A real holiday! Do not deny me these few days of freedom!'

Caro pursed her lips and fluttered a hand. 'If I could believe that was all it was. You could easily have arranged to travel into St Albans with Chalker. But you will please yourself, as always, Alexia.' She sighed, and her voice wavered. 'Why you bother to have me live with you as your companion and chaperon I cannot conceive!'

'Because you add respectability to what are considered to be my rackety ways, Cousin!'

'Which you promptly squander on some new exploit! As though racing your curricle against a gentleman for money were not enough! Now you are off, the dear Lord knows where, all on your own, without even Chalker or Jeffs to keep you company! I do declare, you will be the death of me, Alexia!'

'Nonsense!' Lexie spoke bracingly. 'I am not some poor thing who needs cossetting every moment of her life! I am going to visit a friend!'

Childishly, she crossed her fingers behind her back. Lies did not come easily to her but on this occasion some were unavoidable. Although this one had an element of truth in it.

'She will have a servant to look after me. Now, I trust you to see to things in the house in my absence. Mr Lyme has the estate in hand; I am so glad he is enthusiastic about the changes Lord Stormaston suggested.'

'Anyone might think,' said Caro in a resigned tone, 'that his lordship owned the place, the way he was laying down the law!'

Lexie, remembering the authority Storm had brought to bear on poor John Lyme, secretly agreed. 'But he achieved his ends—which were mine,' she pointed out. 'I asked him to persuade Mr Lyme. He did it for me.'

'It seems to me he would do almost anything for you, Alexia. He certainly behaved as though he had every right... I wonder he has not declared himself yet.'

'Oh, he will never marry,' said Lexie airily, ignoring the pain the assertion gave her.

'Hmm.' Caro eyed her pink face suspiciously. 'It seemed to me— But there...' She cut herself off with another resigned sigh. 'He flirts with every woman he meets, even the Duchess. He cannot help it. So I suppose there was really nothing particular in the way he looked at you.'

Lexie caught her breath. 'Of course there was not,' she maintained.

'But by the way you look at him, my love, you declare your feelings for all to see. You will have to be more careful when we return to London, or gossip will be fuelled anew. And although you are my benefactor and I have no authority over you, Alexia, I do consider myself to have a responsibility towards you. I feel I must warn you.'

'Of course you must, but you are imagining things, Cousin Caro! I look upon his lordship as I would on any gentleman friend!'

'I,' remarked Caro with a shrug, 'have never seen you look at anyone in quite the way you look at his lordship.'

Dear Lord, were her feelings plain for all to see? She had thought herself circumspect in her dealings with Storm. Yet Caro— But Caro had had a clue, had known her to be interested in marriage to the Marquess. So she had imagined the rest.

At least, Lexie hoped so. It would be too mortifying for words were all her acquaintance to realise that she had fallen in love with the most notorious rake in Town.

Aiming to be in St Albans before nine o'clock, Lexie left early the following day, riding a frisky Danny. But, bowing to the anxiety and outrage of Jethro Pascoe, she had agreed to allow Jeffs to accompany her to the outskirts of the city. And had been persuaded to hire a man to ride back with her at the end of her visit.

''Tis not safe for a young woman like yourself to undertake such a journey alone,' he had scolded. 'What be you thinking of, my lady? Get away from everything if you must, but do be sensible and take precautions against being set upon by thieves and vagabonds!'

So Jeffs rode at Danny's rump and Lexie was not sorry for the company. It would have been a long, anxious ride had she been alone, with all kinds of travellers on the road and many a thicket near enough to conceal footpads and robbers.

'There is no need for you to come further than that inn just along the road, Jeffs,' she said as they came upon the first houses. 'You may assure Mr Pascoe that I arrived quite safely. Refresh yourself in the inn before you return.'

She handed Jeffs a coin; he touched his hat and dismounted at the door of the Weary Traveller protesting his gratitude.

Free of his company, Lexie made haste to find her way to the coaching inn where she was to pick up the stage. She did not know the town well and had to ask her way more than once. She arrived with a sense of relief and pride in achievement. She was perfectly able to survive on her own!

Dismounting in the yard, she handed Danny over to an ostler, asking that her packs be removed and the animal stabled and cared for until she returned to claim him. She was about to conclude the arrangements with the man pointed out as in charge when she caught sight of a familiar figure striding purposefully towards her.

Clad in country clothes, twill breeches and stout leather boots, a rough woollen coat and low brown beaver hat, his appearance still managed to stop her heart.

'Did you really imagine I would allow you to travel alone?' he asked, as he nodded a greeting. Formal bows and curtsies would not have been in place, but his eyes, warm and smiling, told her he was pleased to see her. And hers—hers probably revealed her overwhelming joy at the sight of him.

Marlow appeared at his shoulder, dressed simply and wearing a disapproving look. Used as he was to his master's adventures, he still did not have to approve all the cloak-and-dagger intrigue which was accompanying this *affaire*.

'Marlow will deal with the stabling of your horse, you may trust him to see it done right, and he will see your bags put into my carriage,' Storm went on, as Lexie, overwhelmed by his sudden appearance, seemed lost for words. 'We will go inside and partake of some refreshment.' He turned to Marlow. 'Take some yourself when you have made the arrangements,' he instructed.

'Yes, sir,' said Marlow, emphasising the last word.

'He objects,' murmured Storm, as he took Lexie's arm and ushered her towards the inn door, 'to having to call me "sir" instead of "my lord". He considers it *infra dignitatem*.'

'Poor Marlow,' said Lexie, recovering her voice, though it quivered with emotion. 'How our servants do disapprove of our ruses and foibles! Chalker was almost in tears over the few clothes I was proposing to bring and Jethro talked me into allowing Jeffs to escort me to the edge of the town!'

'Sensible fellow, Pascoe. I like him. I believe you could have taken him into your confidence. But thanks to him or not, you have arrived safely and I swear we shall not be parted again until we must return to our separate establishments.'

'You could not promise anything which would content me more,' she assured him.

Having partaken of light refreshments in a rather crowded inn parlour, where the Marquess, despite his unremarkable clothes, was accorded instant attention, his quality being unmistakable, Storm led her out to his waiting equipage. Lexie eyed it with amusement.

'Where on earth did you find that old chariot?' she demanded.

'At the back of the coach house at Stormaston. And the hired horseflesh is scarcely of the standard I normally use. However, one must keep up appearances. If we are to behave as an ordinary couple for a while, we must look the part.'

Trust Storm to enter into the spirit of the enterprise and to do things thoroughly, thought Lexie fondly.

The chariot, although elderly, was well sprung and comfortably cushioned inside. Lexie did not long lament her lost opportunity to take the stage, especially when she saw it arrive already laden with passengers and luggage. She would have found no room inside and been condemned to a seat on top.

'No,' said Storm, handing her into the chariot and nodding meaningfully towards the crowded coach. 'I could not allow you to travel in such discomfort! And knowing you, my dear Lexie, I guessed you would chose to travel that way rather than by post chaise.'

'Post chaises can be dirty and smelly,' Lexie reminded him. 'I thought the stage would be an experience.'

'One you would do well to avoid unless in an extremity! The mail coach would be preferable.'

'Is Marlow to drive?' asked Lexie as Storm followed her into the chariot's interior.

'He is taking the first stage, then we shall drive turn and turn about, all night if necessary. But we should arrive before midnight unless anything untoward happens. The journey should not take much more than ten hours.'

Ten hours, half of them spent in close proximity to Storm in the confines of the coach, the other half spent watching his broad shoulders through the front window as he shared the box with Marlow when he took the ribbons. Definitely better than travelling by the stage.

In fact, for the last part of the journey Marlow did all the driving while Lexie dozed, her head cradled on Storm's shoulder.

They arrived in darkness. Marlow drew the horses up before a neat cottage on the outskirts of the small resort nestling on the shore.

'In daylight you can see the sea,' Storm told her as she staggered out, to be caught fast in his arms.

Lexie yawned, moving to ease her cramped muscles. 'Like Cornwall,' she murmured.

'I doubt it! The coast is quite different here. No cliffs. Flat as a pancake.'

At that moment the door was flung open, revealing a small figure holding a candle high, while behind her more candles and a lamp threw out a welcoming glow.

'Master James!' cried his old nurse. 'I thought I heard you arrive! Do bring the poor young lady in at once!'

'Martha!' Storm moved forward, his arm about Lexie's shoulders. 'This is Mistress Lexie.'

'Any friend of Master James is welcome here,' said Martha, eyeing Lexie approvingly and bobbing a small curtsy.

'Thank you, Mrs Dean.'

'Do call me Martha, my dear. Master James always does.'

No further explanations were necessary. Storm had laid the foundations for the visit with great care. Martha took them up to a large, airy room on the first floor, decorated in cream with cheerful floral drapes and covers, cotton rather than silk, but none the worse for that. A washstand stood in one corner with an ewer of water in the basin and towels hung on a rail.

'You'll want to wash the dirt of the journey off yourselves,' remarked Martha. 'I'll fetch a kettle of hot water, there's one simmering on the stove.'

'I'll go,' said Storm. 'I'll not have you fetching and carrying for us, Martha. Where's Daisy, your help?'

'She's been abed this last hour or more. She'll bring a kettle up in the morning, empty your slops and the like.'

'I won't be long,' promised Storm, dropping a light kiss on Lexie's lips as he passed on his way to follow Martha downstairs.

'I shall probably be asleep,' yawned Lexie.

'Then I shall have to wake you up.'

His eyes laughed into hers. But he meant it.

CHAPTER ELEVEN

SHE had no time to do more than remove her pelisse and bonnet before Storm returned with a huge ewer of hot water.

'We must share this, I fear,' he told her, smiling wickedly. 'Just as we must share everything else while we are here. Do you need help to undress?'

Lexie laughed softly and turned her back. 'Chalker normally undoes the fastenings of my gown. If you would not mind?'

'A privilege, *madame*. Just a moment while I fill the basin and deposit this jug. Now, let me see. . .'

His skilled fingers soon unhooked the back of her gown, which he smoothed forward over her shoulders, brushing the enticing swell of her breasts as it fell to her feet. Lexie stepped out of the crumpled tan serge, an old but sturdy gown doing duty as a summer travelling dress. She bent forward to pick it up, but Storm's arms prevented her. His mouth nuzzled the curve where creamy shoulder met slender neck while his hands cupped her thrusting breasts. 'I haven't finished,' he murmured thickly. 'The ties of your chemise. . .'

Lexie gave a shuddering sigh. 'Stop it, James, or we shall never finish undressing and washing!'

'Do you really want me to?' he asked, mock indignation warring with laughter in his voice.

'No, but—'

'Then I shall not.' His teeth nipped her ear but one of his hands left its erotic fondling to tug at the bows of her garment.

'Do be sensible,' protested Lexie, whose legs were beginning to lose their strength. 'I really must wash the dirt of the journey off before we go to bed.'

Storm sighed. 'Cleanliness before sinfulness, I do declare!'

'Oh, Storm! Do not remind me!'

'My regrets, sweet Lexie, I was only joking. A jest in bad taste, I acknowledge. Pray do not let it spoil things for you.'

His voice held real contrition as he turned her to him and dropped a gentle kiss on her parted lips. His eyes, blue as a summer sky, gazed down into the clouded green depths of hers. 'I will make you forget,' he promised.

Lexie gave herself a mental shake. She had been so delightfully relaxed and happy it would be a crime to allow a careless word to ruin their time together. She had taken the decision to come. She could not allow conscience to intrude now.

Her eyes cleared. 'I was being idiotish,' she admitted.

'Only very slightly. The greater stupidity was mine. And I shall suffer for it,' he announced in resigned tones.

Lexie frowned. 'You, suffer? How?'

'I have appointed myself your lady's maid. I shall undress and wash you and put you to bed. But I have no one to do a similar service for me.'

'Oh, no?' Lexie grinned, all qualms forgotten. 'If your lordship would deign to instruct me in the art, I am perfectly willing to undertake the duties of your man.'

'You are?' He sounded delighted. 'Oh what joy! We shall tend each other like delicate blossoms—'

'Don't be a fool, James!'

But Lexie was laughing, revelling in this new, teasing, light-hearted facet of the man she loved.

Tend her he did, washing her from her forehead to the soles of her feet, drying her with rough, abrasive strokes that set the blood coursing through her veins. When she reached for her nightgown he stayed her hand.

'You do not need that, my love.'

Lexie nodded and, feeling excessively wicked, undressed him and bathed him while herself remaining quite naked.

By the time they tumbled into bed they could not wait. The fusion of their bodies came almost instantaneously. But, tired as she had thought herself, Lexie did not sleep but responded to Storm's lovemaking as often as he was able to revive his own resources. Daylight was streaking round the curtains before they dropped at last into the sleep of utter exhaustion.

The days passed in quick succession, golden days of early autumn as August faded into September. They walked, rode hired horses, lazed on the beach and even made use of the single bathing machine the little resort boasted. But above all they made love. The week they had promised themselves flew by, turned into two and then ran into a third. Lexie wanted their time together never to end.

Storm, surprised that his initial passion seemed not one whit abated by more than two whole weeks of

Lexie's exclusive company and the innumerable occasions upon which he had possessed her, began to assess the possibilities for carrying on the affair once they resumed normal life.

'I really must return to Wiltshire,' he sighed. 'I may not neglect my duties any longer.'

'Duty!' lamented Lexie. 'How I wish we could live like this for ever, simply, our needs small, able to exist on a competence!'

'How bored we should both become without some kind of occupation!'

'You can say that, when you idle about Town for the most part of the year?'

'There, dear Lexie, I must beg to differ! I normally spend far more time at Stormaston Park and travelling around my other estates than I do in Town!'

'So you may. I apologise! But for myself, I could find plenty to do, even in a place like this.'

Looking after our children, she dreamed but did not say.

'But what of the challenges you so much enjoy, the social round you craved when isolated far from Town? No, my love, you would soon tire of playing the milkmaid, just as you tired of Cornwall! Administering my estates takes time and skills which I enjoy deploying. And I should sadly miss experimenting in my laboratory were it taken from me! I am on the very point of completing the design of an engine to work the water pump!'

He had told her of his interest in steam engines, his self-imposed task of discovering how they worked and how best to utilise their power, and Lexie shook her head. Such an interest did not sit well with his reputation, but she was fast discovering that the man she loved was far from the idle rake he appeared to be. 'You will blow yourself up one day!'

'Do not fear for me! But I have been thinking. We need to plan how to go on once we return to the world. I think it best if I find a convenient house or flat in London where we can meet as often as we like. If we are discreet—'

'No!'

Lexie's flat denial cut him off short. He studied her angry face in astonishment.

'But I thought you would want to continue—'

'I denied my conscience to pay my debt.' Disappointment that he could propose nothing more than the continuation of a casual *affaire* after the rapturous time they had spent together roused Lexie's anger. She would not carry on as his mistress. She had far too much pride. If he could not see that his precious freedom meant nothing in the face of what they shared together, then he could enjoy it without her help.

'The length of time I should submit to being your mistress was never mentioned. I am now saying that leaving here marks the end.'

His clipped response made Lexie shiver. 'Very well. If that is your wish. Our liaison ends here.'

Storm was angry, too. Knowing he still wanted her, the creature was no doubt hoping to force him into offering her more. He would not be blackmailed into marriage, the idea of which he both disliked and feared. All his years of adolescence had been circumscribed, his behaviour dictated by others. His freedom was too precious to be surrendered for the sake of mere carnal delight. There were plenty of willing women in the world.

The anguish in Lexie's eyes almost undid him; but her bitter words served to strengthen his resolve.

'I am unused to the courtesies normally observed in a situation like this and bow to your superior knowledge, but if you are expecting me to wait until you tire of me and decide to dispense with my services, then you are sadly mistaken, my lord. I will not be cast aside like soiled linen!'

'Then it is certainly best that we part as soon as possible,' he bit back. 'But we cannot depart now, it is too late. We must wait until tomorrow. Neither can I conveniently vacate your bed. I do not wish to distress Martha. So—' His manner changed as he reached for her hands and smiled his most rakish smile. The smile that ravaged her senses. 'One last night together, eh?' he suggested.

Lexie swallowed. He was attempting to manipulate her and she knew it. She was sorely tempted to accept one last night of Heaven before she need contemplate the bleak future. She had, after all, suspected that he would not offer marriage even had she become pregnant. So nothing had actually changed.

But even as she thought of it her senses rebelled. She could not stand to have him touch her under the circumstances. She shook her head. 'We will share the bed if we must, but I cannot agree to anything more. I will go up now and pack.'

Storm hid his triumph. Tonight he would have a last chance to slake the raging desire the woman roused in him, for she would not be able to resist his skilled wooing. Then, after they parted next day, he would put her from his mind.

It did not quite work out that way. He had forgotten Lexie's will, her ability to deny her own desires. He should have remembered that occasion in the flat.

At his first overture, Lexie stiffened.

'No, Storm. You will have to force me.'

'I think not, my dear. You may not wish to continue the relationship, but your craving for me is not yet dead.'

She did not deny his charge. 'But my willingness to indulge it is! Our intimate relationship is over. It should never have been. Leave me alone, Storm, or I shall have to seek refuge with Martha.'

How long she could have withstood the searing demands of her body Lexie did not know. But her threat sobered him and he desisted.

'You are a fool, Lexie,' he gritted. 'But I am not an animal, whatever you may think. I shall not attempt to force you against your will. I wish you a good night.'

He turned his back, grappling with his need. Lexie's breathing became steady behind him. How easily she had fallen asleep! Had he really failed to stir her?

He lay for a long time contemplating a future without the warmth of her near him and did not like it. But he would recover.

He almost got up to walk off his frustration, but before he had quite decided on that course he fell asleep. Only as he edged into oblivion did his mind register that the things he valued most about her, her courage and pride, her determination, her principles, even her refusal to be entirely restricted by convention, remained intact. And had defeated his rash assumption that she would be willing to countenance anything he might desire.

He should have been more circumspect. He would try a more subtle approach in the morning.

But when he woke he found her side of the bed empty.

At first he did not worry. She had woken early and gone for a walk. Or gone down to make herself a drink in the kitchen, something she had taken to doing whenever either of them felt thirsty, for she enjoyed a cose with Martha, with whom she got on famously.

But when he rose and went downstairs there was no sign of her.

'Has Mistress Lexie gone out?' he asked Daisy, who was busy clearing the grate preparatory to boiling up water for washing.

'I haven't seen her, sir,' said Daisy, her rosy face beaming up at the handsome gentleman.

Martha was still abed. Storm returned to the room they had shared and only then did he notice that all Lexie's things had gone.

'The Devil! She has walked out on me!'

Nothing remotely like it had ever happened to him before. He had always been the one to end an *affaire*. Rejection tasted bitter.

But then he shrugged. What did it matter? They were to part today in any case. The end of an *affaire*. Nothing new in that. And perhaps she had merely woken early and gone to wake Marlow to have him prepare the chariot for the journey. That must be it.

But why take all her things?

Frowning, Storm descended the stairs again. 'I am

going to the inn to speak to Marlow,' he informed Daisy, who was by now scrubbing the floor.

The small place boasted only the one stables and post house, which were attached to the inn. The stables showed signs of life, but Marlow was nowhere to be seen.

'Not down yet, sir,' a pot boy told him upon enquiry.

'Have you seen the lady who normally accompanies me?'

'I seen her, sir. Hired the post chaise an hour ago. Had to wake the post boy. Grumpy, he were, at being roused so early from his bed.'

Storm cursed under his breath. He could probably catch her up, but why trouble? She wanted to go and should be safe enough in a hired chaise. He would knock Marlow up, tell him they were returning to Stormaston Park forthwith, and after submitting to Marlow's razor, go back for breakfast and bid Martha farewell.

Lady Amber would soon be forgotten once he returned to his estates, his duties and his experiments.

Lexie scarcely noticed the discomfort and poor state of the series of chaises which carried her to St Albans. Forced to change carriages at every stage, she was glad to have only scanty luggage with her. She arrived, after hours spent dully watching the rise and fall of a succession of postilions' bottoms, with just enough time to make the journey to Merryfield before dark. Or—should she take accommodation for the night and ride back tomorrow, at a respectable hour?

She decided on the latter course. She had slept scarcely a wink last night, though she had pretended to while the hot tears ran silently down to soak her pillow. Storm, she knew, had lain awake, too, though she sensed immediately when at last his breathing changed to the steady rhythm that told her he was asleep.

As the first streaks of dawn lit the sky she had slipped out of bed, silently donned her travelling gown, fearful of waking him with every rustle, picked up her bags and crept from the house. She regretted not being able to say goodbye to Martha but the old lady already knew how grateful she was for her hospitality. She would write her thanks the moment she reached home.

Now she needed time to recover her composure, to rehearse the story she would tell, to garner enough courage to smile, smile, smile, when she wanted to hide away and cry her heartache away.

Told who she was and having been shown several gold coins, the innkeeper discovered that he did have a small, private room the lady could have for the night. The head ostler would be pleased to allow her to inspect her animal and he could arrange for one of his stable hands to ride out to Merryfield with her the next day.

If the story spread that Lady Amber had slept at the Post House alone and unaccompanied, she would think of some explanation. A sudden emergency at her friend's—anything would do. She was, at that time, past caring what anyone thought. Except that she must hide her hurt. She could not bear to be looked upon with pity.

So she rode into the stable yard at Merryfield, paid off the man who had accompanied her, and returned Jethro's greeting with every appearance of cheerful good humour. Danny did not seem to have suffered unduly from his period in stables, though Jethro looked askance at his rough coat and slightly tangled mane.

'We'll soon have him trimmed and gleaming again,' he promised. 'I trust you enjoyed your visit, my lady?'

'Very much, thank you,' answered Lexie, truthfully. She would always have those golden days to remember as she drifted into elderly widowhood.

But as she settled back into the routine at Merryfield she found the unadulterated company of her cousin somewhat tedious. It certainly did nothing to relieve her misery. Caro's presence had been fine in London, when she was out most of the time and entertaining for much of the remainder, with Caro organising her household. She had scarcely noticed Caro's incessant chatter about trifling matters.

The truth was, she was missing Storm. His company had made all else bearable. Without it, life had become a wasteland.

She could not allow herself to drift into an uncaring decline. She did not need to marry, yet she had gone to London wanting to, for life was not pleasant or easy for a woman alone, however well situated. She had not looked for love before she met Storm. Just affection and compatibility. Having fallen disastrously in love, she had thought she could never marry anyone else, but. . .

If only there were some decent gentleman of suitable rank able to fill the empty places in her life, he might manage to change her mind. She needed children to love, to take away the ache the loss of Storm had left in her heart. Every time she had used her sponge and vinegar, she had had to grit her teeth.

It had been effective, for her monthly show had arrived spot on time almost as soon as she returned to Merryfield, relieving her of anxiety in that quarter, yet bringing a new cause for grief. Storm had passed no comment on her precautions. She wondered whether he had noticed. But having his child outside wedlock would not have been the answer.

Perhaps there would be different gentlemen in London looking for wives during the Little Season before Christmas. From what he had said, she did not think Storm would be returning to Town before the New Year, except for short business visits. He had no plan to circulate in Society. So she could take up residence in Bruton Street without fear of running into him at every turn.

'We are returning to London,' she told Caro that evening. 'I need to do some shopping.'

To her surprise, Caro beamed. 'I shall not be sorry, Alexia. Life here seems rather dull, does it not?'

'I did not think you would find it so!'

'I enjoy running the household here, of course, but—' Caro gave Lexie a guilty look '—I do miss a comfortable cose with Mrs Seacombe.'

'So you must! Well, I am glad we are agreed. Shall we leave at the end of next week?'

'I will go ahead and make certain that all is in readiness to receive you!'

'That will scarcely be necessary, Cousin. A note to Mr Dymock should be sufficient. Mrs Walker is quite capable of catering for us without supervision. We may travel together in the coach. Pascoe can arrange for my horses and curricle to follow.'

'You'll be dashing about in that again, I collect. Will you never change, Alexia?'

'Not if I can help it,' said Lexie grimly, envisioning some future husband frowning at her capers and forbidding them. She would have to be very sure of her man before she consented to relinquish her freedom.

For the first time, she appreciated Storm's reluctance to abandon his. But surely he knew that she would not attempt to restrict him? At least, not in ways unconnected with women! Just as she was certain he would not seek to restrain her?

Resolutely, she put such thought from her mind. She would forget. One day, as she watched her children grow up, she would wonder why she had allowed herself to be made so unhappy.

But tears gathered in her eyes as she acknowledged that they would not be James's children.

Once back in Bruton Street Lexie set about visiting acquaintances who were in residence and leaving her card. To her surprise, the Downshires were back in Grosvenor Square.

'My dear,' said the Duchess, eyeing Lexie critically. 'How delightful to see you again so soon. I did not expect you to return to Town until the main Season next year.'

'Neither did I,' admitted Lexie. 'But the estate does not need my attention and I missed the social life to be found here. A number of acquaintances seem to have either remained or returned to Town. My diary will soon be full! I trust I shall see both you and Fanny at many of the functions.'

'Probably not,' said the Duchess, her expression sobering. 'We are here to enable the Duke to consult a heart specialist. He is bein' forced to adhere to a strict regime, which I am certain he would soon abandon should we return to Downshire. He declares that he is not ready to quit his lease just yet, but we are all most concerned over his health. James has returned to Town to be on hand should his presence be required.'

'Oh, how sorry I am!' cried Lexie. 'I did so enjoy entertaining His Grace at Merryfield. He is one of the few gentlemen who would not condemn me for racing my curricle against his grandson!'

'Considers you a rare plucked 'un. Don't censure James for allowin' the wager, either. There are those who think it most reprehensible of my grandson to take money from a lady as a result of winnin'. But he is well used to weatherin' such criticism. He seems to court it. How are you, my dear? You do not look in plump currant at the moment.'

The Duchess's sudden change of topic took Lexie by surprise. She had been sleeping badly and eating little. She knew she looked tired and drawn and mention of James had almost overset her. But she turned to Fanny with a laugh. 'Just because I have grown thin everyone thinks I am ill!'

Fanny nodded. 'I seem to be adding flesh and everyone tells me how well I look. As though weight had anything to do with it!'

'Do call again, my dear,' pressed the Duchess as

Lexie took her leave. 'You know we shall always be pleased to receive you.'

To Lexie's relief, Storm appeared to be retired from Society for the moment. As far as she could gather, he spent most of his time at White's. A much improved Hugo appeared at Grosvenor Square, splendid in his uniform. He had been granted compassionate leave to visit his grandfather.

'Best thing I ever did,' he informed Lexie when they met. 'Havin' a splendid time in the army, enjoyin' the life immensely. Fine crowd of fellows in my mess, don't you know. We get up to all kinds of larks.'

'Innocent ones, I trust?' murmured Lexie sweetly, seething that he had put it forward as his idea to purchase a pair of colours and anxious that the good name of Graham should not suffer by his pranks.

'Oh, no harm in it, no harm at all. We hunt every day, ride like fury. Tally ho!'

He did seem pleased with himself and with life, which must be a relief to Storm. And to his grandparents.

'He is much changed,' the Duchess confided in the privacy of her boudoir, to which, some weeks later, Lexie had been invited. 'We was becomin' worried over him. Threatened to become frivolous, vain and spiteful. The discipline seems to be knockin' those unfortunate traits out of him. James bought his commission, y'know. Wanted to join the army himself years ago, but Downshire and I managed to persuade him against. Have you seen him lately?'

Lexie's heart continued to hammer, as it always did when Storm was mentioned. She clasped her hands in her lap, then plucked at the wool and silk mixture of her soft violet morning gown. 'No, ma'am. He is not attending many functions. We have not met since my return to London.'

'Hmm.' The knotted fingers arranged her grey skirts more comfortably as the Duchess lay back on her *chaise longue*. 'Just as well, the mood he is in. Never known him so morose. Nothing right.' She raised her lorgnette. 'Have you quarrelled?'

Lexie flushed. 'We are no longer on the best of terms.'

'Won't ask why.' She dropped the glasses to her lap. 'Reprobate won't wed you, I collect. Do him good not to get his own way in everythin'.'

'He did not get it over joining the army,' Lexie reminded the Duchess quietly.

'No, but there ain't been many things he's been denied since he came of age. Especially women. Runs through 'em like smoke.'

Lexie winced.

'But there don't seem to be anyone at the moment,' went on the Duchess disingenuously. 'Treat him kindly when you meet. You can never tell, with James. He don't give in easily, but when he does, he does it handsomely.'

Unable to stand any more of the Duchess's hints, Lexie turned the subject. 'Has Fanny any new suitors?'

'One or two. But she don't take any notice of 'em. She's like James in that. Won't do what she don't want to. But she's young. I've heard that Cranley is after you. What do you think of him, eh?'

Lexie chose her words carefully. 'He seems a kind, decent sort of gentleman. Pleasant enough.' But wildly boring.

'Will never set the Thames on fire, but he's well placed. You could do worse than consider him if James refuses to come up to scratch. Cranley is turned forty. He won't wait much longer to find himself a wife.'

'No.'

The Duchess took the hint and the conversation turned to fashion for the winter ahead. It was already chilly and damp, with fogs rising off the Thames. Fanny came in and joined the conversation. She was looking particularly wan, in Lexie's opinion, despite her rounded figure. She wondered how much she was seeing of Lord Dexter, for Felix was in Town.

A couple of days later she was surprised to be told that Lady Fanny Graham was below, asking if her ladyship would receive her.

'Alone?' asked Lexie in surprise. Fanny usually came with the Duchess.

'Apart from her servant, my lady.'

'Send her up immediately!'

Lexie had no other callers that morning and received Fanny in the morning-room, where she had been sitting at her writing table composing letters to her mother in Ireland and John Lyme at Merryfield.

'Fanny!' she greeted her friend. 'How nice to see you! Do sit down.'

She indicated a comfortable winged armchair and Fanny perched on the edge of the seat, clearly in a considerable state of agitation.

'Oh, Lexie!' she exclaimed. 'I do hope you may be able to help us!'

Lexie lifted enquiring golden eyebrows. 'Us?'

'Felix and me.' Fanny swallowed. 'I am pregnant.'

Lexie, who had subsided into the depths of her comfortable chair, sat up straight.

'By Felix?' As though she needed to ask! The rake!

'Yes, but it is not what you think! I begged him to make love to me. We were desperate, you see. We love each other so, but we both knew from things James has said that he would never approve the match. He has as good as warned Felix off. Yet Felix has changed, he does not even look at other women and would abandon everything for me! But I will not allow that.'

Now that the flood-gates had opened, Fanny seemed unable to stop her rush of words. Her hands were twisting together in her lap. 'We could elope but just think of the scandal! And I believe that once he is faced with the fact of my condition, James will have to permit our marriage. That is why I did it,' she finished on a gulp.

'I cannot deny that you astonish me, Fanny! When did you conceive this desperate plan?'

'At Merryfield. Felix came to me there. It was easy. And I began increasing immediately. I wasn't certain at first, I have never been very regular, you know, but I am quite sure now. I must be three months on and I shall begin to show soon. We must act immediately. Oh! Lexie, could you tell James and persuade him to let us marry? He respects your judgment. Please, Lexie!'

'Your condition explains your added pounds,' said Lexie wryly. Ask James? How could she? 'Do your grandparents know?' she asked, to gain more time.

Fanny shook her head. 'I would rather they need not. I have no wish to hurt them. But James is my guardian. I must have his permission if I am not to elope. Do say you'll break the news to him, Lexie!'

'They can count, Fanny. They will guess when your baby is born so very early.'

'Well, we shall go on a tour abroad. We can, now Napoleon is defeated. No one will know exactly when the infant is born.'

'You would lie about his birthday? Celebrate the wrong date?'

'What would it matter?'

'Not much, I suppose. But Fanny, I have to tell you that Storm and I are no longer so friendly as we were. I have not seem him this age.'

'Oh.' Fanny's countenance fell. 'I did wonder, for he has stopped circulating in Society while you have not. But I am certain he still holds you in high regard! He always mentions you when he comes to visit Grandfather.'

Lexie sighed. No doubt he was covering up his discomfiture over being abandoned in Essex. He would never admit to what he would see as her rejection. She could understand that.

She spoke of him to his grandmother, for the Duchess related all the latest gossip. Much good it did her to hear it, for he seemed to be behaving with remarkable restraint despite his reported ill-temper, and that made her love him all the more; but just to speak of him seemed some kind of comfort, even though it caused immense agitation of the spirit. Dared she hope he felt the same?

No, that would be foolish. He had never loved her, simply desired her. Perhaps he wished to hear that she was in a fit of the dismals so that he could know the satisfaction of thinking that it served her right. Or to ascertain whether her unhappiness was liable to throw her back into his arms. Or whether desperation to wed would result in her accepting some dullard like Cranley. She hoped that, if she did, he would be a little upset.

But Fanny was waiting eagerly for her response. How could she refuse to try to help? She did not really know how Storm now felt about her. Her intervention might set him further against the match rather than influence him towards it, but she felt compelled to try. She had grown fond of Fanny, she liked Felix enormously, she liked and respected the Duke and Duchess and would save them from hurt if she could.

In the end she reached out and took one of Fanny's restless hands in hers. 'I will speak to him, Fanny, but do not rely too heavily on my proving successful.'

Fanny departed full of profuse thanks. Lexie resumed her seat at her writing table and embarked upon the difficult task of sending Storm a note asking him to call the following morning to discuss a delicate but important matter.

When she was satisfied with the wording she sent a footman round to his rooms to deliver the note. Storm was out and so she had to wait in some trepidation for either an answer or for his advent the next day.

She wished that the prospect of seeing him again did not cause her so much agitation. He might refuse to come. In that case she would have done her best, her conscience would be clear.

But her heart would feel heavier than ever.

CHAPTER TWELVE

LEXIE dressed with especial care the next morning. A
note had arrived early to say that his lordship would
call at eleven o'clock and she did not want him to
think her pining.

'There, my lady,' said Chalker. 'You are looking
splendid, this morning. It is a long time since his
lordship called, is it not? Will he be your escort again
next Season?'

Lexie suspected that Chalker had her own ideas as
to what had happened while she was on holiday. But
Lexie had not confided in either her or Caro. Better to
keep her secret locked in her heart.

'I do not expect so,' she responded. She smiled.
'Lord Cranley would be certain to object.'

Chalker looked disapproving. 'Oh, him.'

'What is it, Florence? Do you not like Lord
Cranley?'

'He's not for you, my lady,' burst out Chalker, then
blushed a furious red. 'Forgive me, my lady! I should
not have said that.'

'No,' agreed Lexie repressively, 'you should not.
However, I incline to agree with you.'

'You do? I'm that glad, your ladyship! Couldn't bear
the thought of you marrying that dull stick of a
gentleman! You and Lord Stormaston were meant for
each other!'

'The Marquess does not think so,' said Lexie drily.

She did not reprove her maid further. She had given Chalker the opening and, in truth, was glad to have her own opinion confirmed. She would have to discourage the man or he would gain the wrong impression. Unlike Storm he was serious in his intentions. Perhaps if she did something really outrageous. . .

The hint of a smile played at the corners of Lexie's mouth. Her green eyes sparkled back at her from the mirror. Yes, she looked in fine fettle, thank goodness! If only she were not so nervous! But the heat generated by her tension had put a healthy-looking flush on her cheeks. She hoped he would be punctual. He usually was.

Dymock announced his arrival as the clock on the mantelpiece in the morning-room struck the hour. Lexie remained seated as he made his bow.

Against all propriety, Caro was not present to act as chaperon and Lexie gestured to Dymock to close the door of the morning-room behind him.

Storm did not take the proffered seat and had a faint sneer on his face as he spoke.

'If you hope to compromise me by conducting this interview in seclusion, ma'am, you will fail.'

Lexie gasped and the faint colour in her cheeks fled, leaving her looking pinched. 'You are unkind! I had no such idea in mind, my lord! I merely wished for privacy. I would not like others to overhear our conversation this morning.'

'No? I must admit you surprise me. If you are to tell me you are pregnant despite all your care, an audience would appear an advantage.'

He was, she sensed, in a towering temper, which he

was unleashing on her, although his quite unwarranted scorn seemed to hold an element of hurt in it, too. But she had no time to search out the reason for this. She composed herself to face his anger, his contempt, without quailing. For Fanny's sake.

'I am not pregnant,' she informed him steadily, her knuckles white on the hands clasped in her lap. 'I would not have requested an interview on my own behalf. I wished to speak with you about your sister, Lady Fanny.'

'Fanny!'

The explosive exclamation illuminated Lexie's understanding. He already knew! And thought she was about to attempt a similar form of blackmail! She heaved a sigh, partly of relief, partly to bolster her courage.

'She came to see me yesterday in great distress. She and Felix—'

Storm interrupted her with a smothered curse. 'Have behaved in the most scandalous manner!' he finished her sentence for her in his own words. 'And Felix has the gall to tell me that he wishes to wed the chit! No doubt some would regard this as an honourable intention, but I know better! He seduced an innocent girl for his own ends. I will not have it. I have called him out. My seconds are meeting his today.'

'James! You cannot mean it! They are so in love! Are you blind, that you have not noticed how they adore each other? But they knew you would not approve the match and so Fanny begged—yes—' as Storm gave a snort of disbelief '—Fanny begged Felix to lie with her! I had it from her own mouth!'

'Fanny would never—'

'Have you spoken to her, James? Does her happiness mean nothing to you? Oh, I know Felix has a bad reputation with women, but any man can change. Fanny is convinced he is devoted to her. And if you deny them the chance to wed, what becomes of the child she is to bear?'

'It will be taken care of.'

'Poor little soul!' Then, 'Did Felix speak to you?' wondered Lexie again. 'Fanny pleaded with me to intercede—'

'I cannot imagine what good she imagined you might achieve.'

'She did not know of the extent of our estrangement. I told her you probably would not listen to me, but she still pleaded with me to approach you. Did Felix. . .?' She left her repeated question trailing.

'No, he did not have that much nerve! I had to discover the truth from Hugo.'

'Hugo! Is he in Town again?' And up to his old tricks? 'How did he find out?'

'Put two and two together and made four, I collect. He is her brother, they are more of an age and he knows her better than I do.' Storm sounded resentful rather than regretful. 'His conclusions were confirmed by a weeping Fanny and he took the greatest of pleasure in informing me, coming straight round last evening to my rooms to suggest that I was to blame for introducing her to my disreputable friends. I suppose I am, but I thought she had more sense!'

'Love,' pronounced Lexie sadly, 'takes no account of common sense. So you tackled Felix, who admitted the offence, and you called him out!'

'Exactly.'

'And what good will that do, except to prove who is the better shot? Or is it to be swords? Really, Storm, I thought you had better judgement! They will make a well-matched pair—'

'Fanny is well dowered, Felix lacks funds. So much for your so-called love!'

'I do not believe that to be his motive. From what I have observed, he is truly enamoured of your sister. And why not? She is a fine young woman.'

'Hugo told me you encouraged the match!' Hurt and anger mingled in his voice as he made the accusation. 'That was why you brought them together at Merryfield, no doubt—to give them the chance to misbehave. I saw Felix returning to his room one night and thought he had been with the parlour maid!'

'You, my lord, sound like the pot calling the kettle black! Where had you been?'

'That was an entirely different matter! You are a widow, not a green girl scarcely out of the schoolroom!'

'To you, perhaps it is. Not to others, should they learn of it. But why don't you speak with Fanny? Let her plead her cause?'

Storm threw back his head and regarded Lexie down his aristocratic nose. 'The matter will be settled between Dexter and myself.'

Lexie found it impossible to remain seated a moment longer. She sprang to her feet.

'Is Fanny to have no say in the matter? Is her opinion to be treated as of no account? Really, Lord Stormaston, I thought you more enlightened than to behave like a despot!'

'I will not argue with you, Lady Amber. I will bid you good day.'

He bowed and, without waiting for the butler to show him out, marched from the house. Lexie watched his retreating form, the stiff set of his shoulders and wept for Fanny. And for herself.

Where was the James Graham she had come to know over those wonderful weeks by the sea? If the Marquess did not watch his behaviour, he would soon become as dry a stick as Lord Cranley.

Storm, striding back to his rooms, felt all the bitterness of defeat.

Unable to bear the thought of his life without her, he had been on the point of abandoning his resolve, lowering his pride and declaring himself to Lexie, asking her to marry him. And then Hugo had come along to trample on his hopes.

Fanny and Dexter had deceived him. This alone he could have borne. But for Lexie, his high-spirited, green-eyed, golden nymph, to conspire in their deceit, had hurt him more than he would care to acknowledge.

He had thought her eminently honest and open. But all females were the same. Every one of them would betray a man at the drop of a hat. Just when he thought he had at last found a woman he could both love and trust, the creature had to prove otherwise.

But it simply confirmed him in his earlier opinion. He must make a marriage of convenience to beget an heir, but not until he could no longer put off the evil moment. That was all he had left to hope for in the way of domestic felicity. The woman whose company he craved had proved false.

Upon his return, Marlow greeted him dourly.

'Lord Hugo called to tell you that the duel is arranged for just after dawn tomorrow. That is, at six-thirty of the clock. I have cleaned your pistols.'

'What is it, man? You look as though you had just lost a fortune.'

'Never having had one to lose, I wouldn't know what that was like, begging your pardon, my lord. But what I do know is that this affair is foolish. Lord Dexter is your friend. He is a lively young man, but there is no real vice in him. If Lady Fanny—'

'Remember your place, Marlow!' barked Storm. 'Are you daring to question my actions?'

'No, sir.' Marlow failed to look abashed. 'Only your sense. You cannot fight your best friend, sir!'

'You think not? We shall see!'

Storm's displeasure with Fanny and Felix had cooled somewhat overnight. He knew the temptation desire could put in a man's way, and in a woman's, too, if they were only allowed to admit it. But the pair should have confided in him earlier.

Felix should have requested his permission to address Fanny. That he would probably have refused did not signify. He might, in the end, have been persuaded, for Felix had been his companion in sin for many years and he knew perfectly well that, like his own, Felix's behaviour was not as disgraceful as many thought.

He himself had been contemplating marrying a modest young woman he had seduced by a trick, against her will. His conscience smote him at the thought, but he quickly pushed it aside, telling himself again that she had, after all, agreed to the wager, as he followed his line of reasoning. If he had considered himself a suitable husband for Lexie, why should not Felix make Fanny a desirable spouse?

He had acted from outrage and pique, anger against the erring couple, and disgust and disappointment over Lexie's betrayal, all fuelled by her note, which he had immediately taken to be another attempt to blackmail him into a course of action he would never choose. Or rather, that Lexie believed he would never choose.

But that had not been so. He could not doubt the sincerity of her denial. At least he had that comfort. If comfort it was.

But, death and hell, he had committed himself to a confounded duel and could not back out now! He had no desire to either kill or injure Felix. He was the better shot, but Felix was pretty accurate and could not be relied upon to miss. It seemed likely that one or the other or both would end up with a bullet in him. He hoped Hugo had engaged a competent surgeon.

Hugo was relishing this. The army had made him somewhat bloodthirsty. But on the whole his behaviour had been greatly improved by the discipline, everyone had remarked upon it. And most of the time he was away, swept from under the feet of his family, unable to cause embarrassment.

It was as well he had been home yesterday. Otherwise Lexie might have pulled the wool over his eyes, might have pleaded Fanny's cause without his ever knowing the despicable part she had played in the drama.

That, he considered, was quite the most hurtful aspect of the entire affair. Even a bullet in the shoulder would not occasion him so much pain.

* * *

Fanny came tearing round to Bruton Street quite unable to restrain her tears, even in public.

'Oh, Lexie!' she cried. 'Hugo guessed! He made me confess and went straight round to inform James, and James went to see Felix and they are to fight a duel! Felix will be killed, I know it, for he is not as accurate a shot as James, although he is better with a pistol than a sword, which is why he chose it—'

'I know, my dear,' said Lexie, the moment she could get a word in edgeways. 'Lord Stormaston came round here in a towering rage. He accused me of conspiring with you to arrange a suitable venue for your fornication!' she added grimly.

'Oh, how could he! I must see him, but he is keeping out of the way, he has not been to Grosvenor Square today. Why will he not listen to what I have to say?'

'Because he is arrogant and pig-headed. But do not despair. Felix may fire a lucky shot. James may be killed.'

Her voice shook but Fanny, wrapped up in her own grief, did not notice.

'Oh, do not say so! I could not bear that, either! How could I marry the man who had killed my brother?'

'An impasse, I agree,' said Lexie drily. How could she still wish to wed a man who considered her a liar and a cheat? 'But I cannot conceive of any way to stop this foolishness. We do not even know where the duel is to be fought, or the time that has been fixed. Although Hugo probably knows. Could you winkle the information from him?'

Fanny shook her head. 'I have not seen him since yesterday, either. Now he is in the army he is staying at the Guards' Club with fellow officers, as guest of a friend in the Foot Guards. I cannot visit him there.'

'Neither can I. But you could send a note asking him to call.'

'Which, knowing Hugo, he would ignore, guessing I would want to drag the details of the meeting from him.'

'So we must wait in ignorance, the lot of women down the ages, it seems to me. But you know, Fanny, I do not think either man will attempt to kill his opponent. They have been too close.'

'I do pray you are right! And there is another thing. Grandmama is beginning to suspect that there is something wrong. I dread her quizzing me when I return!'

'It would take a moron not to notice that something is upsetting you, Fanny! Of course your grandmother can see something is wrong! I think you should make a clean breast of the entire thing. She may be able to influence your brother where I cannot. He does listen to her.'

'Only when he wants to,' said Fanny gloomily. But her tears had dried up. 'It would be a comfort to tell her everything. But she will be so upset!'

'Perhaps not as much as you might expect. She is an unusual lady, my dear Fanny. And, you know, she favours Lord Dexter.'

'You think she does?' Fanny responded eagerly.

'I am certain she has a fondness for him. Whether that extends to approving a match between you I could not say. But do not despair, Fanny. Things may not be as black as you believe them to be.'

Lexie sent Fanny on her way in a more sanguine

state of mind than when she had arrived. As for herself, she could only pray that neither Storm nor Felix would wish to seriously harm the other.

But she could not sit about waiting for news to be brought to her! Had she been in Fanny's shoes she would have defied convention, scandalised Society and charged round to the Guards' Club to demand to see Hugo. However, the duel was not to be fought over her; she had no official reason to be concerned in the affair. So her involvement must be discreet, secret.

Somehow, she must contrive to be present. She would not be able to prevent the exchange of fire, but she had to know the worst the instant it happened. For if Storm were badly injured she would indeed defy convention once more and rush to his side. That should prove outrageous enough to deter Cranley, she thought, enjoying a momentary gleam of humour. And should Felix be the victim she would like to be in a position to carry the news to Fanny.

Her thoughts were much occupied for the remainder of the day. By evening she had formed a plan.

Chalker was used to her irregular ways and evinced little surprise at being asked to call her mistress at five and dress her for riding. The yawning stable boy saddled Danny without demur. And Lexie set off alone just before dawn broke to loiter in the shadows at the end of St James's Street, hoping that Storm and his seconds had not already left for the rendezvous.

She saw Hugo and another man arrive and relaxed. She watched them leave shortly afterwards with Storm, followed by Marlow carrying his master's gun case. All four travelled inside the unidentifiable coach Storm had used to abduct her.

It was easy enough to follow them to Hampstead Heath. Felix and his party arrived almost simultaneously and another carriage drove up shortly afterwards, apparently carrying the surgeon and umpire.

Lexie, dismounted, holding Danny's headstall, and watched from the shelter of nearby bushes. If only she could do something to stop the madness! But the men would never allow a woman to intervene, to prevent them carrying out an idiotic ritual which a misguided sense of honour demanded they enact. They would simply set her to one side and carry on.

So she waited, silent, tense, her mind offering up unformed prayers for some intervention from the Almighty, while the seconds went through the motions of arranging the details of the duel to everyone's satisfaction.

Storm stood ready, remembering that first duel he had fought with rapiers, his sense of utter disillusion when he had discovered his defence of the lady's honour to have been ill-advised. He had vowed never to love another woman, false creatures that they were, and had treated Lexie badly because of his bitterness but, despite his vow, had allowed himself to be drawn into its meshes again. He had, against all his principles and wishes, fallen in love with Lexie. And she, too, had proved false.

And now he was about to fight his best friend for deflowering his sister. He did not want to believe that Fanny had been the instigator of the affair. She was no wanton, while Felix was a proven rake. He must be the guilty party. But women were unreliable creatures. He should have tackled Fanny. But it was a delicate matter and he had not managed to steel himself for the task.

Honour demanded he seek satisfaction from Felix, who had wronged his sister, his ward. But his heart was not in it. Storm stood back to back with his friend, who looked haggard and anxious—as well he might, since he was by far the worse shot, proved time after time in Manton's shooting gallery.

The umpire began to count. His mind clear as crystal, his hand perfectly steady, Storm strode forward the fifteen paces demanded, turned and fired. He heard Felix's almost simultaneous shot and waited for the jolt and the pain as the round tore into his flesh. Or for oblivion.

Lexie watched, holding her breath, as they strode apart, turned and fired. Incredulous, she saw puffs of dust rise a yard or so in front of Storm and a yard to one side of Felix. Choked by overwhelming relief, she saw them come together and shake hands. Then she was on Danny's back, riding like fury to Grosvenor Square in order to give Fanny the news of both men's safety.

When she arrived at Downshire House and asked to see Lady Fanny, she was shown into the Duchess's bedchamber. The elderly lady was still in bed, propped up against a mound of pillows, with Fanny sitting beside her. Her Grace sat very still. The old eyes, slightly watery, fixed themselves on Lexie's face.

Lexie made a quick curtsy and while she did so, without preamble, she announced, 'They are both unharmed.'

She saw the stiffly held shoulders of the Duchess

relax. Fanny gave a gasp of surprise and pleasure and threw herself at Lexie, clasping her so tightly in her exuberant relief that Lexie, laughing, protested.

'I pray you will not strangle me, Fanny!'

'But how did you find out?' demanded the cause of all the trouble breathlessly.

'I followed the Marquess to the meeting place and watched. Both gentlemen aimed their shots at the ground.'

A snort from the bed brought Lexie's attention back to the Duchess. Her lace-covered head had subsided against the pillows but her eyes held a new alertness.

'What a sad roil you made of this, Fanny! Why could you not have spoken to me earlier? I would have made James see sense. All these dramatics were quite unnecessary!'

Fanny, abashed, hung her head. 'I told you, Grandmama, at first I believed that you would side with James. You did wish me to wed Oswald Cresswell, did you not?' The question was rhetorical and, ignoring the Duchess's impatient grunt, Fanny rushed on.

'Then, later, when I discovered my condition, I did not wish to upset you or Grandpapa. Lexie said you liked Felix and had influence with James, but I was afraid to test the truth of it in case I caused a quarrel between you. Even now,' she added gloomily, 'I suppose James will oppose the match.'

'Probably,' agreed her grandparent. 'But he will allow it. And as for you, young woman,' turning to Lexie, 'we owe you a debt of gratitude. You have saved us from hours of lowerin' suspense, for I doubt if either participant will make haste to present himself here.'

'I could not bear to wait idly for news and knew you would be equally anxious.'

'And so, being the enterprisin' creature you are, you took matters into your own hands! Did it by yourself, no doubt, eh? Didn't take a groom with you, I'll wager!'

Lexie made a regretful face. 'No, ma'am.'

'You must take breakfast with us. They are sendin' up trays. Then I'll instruct one of my grooms to ride back with you, after you've paid your respects to Downshire. Might as well make some show of behavin' with proper decorum.'

'Yes, ma'am,' said Lexie meekly, her eyes dancing as they met those of the Duchess.

'Did James know you were present?' demanded that lady.

Lexie shook her head. 'I took care not to be seen. Since they were engaged in an affair of honour, I did not wish either gentleman to think me an interfering female.'

'Hmm. So he will not realise that we know what transpired. Excellent. Fanny, you will not admit to knowing the result of this farce, d'you hear me?'

'Very well, Grandmama.'

The Duchess greeted the appearance of the breakfast trays with a smug expression on her lined face. All three set about demolishing their contents with good appetite. An hour ago Lexie would not have thought herself capable of eating a bite. As for Fanny. 'I'm eating for two,' she giggled.

That giggle was a sign of her relief. Lexie felt like joining her in senseless merriment. James was safe. But she wondered what kind of reception he could expect when he presented himself later, as he must, to tackle the problem of Fanny's future.

Storm had not yet given Felix permission to marry his ward. He had not killed him or even maimed him for daring to aspire to winning Fanny's hand, or for robbing her of her virginity. Yet Felix had felt equally unable to try to further his cause by killing or maiming the man who stood in the way of his ambition.

'I will think about it,' was all Storm would promise as they parted after shaking hands. 'And you will not communicate with my sister until after I have seen her and you have my permission. Is that understood?

Felix had looked about to argue, but seeing the steely glint in his friend's eyes, had compressed his lips and desisted. 'She will wish to hear from me,' was all he had said.

Storm had heard the sound of hoofbeats retreating at a gallop and looked up to glimpse a shadowy figure on a chestnut horse, its coat shining copper in the first of the sun's rays, and his heart had lurched.

It could not have been Lexie. She could not have known where the meeting was to be held. And even she would surely not venture out alone to attend a duel. Yet the impression persisted as he made his way back to St James's. Had she, somehow, discovered the venue and come to watch?

Was her conscience troubling her, that tender conscience which had caused him such frustration over the last months? Despite her denials, she must have encouraged the pair, have contributed to the situation which had led to the meeting. No doubt she wanted to witness the result of her intrigues. Would she have been troubled had it resulted in death or injury? To either man?

His uneasy ruminations did not prevent his eating a hearty breakfast and, thereafter, he took over an hour to dress in full fig in preparation for an interview with Fanny and the Duchess. He had no doubt at all that his grandmother was by now privy to all that had transpired and of his challenge to Felix. And if that had been Lexie galloping off, then she probably already knew he was safe and sound, too.

So let her wait while he donned the togs of the consummate man about Town. Weston's tailoring was superb, he admitted, inspecting the fit of his black superfine coat with satisfaction, the hang of his fashionable trousers with approval. Pantaloons were going out and he did not regret the change. He knew he looked the epitome of restrained elegance as he later made his way, at a leisurely stroll, to Grosvenor Square.

He needed no announcement in what would one day be his own domain. He deposited his hat and stick, nodded dismissively to the butler, who had informed him that Her Grace and Lady Fanny were in the morning-room while His Grace was resting in bed, and made his way upstairs.

At sight of him Fanny jumped to her feet and flew across the room.

'James!' she cried, flinging herself into his arms. 'You are safe! Oh, I am so glad!'

Fanny was not a good actress. Her surprise and pleasure at seeing him safe were obviously feigned. She had not asked about Felix's fate. Storm grinned with false amiability.

'I collect that Lady Amber has already conveyed the

news of Lord Dexter's survival,' he remarked drily, and noted the look of frustrated annoyance which crossed his grandparent's face.

His mood lightened. The Duchess had been about to pretend she knew nothing of the outcome of the affair. No doubt she would have made dragging the details from him an embarrassing business. He was almost grateful to Lexie for forestalling him.

'And now, if you please, I would wish to speak with my ward in private. Come, Fanny. Let us retire to the library.'

The Duchess tapped her stick on the floor, a single, loud, authoritative thump. 'You will conduct the interview here, James. I will not have Fanny intimidated or upset by your prejudices!'

'You agree to the match, I collect, ma'am. I have to inform you that, although I have no dislike for Lord Dexter and find him an agreeable companion, I do not consider him a suitable husband for my sister. He is, to put it bluntly, a confirmed womaniser and reckless gambler. Fanny would soon discover her mistake when she had to suffer the humiliation of countless infidelities and discovered that all her dower had been frittered away.'

'He would not—' began Fanny, only to be interrupted by the Duchess.

'Fustian, James! I am surprised at you! Ain't you noticed a change in Dexter's behaviour this Season? Even my old eyes could see how attached he and Fanny have become!'

'Your eyes are sharp enough when you wish, Grandmama.'

'And they ain't quite so concentrated on my own affairs and misdeeds as yours, my boy!'

'So,' said Storm, dropping languidly into a chair, since it seemed he must conduct his interview with Fanny in the presence of his grandparent, 'do I collect that you approve of Fanny's misconduct?'

The Duchess snorted. 'Foolish child! Of course I do not! But it was your attitude which drove her to it, James. Told her, should have asked me. But there you are, young people these days will go their own way. You can't fight this, James. There's the baby to consider. This great-grandchild—' she shot a withering glance at her grandson '—won't have it born a bastard. So get Dexter along here immediately. Settle the matter. Make the child happy.'

'I want nothing more than Fanny's happiness, believe me. I just cannot conceive that marriage to Dexter will bring it.'

'Just as no mama can imagine their daughter finding happiness with you. Yet you have it in you to make an excellent husband. If you wed the right woman.'

Storm made an impatient gesture. 'Leave me out of this! It is Fanny's future happiness we are discussing! As her guardian, I cannot approve the match.'

'Oh, James!' wailed Fanny. 'Must you be so difficult? Felix and I love each other! We must marry!'

'You have made it imperative and left me small room for manoeuvre, that I concede. I cannot give the match my absolute blessing: however, neither can I prevent it.'

'Oh, I knew you could not be so hard-hearted! Thank you, oh! thank you, James!'

'Had you chosen to marry Mr Cresswell—'

'But we neither of us wanted the match! Why, he helped Felix and me! We would all go off together and he would leave us alone somewhere and then escort us back again!'

'Oswald Cresswell did that?'

The incredulous note in Storm's voice made Fanny giggle. 'Oswald is so sweet! And not nearly as much under his mama's thumb as you might imagine!'

'But it was Lady Amber who encouraged you to lie together to enable you to blackmail me!'

'No, she didn't know a thing about that. Lexie is far too scrupulous to do anything to encourage impropriety!' The blank stare Storm gave her could not stop Fanny now she had begun her confession. 'It was entirely my idea, James, and I had to threaten Felix that I would abide by your wishes and wed Oswald if he wouldn't compromise me!'

Storm's eyes sharpened. 'You gave me to understand Cresswell had no wish to marry you!'

'Neither had he! Felix didn't really believe I was serious, but it made him realise how determined I was. Oswald cherishes a *tendre* for Lexie, you know, although he knows it is hopeless. But I believe he is growing fond of Miss Daventry. Once Lexie is wed—'

Storm crossed his long legs and fiddled with the set of his trousers. 'Lady Amber is considerin' marryin' again, is she?'

'Lord Cranley, if she has any sense,' interrupted the Duchess. 'I am confident he is on the point of offerin' for her.' Ignoring Storm's sudden frown, quite at odds with the studied nonchalance of his manner, she waved an imperious hand. 'There is a pen and paper on the table. Send a note to Lord Dexter this moment! Put the poor creature out of his misery. Had I been he, I'd have winged you, James, for bein' such a numbskull.'

Storm was left wondering in which direction the Duchess thought he had been foolish. Or whether she considered his every action had been that of a dolt. He was beginning to doubt his acumen himself.

'Fanny,' said the Duchess when the note had been dispatched, 'go and make yourself tidy for when Felix arrives. You will not wish to greet your betrothed looking all of a scramble. And I wish to exchange a few private words with your brother.'

CHAPTER THIRTEEN

STORM'S, heart sank at his grandmother's words. He could guess what was coming and had no wish to discuss his own affairs until he had sorted out his feelings.

Lexie had not been culpable. He had accused her wrongly. She might refuse to forgive him, and he could not blame her if she did.

But more to the point, he had a large bone to pick with his dearly beloved brother. Without doubt, Hugo had been up to his tricks again, sowing distrust and discord in his elder brother's path. Would the fool never learn that jealousy such as his could sour his entire life? He had been given the chance to make something of himself and on the surface had profited from the experience.

But the heart beneath that red jacket with the blue facings and gold lace had not changed. Hugo's resentment at being born the younger son still lived and he would seek to damage his brother in any way he could.

A lesson Storm would not soon forget. He should have realised that Hugo was not to be trusted. Hugo had sold him a pack of lies about Lexie.

'Forgive me, Grandmama, but I really must leave,' he said, rising as Fanny left the room. 'I have to see Hugo. Make sure everythin' is settled, no loose ends left after the affair this mornin'.'

'Of course everything is settled, James! You shook

hands with Felix, neither of you was hurt and if the doctor has not been paid he will send in his account! Oblige me by sittin' down.'

With a resigned shrug, Storm did as bidden. When his grandparent was in this mood, there could be no gainsaying her without being discourteous.

'Hugo,' pronounced his discerning relative, 'doubtless engineered the duel. Thought the boy was gettin' over his resentment and envy of you, but it seems he still bears a grudge. Told you about Fanny and Dexter in such a way as to put you out of temper, I'd wager.'

Storm had to admit that the Duchess was right.

'I believe he told you lies about Lady Alexia, as well. Poor child, your lack of trust upset her dreadfully.'

Storm was not going to admit, even to the old lady giving him a well-deserved set-down, that he had also accused Lexie of an intention to use a similar excuse to blackmail him into marriage. He remained silent.

'How could you believe Hugo's version without question?' went on his inexorable critic. 'You've known the boy as long as the rest of us! Fond as I am of him—for he is, after all, my grandson—I have never blinded myself to his faults. If he can hurt you, James, he will. Never forget it.'

'I have excellent reason to remember, ma'am.'

'You have behaved like a pot-head, James. There was no need for all this pother, let alone the farce this mornin'.' She glared at him, pointing at his cheek. 'I thought you'd had enough of duels to last you a lifetime!'

Storm lifted his brows and gave a slight, deprecating smile. 'I have fought others. Surely you knew?'

The Duchess glared down her nose and sniffed. 'I heard. You were not hurt. Gentlemen indulgin' in sword fights or shootin' each other's heads off over a stupid point of honour don't concern me.'

Storm's brows quirked and his eyes laughed in wicked contradiction.

'Even when you are involved,' continued the Duchess repressively, 'know you can take care of yourself and it's usually all over by the time I hear. Besides, you're not likely to kill or be killed, the penalty is too harsh. Even if you escaped with your life you'd be condemned to live abroad, have to forfeit your estates and inheritance. Too much sense for that, thank God. And so have your likely opponents. But when Fanny is involved, then I do consider it my business. Hurt Dexter and she'd be devastated. And Society would be flooded with gossip and innuendo. She would have been ruined. She may well be now, if the affair becomes broadcast.'

Slowly, Storm sat up straight. He looked his grandmother in the eye, his expression horrified. 'Can you believe, Grandmama, that that consequence never entered my head?'

'Easily! Nothin' sensible has entered your head for months!' declared the Duchess. She shook her head in disgust, setting the ribbons and lace of her cap fluttering.

'Would never have believed a son of mine could have reared such a witless brood. Hugo doin' his best to ruin himself and take you with him, Fanny goin' off at half cock because she thinks she won't get her own way, and you, my boy, have offered over the past months as prime an example of dimwitted behaviour as I ever hope to witness!'

Storm lifted his eye-glass and eyed his grandparent through it in his most arrogant manner. 'In what way exactly, may I ask?'

'No need to glare at me through that thing! Don't signify with me! Why haven't you offered for Alexia Hamilton?'

Storm's fingers tightened about the slender handle of the glass. His grandmother heard the snap of the delicate silver stem. She gave a wolfish grin.

'That came near the bone, eh? There's been somethin' goin' on between you for months. She refused to warm your bed for you, and so she should, a respectable widow like the Countess of Amber. So what did you do? Give up? Or continue to pester her? And what was that curricle race at Merryfield really about? Who suggested it?'

'Lady Amber herself.' Storm had recovered himself. He spoke with a careless shrug of his impeccably tailored shoulders. 'She wished to prove her skill at drivin' to be superior to mine. Unfortunately, she couldn't and lost the wager.'

'And looked uncommonly disconcerted at doin' so. Until the followin' day. I'd swear she'd lost a lot of sleep during the night, but to me she looked like a woman who had been comprehensively ravished.'

'She did?' murmured Storm lazily, still attempting to avoid admitting the true terms of the bet, but immodestly conceding the truth of the Duchess's words. They had, however, brought back to vivid memory the satisfaction, the delight of shared passion during those hours spent in Lexie's bed. He crossed his legs. The old lady's eyes were still sharp.

'I gather,' said that lady with another wolfish grin, 'that you took your reward in her bed. No one else is likely to have been responsible. So you won all round, did you not?'

'I do not usually lose, Grandmama.'

'Ha! So you admit it! I knew as much. And when my agent could not reach you at Stormaston and Chalker told my girl that her mistress had given her a couple of weeks off because she wouldn't be needin' her services, I concluded you'd gone off somewhere together. I trust you had an agreeable time.'

'Capital, I thank you.'

'Where'd you go?'

The disclosure was inevitable. Storm grinned, daring his grandmother to disapprove. 'To stay with Nanny Dean in Frinton.'

'Of course. She always indulged you dreadfully, James. So why are the two of you at odds now?'

Reluctantly, Storm admitted, 'Because Lexie would not continue our *affaire* once we returned.' Unconsciously, his voice took on a bitter tone. 'She had paid her debt and, for her, that was the end of it.'

'She wasn't happy indulgin' in love outside marriage, I collect. You should have wed her, James.'

'You have informed me of your opinion before, ma'am. But I have no wish to wed.'

Which was still essentially true. He did not relish the idea of surrendering his freedom; yet, living with Lexie, even for so short a time, had made his present existence seem peculiarly unsatisfactory. Even Stormaston and his laboratory had not been able to lift him from the dark mood her rejection had plunged him into.

'So you have been goin' around like a bear with a sore head because she has withdrawn her favours, and she's been pinin' because she can't square her conscience. And you refuse to wed her.'

'She did not look as though she was pining to me.' Still bitter.

The Duchess's snort could have been heard outside the door. And at that moment a footman entered to announce that Lord Dexter had called and to ask whether Her Grace would receive him.

In fact, since he had been summoned, Felix had followed hard on the fellow's heels. The Duchess saw him hovering beyond the door and called out to him to come in.

Felix did so and then, seeing Storm, who had risen to his feet, halted just inside the room. The men eyed one another, still not back on the old, easy terms.

'Come in, come here, Dexter! James has somethin' to say to you.'

The imperious tones of the Duchess cut through the uneasy atmosphere. Storm gave a slight shrug and made his bow. Felix made his devoirs to them both and looked questioningly at Storm.

Storm eyed his friend of so many years and saw what Fanny and the Duchess had seen, a personable young man with an engaging manner, upon whose handsome features his so-called vices had left no mark. They'd both rattled about Town, raised hell on occasion, drunk too much, gambled too deeply, known too many women. But Felix was an honourable man, well-liked, without a vicious bone in his body. And one day would inherit an earldom. If Fanny loved him, well, Storm supposed that could be the making of him.

'Have you mentioned your aspiration to my sister's hand to St Clare?' Storm demanded.

Felix looked surprised at the question. 'Of course.'

'Then why in damnation—' he cut off, bowed to his grandmother '—my apologies! Why did not one of you approach me? Am I so d— so unapproachable as you make me appear?'

Felix faced up to him with a wry smile. 'On some matters, yes. You made my unacceptability as a suitor for Fanny's hand abundantly clear on several occasions.'

'I am still not entirely happy with the match. However, since Fanny's happiness apparently depends upon it and the Duchess approves, I must allow it.'

Felix bowed gravely. 'I can assure you of my most earnest intention to make her happy.'

Suddenly, Storm relaxed, and laughed, if a trifle ruefully. 'My friend, the trouble is I know you too well. We have caroused together too often for me to feel entirely convinced of your ability to do so for long. Yet if you can reform, then I must believe that there is hope for me yet! Go along to the library. Fanny will join you there. My solicitors will meet with yours as soon as can be arranged.'

Felix laughed, too, and once more held out his hand. 'I thank you from the bottom of my heart, brother! The wedding must be soon, as you will appreciate.'

'But don't arrange some hole-and-corner affair.' The Duchess spoke up again, holding out her hand for Felix to take. 'Welcome to the family, Felix,' she murmured as he kissed it, then went on. 'That would not be sensible. Fanny's reputation must be guarded at all costs. If you go abroad immediately afterwards, the ceremony may be delayed for as much as a month, I think. That will give us and the lawyers time to make all the necessary arrangements.'

'We do not wish for a grand affair, Your Grace,' said Felix. 'A simple ceremony with close family and friends present would suit us both excellently.'

'You've discussed the matter and have it all arranged, I collect,' interjected Storm. He sighed. 'I really was fighting a losing battle, was I not?' he remarked in a histrionically resigned voice.

'I fear we were ready to elope had you not come round,' Felix told him with an apologetic smile. 'But for everyone's sake, and especially Fanny's, I was reluctant. I had no wish to begin our life together with such a cloud hanging over us.'

'Very sensible of you, my boy,' said the Duchess. 'And now, run along. I have not finished what I have to say to my grandson.'

As he passed, Felix clapped Storm on the back. 'No hard feelings, I trust?' he asked.

'None, brother,' responded Storm, and meant it.

'And now,' said the Duchess when once again they were alone together, 'what of Alexia? You love the child, do you not?'

Storm, who had been about to sink down into his chair, straightened up again.

'I have no wish to discuss Lady Amber.'

'But I have. It is time you wed, I've told you so before.'

'Many times,' interjected Storm in a bored tone.

The Duchess ignored him. 'You'll never find a more fittin' bride. You suit each other admirably. I cannot conceive what is stoppin' you from askin' her.'

'A constitutional objection to the state of matrimony, Grandmama.'

'Then you are more idiotish than I thought you, James. Look about you, boy! Do you see every marriage in terms of those famous examples of failure to which the Regent subscribes? What of my marriage? What of your parents'? Reasonably felicitous marriages outnumber bad ones, even amongst those that are arranged. And you need an heir.'

'As you have informed me *ad nauseum*. But either I shall marry where mutual love exists, or I shall make a marriage of convenience when it is no longer avoidable.'

'Then what in Hades are you waitin' for, boy? You love her and she loves you. Get on with it!'

'Really, Grandmama, your language sometimes requires moderating!'

'Fiddlesticks! You are prevaricatin'. Go and beg the girl to marry you and thank Providence for sendin' her your way!'

Slowly, Storm sat down, elegant as ever, but with an abstracted air. 'Lexie does not love me.'

'Nonsense! Of course she does! Anyone but a fool could see she's head over heels in love with you by the way she looks at you. It is just as obvious that she is in love with you as it is that you are besotted with her. Why else has she been in the dismals ever since she returned to Town?'

Storm glared at his relative. He did not like being told he was besotted. He was not. 'Simply because she failed to manoeuvre me into Parson's mousetrap?' he enquired cynically.

'Not Lady Alexia.' The Duchess defended her protégée firmly. 'She would put you behind her and concentrate on findin' someone else to marry.'

'Which she appears to have done,' pointed out Storm dryly. 'Lord Cranley, I understand, is on the point of offerin' for her.'

'But, mark my words, she'll never accept him. Might think she could, but when it comes to the point she'll not bring herself to do it.'

'Our desire may be mutual—you see, I am being honest—but I doubt she loves me. She wishes to wed me for more worldly reasons. Cranley is heir to a marquessate and is very rich. He will do her very well.'

'Ask her,' suggested his grandmother.

Storm left Downshire House with his emotions in turmoil. Could he believe his grandparent's word? Did Lexie love him? She had behaved as though she did, but then, so had plenty of other women. Before all this furore he had intended to seek her hand. But. . .

Lexie had, only half an hour earlier, proved the Duchess right. Lord Cranley had presented himself requesting a private interview with Lady Amber. Although feeling far from ready to cope with what she guessed he had come to say, Lexie could not refuse to see him. She had left it too late to remedy the false impression she must have given.

He had, he said, having greeted her with elaborate courtesy, naturally heard that the Countess had appeared attached to Another during the summer, but since she had not recently been seen in His Lordship's company and had accepted his own attentions, Lord Cranley ventured to hope that she might welcome his suit. He had come to request her agreement to his approaching her father, the Earl of Webley, to seek permission to address her with a view to uniting their lives to their mutual advantage.

Lexie, her feelings of guilt almost overcome by the inclination to fall into a strong fit of hysterics at the form of his declaration, had managed to command herself sufficiently to send the slightly-corpulent gentleman away with his pride and temper intact. She had apologised profusely for any wrong impression she had given but, highly as she regarded him, she did not love him, and therefore could not marry him.

More protestations had followed but Lexie had, in the end, managed to extricate herself from a difficult situation and, on his departure, breathed a sigh of relief. At least that problem was now solved.

She hoped Fanny's dilemma had been resolved to mutual satisfaction all round: that Storm had given in graciously and was no longer at odds with Fanny and Felix. She longed for news, but knew she would have to wait until she saw Fanny again to learn the outcome.

She did not have long to fret. A radiant Fanny, escorted by an equally happy Felix, called the following morning.

'And we are to be wed on the first day of December,' Fanny told her. 'You will come, will you not, Lexie? Be my Matron of Honour?'

This compliment Lexie graciously declined. Storm, she gathered, was to support Felix—when he gave in, he did so handsomely, as the Duchess had said—and she could not bear the thought of being so intimately involved with him at the wedding. It was to be a modest, quiet affair, and this she made her excuse.

Fanny was disappointed, but not downcast. Melissa Daventry would almost certainly agree to support her. And in the excitement of discussing the forthcoming wedding, no mention was made of Lord Cranley's proposal and Lexie's refusal of his suit.

Over the next few days Lexie tried to behave as normally as possible. She could not hide herself away from the criticism she knew would greet the news that she had refused Cranley. She had behaved badly, she could not deny it. But it seemed a small offence to live down compared to some of the others she had committed.

News of the engagement spread and Fanny and Felix received so many invitations they could not possibly accept even half of them. However, they did appear together at a musical soiré with Lexie, improbably, acting as Fanny's chaperon. The Duchess did not wish to leave her husband's side, for although his condition had improved she was still concerned for his health.

'Angina don't often kill accordin' to the doctor,' she had said, 'but it is a distressin' complaint. If Downshire is goin' to have an attack, I want to be there.'

It was at this social occasion that Fanny and Felix heard of Lexie's shocking treatment of poor Lord Cranley, who had gone off to his estates to digest his disappointment. And when Felix saw Storm a couple of days after that, Storm, who had not even visited his club in the meanwhile—he had been paying a flying visit to Wiltshire, certain business matters at

Stormaston having demanded his immediate attention—was also made aware of the facts.

The information crystallised in his mind the decision he had already subconsciously taken.

'You're all goin' to the ball tomorrow evenin', you say? I received my invitation and declined to attend, but I'm certain Lady Castlereagh will not object if I change my mind. I shall look to see you there.'

Lexie did not know of Storm's intention to attend the ball, one of the few to be held in the last month before people returned to their estates and Christmas house parties. She had been invited to spend the festive season with the Duke and Duchess of Downshire but had so far avoided giving a definite answer.

Fanny would not be there but Storm and Hugo probably would. If she heard that Storm intended spending Christmas elsewhere, then she might consider travelling to Kent with them. Provided the Duke was fit enough to travel. Otherwise the Duchess planned to remain in London.

Lexie had already danced several times when a stir at the door made her glance across. Storm's dark head shone in the light thrown by thousands of candles in chandelier and sconce. His unexpected arrival had created an excitement akin to that normally occasioned by the presence of the Regent. Lexie's heart thumped its way to her throat. She had not expected to see him and the shock made her stumble.

'Ouch!' exclaimed Oswald in an ungentlemanly manner. 'That was my toe, Lady Alexia!'

No poetic superlatives from the young man tonight, Lexie noted, amused despite her distraction. He had matured beyond measure since his visit to Merryfield and his calf-love was fast turning into genuine, friendly affection. Miss Daventry appeared to be waging a successful campaign to win his heart, which pleased Lexie. They made a suitable pair.

'Oh,' said Oswald when next they came together, oblivious of the cause of Lexie's earlier clumsiness. 'There's Stormaston! Ain't seen him in weeks! Alone, too. Ain't gone back to his crowd of cronies now he ain't escortin' you.'

'Felix St Clare is here,' Lexie observed.

'But he don't mix with 'em any more either, since he fell in love with Lady Fanny.'

The set ended and Oswald escorted Lexie back to join Fanny and Felix. Storm had already sought out his sister.

'Grandmama has remained at home with Grandpapa,' Fanny was explaining as Lexie came up. 'Lexie! See who is here!'

'Greetings, Storm,' said Lexie evenly, as she curtsied in response to his bow. 'We had become resigned to your continued absence from Society. To what do we owe the honour of your company this evening?'

'Why, Lady Alexia, what else but the pleasure of dancing with you again?'

Lexie's gay laugh held only the faintest of false rings. 'La, sir! What flattery! Was it not that you had become bored with your retired life?'

Storm ignored this. 'They are striking up for a waltz. Shall we take to the floor?'

He crooked his arm and offered it. Lexie, more flustered than she would have liked to admit, glanced down at her card. 'But this dance is taken—'

'I will deal with the disappointed gentleman. Who is it?'

'The Duke of Clarence.'

'Ah!'

He turned as the Sailor Duke barged his way towards Lexie, and made him an elegant, deferential leg. 'Your Grace, I am convinced you will not object to my claimin' the Countess for this dance. It has been so long since we have had occasion to waltz together.'

The Duke, good-humoured as ever, gave a guffaw of laughter.

'Back in circulation again, eh, Stormaston? How's the Duke?'

'I am happy to report that my grandfather's condition is greatly improved. We anticipate his being able to return to Kent for Christmas.'

'Be able to attend little Fanny's wedding, eh? Sly dog, Dexter! Congratulations. Heard you'd become engaged.'

'Thank you, Your Grace.'

Felix and Fanny made their devoirs and Storm took the opportunity to steer Lexie out onto the floor, where the waltz had just begun.

'Such impudence! How can you treat the Duke so disrespectfully!'

His arm came about her waist. 'My dear Lexie, I would brave worse fates than the displeasure of a Royal Duke in order to dance again with you.'

Lexie moved into his arms like one in a dream. A dream come true. But before she could believe that she must discover exactly what were his lordship's intentions toward her.

But dancing a waltz with him was not the best

moment to inquire. Her mind was spinning in time with her feet. She danced in blissful, if dubious, silence.

At the end, Storm escorted her back to her friends. He had not spoken, either. He bowed.

'I shall give myself the pleasure of calling upon you tomorrow morning, Lexie. I trust you will be able to receive me?'

Lexie had intended to go calling herself. But she nodded.

'I shall be at home all the morning,' she told him.

'Then you may expect me at midday.'

He left her then. And shortly afterwards he departed the ball. It was evident that he had come only to speak with her. Lexie, her heart aflutter, slept very little that night.

CHAPTER FOURTEEN

LEXIE could stomach no breakfast next day, but drank
several cups of chocolate. Waiting alone in the morning-room in a demure but becoming gown of damask
rose and with Caro banished to the small parlour, her
eyes kept straying to the clock on the mantel. Its
ornate hands seemed to move at a snail's pace, the
pendulum's tick-tock to become slower and slower.
However, the quarters did chime, the hours struck and
eventually the hands met in upright triumph over the
twelve.

And Dymock himself announced the Marquess of
Stormaston as the last stroke faded into the silence.

Lexie did not rise—her legs did not feel strong
enough—or speak. She waited until Storm stood in
front of her and then offered her hand.

He bowed over it before, gently, kissing the knuckles. Instead of releasing her he turned the hand palm
upward and touched it again with his lips.

Lexie's breathing quickened in time with her pulse.
He was playing the suitor. But what was the nature of
his suit?

'Do sit down,' she managed to say, remembering her
duties as a hostess. 'May I offer you a drink?'

Storm, equally tense, but determined not to show it,
sank lazily into the indicated chair and said, 'A glass
of Madeira would not be unwelcome.'

'Dymock?' The butler had not yet left the room. 'A decanter and two glasses, if you please.'

He brought the tray holding the requisite items from a cupboard and placed it on the table near Storm before pouring the wine and handing each a glass.

'Thank you.' Lexie accepted hers. 'Shut the door as you leave.'

Dymock bowed. 'Yes, my lady.'

They drank in silence. Storm's glass was soon empty. 'Excellent vintage,' he remarked.

'Help yourself to another,' invited Lexie.

'And you?'

'I have enough, I thank you.'

She needed to have her morale boosted, but not to have her mind fuddled. It was quite confused enough as it was.

He poured his second glass and sat holding the dark tawny liquid to the light. He was, realised Lexie, exhibiting an unusual degree of reluctance to come to the point. His lordly self-assurance normally carried him through any difficulty without any sign of uncertainty. He had not hesitated a moment before attempting to seduce her.

'Why did you wish to see me?' she asked at last. Incredibly, he seemed to require help in coming to the point.

'I've missed you,' he said simply.

'Indeed?' Lexie congratulated herself on the coolness of her tone.

Storm swallowed a mouthful of wine before he went on, frowning. The love of his life appeared remarkably cool, which made his task the more difficult. 'You should not have walked out, Lexie. I intended to apologise for my conceit in taking it for granted that you would wish to continue our liaison. But, since I believed you enjoyed our love-making, I did not think to question it.'

'I did enjoy it.'

'But not enough to want it to continue.'

'More than enough, Storm. But not under those circumstances.'

'Quite.' The silence echoed for a long moment. Then Storm said, harshly for him, 'For reasons known only to yourself, you wished to trap me into marriage.'

Lexie shook her head. 'Not trap. Persuade. There were many excellent reasons for us to form an alliance.'

He swirled the remaining Madeira round in his glass and inhaled the bouquet. 'Whatever your reason may have been for suggesting it, I have been considerin' that race. It was a close run thing. Had your drive been twenty yards shorter you would have emerged the victor.'

'But it was not and you beat me by a head.'

'Almost a dead heat,' mused Storm. 'And I took my winnings, as you so pointedly remarked before you left Frinton. But—I think you are entitled to claim yours, too.'

'Mine?' Lexie had calmed down now. This was a game of cat and mouse. He was not going to admit to wanting to wed her. She hid a smile. 'But I won nothing.'

'True. But a dead heat would have proved a fair result. We would both have won. What would we have done had that occurred?'

Lexie looked at him, wide-eyed. 'You tell me.'

He grinned, suddenly sure of himself again. 'I would have warmed your bed immediately, but at the same time we would have announced our engagement.'

'So,' said Lexie calmly. 'What are you suggesting?'

'Why, that we treat the result as a draw. We both win. In other words, Lexie, I will marry you, despite the fact that you have no true love for me and do not relish bearing me an heir. But in the event of our marriage that would become your duty.'

'Duty?' Lexie coloured hotly. Not love him! But he had not admitted to loving her. She would let that go. 'What makes you think that I would consider it a duty?'

'All those elaborate precautions you took during our time together to avoid conceiving my child. Did you think me so green that I did not realise?'

'I hoped you had not. I did not wish to offend you.' Lexie clenched her fists in her lap and drew a deep breath. 'Shall I tell you exactly why I took care not to become pregnant? I would have borne a bastard, labelled for life as such whatever his or her upbringing. A boy child would have had no claim on your inheritance. He would have been in a worse situation than Hugo, who at least has the right to use the family name and to expect help and support from his relations.'

Storm looked taken aback by this tirade. The arrogance returned as he met her challenge. 'I have always seen my children well cared for. Surprising as it may seem to you, my dear, I take an interest in their welfare.'

Lexie could accept without rancour the fact of his having already sired children. In that respect he was no different to a widower with an existing family. 'But you would not contemplate making one of them your heir, I collect.'

'Their mothers' quality would scarcely support such a notion.'

'I see. And would mine have made a scrap of difference? I think not. And what of me, Storm? Look at the furore over Fanny's conceiving a child out of wedlock! Imagine the sensation if the outrageous Countess of Amber were to appear with a bastard in leading-strings!'

'You would have had no need—'

Lexie cut him off. 'No need to keep it. I agree. But I am not made like that, my lord. I should have wanted to nurture the child, to bring it up myself. Which would have meant complete retirement from Society. And the chance of making a decent second marriage would have been gone for ever.'

Storm regarded her broodingly. 'Did it never occur to you that, had you conceived, I would have married you?'

'I could not depend upon it, my lord. You have never felt the necessity before. Besides, I did not want to pressure you once my venture with the wager failed. I accepted defeat.'

Storm was, suddenly, kneeling by her side, both her hands clasped in his. 'My dear girl, I had no idea you would feel like that. My masculine mind could not conceive... My former mistresses, the two who each bore me a child, accepted the situation without regret. It meant they would be kept in comfortable circumstances for life, that their child would never want. I had forgot that your outlook would be different.'

Lexie had begun to tremble. Reaction, his nearness,

a myriad of emotions jostled for predominance. The one that won was love.

She released one of her hands from his grasp and ran her fingers through a stray lock that had fallen over his forehead, smoothing it back, and looked deeply into blue eyes which, for the first time that she could recall, were limpid, clear of all pretence or artifice.

'Do not imagine I did not long to bear your child, my dear James. It was simply more practical to ensure that I did not.'

'You mean it would not be a mere duty to carry my heir?'

She shook her head. At last she felt free to say it. 'I love you, James. I have done so for a long time. Only at the very first did I want you because of other things, and they were not money or title, but compatibility, pleasure in your company. By the time I suggested the wager, it was in order to win my heart's desire.'

Storm sat back on his heels, studying her captivating face. Rosy now to match her gown, her golden curls escaping from her little cap to frame it. And her eyes, greener than he had ever seen them before, were regarding him with such a look in them that his heart begun to thud.

'Grandmama said you loved me,' he said with a breathless laugh. 'I did not dare to believe her.'

'She is perceptive and wise. I find her quite delightful.'

'She also informed me that I was besotted with you,' he went on wryly. 'I would not admit it, even to myself, but she was right, as usual. Lexie, my dearest love, I declare myself your slave for life. Dare I hope that you will marry me?'

Lexie's eyes closed as a sweep of relief stopped her breath. Then her face broke into a radiant smile.

'Oh, yes, James!'

He lifted both her hands to his lips and then looked up, all the old, mocking laughter back in his eyes. Only this time it was self-mocking.

'I never anticipated that I would find myself declaring my love on my knees, despite a regrettable expectation among most green girls that no suitor could mean it unless he did!' With which he lifted her to her feet the better to take her in his arms and kiss her until she had no choice but to cling to him for support.

'When will you marry me?' he demanded at last, seating her on the sofa and dropping beside her to take her back into his arms. 'It must be soon. I am impatient to have you back in my bed.'

'You think we should wait?' murmured Lexie naughtily.

'Most certainly. I am determined upon observing the utmost propriety.' His hand found her breast and cupped it, his thumb teasing through the layers of cloth.

'Really?' murmured Lexie, revelling in the thrill of his touch. 'I believe you are behaving in a most forward manner, my lord!'

He chuckled. 'Allow my hands a little licence, do not starve me entirely. But I shall not make the mistake of seducing you again before our wedding. You were not designed for such intrigues, my darling.'

They were still engaged in savouring their new-found happiness, mostly without the aid of words, when Dymock rapped on the door and coughed discreetly before entering.

Storm kept Lexie firmly in his arms.

'Yes, Dymock? What is it?'

Dymock coughed. 'May I be the first to congratulate you, my lord? And to wish you happy, my lady?'

Reluctantly, Lexie extricated herself from Storm's embrace.

'I suppose finding us like this could have but one explanation,' she admitted. 'Thank you, Dymock. See that there is plenty of ale in the servants' quarters this evening with which to drink our health.'

'With pleasure, my lady. I came to inform you that Lord Dexter and Lady Fanny Graham are below. Are you at home?'

'Send them up!'

As Dymock bowed and withdrew, Storm stood, too.

'They will be surprised to hear our news.'

'Perhaps. But pleased, too. You will put an announcement in the papers?'

'That an engagement has been entered into, yes. And the date of the ceremony, if we can agree it.'

'I am so thankful that you did not come merely to ask permission to approach my father, like Lord Cranley! I am no longer dependent upon his approval for anything I do!'

At that moment Fanny came into the room, closely followed by Felix.

'James!' she cried in surprise. 'I did not expect to discover you here!'

'Did you not, my love?' wondered Felix. 'I cannot say I am surprised, after your appearance at the ball last evening, Storm. Are we to congratulate you?'

'Indeed you may! Lady Alexia has agreed to marry me.'

'Oh, James!' Fanny rushed over to kiss him and then Lexie. 'Grandmama will be so pleased! She positively dotes on Lexie!'

'So,' observed the Marquess, 'does the Duke. Lexie won his admiration during his stay at Merryfield. He has not stopped singing her praises since.'

Lexie walked over and put her hand through Storm's arm. 'Poor James! When you were trying so hard to put me out of your thoughts!'

'An impossible task, my love.'

'When are you to wed?' demanded Fanny. 'Is it decided?'

'Not yet. Give us a chance, dear sister! We only agreed on it half an hour ago!'

'Then we are the first to know! How enchanting! Felix, my love, I have an idea! How amusing to have a double wedding!'

'A charming idea, my love. Storm, what do you say? You and your sister wed on the same day! That should give the gabble-grinders something to speculate about!'

'But I am supposed to be supporting you, my friend.'

'I can easily find someone else to fill that role.'

Storm looked at Lexie. 'What do you say, my love? Could you be ready in time?'

'What do I need but a new gown? And if we harry the solicitors. . . But the notice may be too short to allow of my parents travelling.'

'Does that concern you?'

Lexie shook her head. 'They abandoned me to Amber, caring little whether I was happy or not. We correspond only occasionally and I do not pine to see them again. But we must inform Cousin Caro!' She pulled the bell cord and when Dymock appeared told him to inform Mrs Baldwin that she was wanted in the morning-room.

Caro was predictably effusive in her congratulations and excited at the prospect of a double wedding. But Lexie noticed a look of concern on the older woman's face when she thought no one was looking.

'You will remain with me, of course, Cousin,' she hastened to reassure her. 'I shall be in need of someone to take care of both this establishment and Merryfield when we take up residence at Stormaston Park. Would that responsibility suit you?'

Caro's face immediately cleared. 'I am honoured that you should trust me with it, dearest Alexia,' she fluttered.

And talk returned to the forthcoming nuptials.

In the event the double wedding became the highlight of the Little Season. Every effort was made to keep the ceremony simple, the attendance restricted, but this proved impossible, despite the shortage of time left to make the arrangements.

The days passed in a whirl of activity, of planning, not only for the wedding but for life afterwards.

'Come to the Continent with us!' suggested Fanny one day as she and Lexie were discussing the wedding. 'You surely do not wish to spend your honeymoon at Stormaston Park! And if you do not, I shall have no companion but my husband after we are wed!'

'My dear Fanny,' laughed Lexie, to whom this wholly unattractive proposition had been put. 'I am more than happy to go to Stormaston Park—remember, I have not yet seen my new home! And you will need no other companion but Felix! You will have your maid and his man with you. You will not wish to travel with a larger party.'

Fanny appeared uncertain. 'But it is usual for new brides to take a companion on honeymoon.'

'Green girls who scarcely know the man they have married! Who have no notion of what goes on in the bedroom! You have no need of the missish misgivings which bedevil those poor creatures. You know Felix in every way. You may trust him to see that you want for nothing while you are away.'

'But the baby,' murmured Fanny. 'Supposing something goes wrong?'

'Your maid is an experienced woman of the world. And if you are truly in trouble later on, you may always send for help. But I do not think either James or Felix would approve your plan. And I confess, Fanny, I would rather have James to myself during the first weeks of our marriage.'

'Well, of course, I would prefer to be alone with Felix. But. . .'

'But you are suffering from bridal nerves! Bear up, Fanny! You have no need to be nervous. You will return in a years' time with a bonny infant to bring your nursery to life.'

Fanny went away reassured, leaving Lexie with her own worries. When Storm next called, which he did daily, she confided them to him.

'James, I wonder whether I am doing right in marrying you,' she began as he released her from his embrace.

His expression of outrage almost overset her composure. His words did.

'Right? My dear girl, who was it who urged the match from the beginning of our re-acquaintance? It is a little late to begin to have doubts now! Unless, of course, you have discovered that you do not love me after all?'

Considering the ardour with which she had returned his kiss, he could not truthfully believe that! 'Don't be silly, James!' Her voice trembled, but whether with laughter or apprehension even she did not know. 'Of course I still love you! And it is because I love you so much that this thing has been worrying me recently.'

James, collecting his patience and wondering what worm was eating his beloved now, asked, 'What thing, my love?'

'I failed to provide Amber with an heir,' she whispered miserably. 'Old Demelza in Cornwall said it was because my husband was too old. But supposing she was wrong? Supposing I prove barren?'

He gathered her into his arms again and pressed her hot face into his shoulder.

'That would be unfortunate. But not reason enough for me to regret marrying you. There is always Hugo and his progeny to fall back on. Or even,' he added, half-mischievously, 'one of my by-blows.'

'You truly would not hate me for not being fruitful?'

The anxious expression on her face brought a tender smile to James's, a soft light to his eyes. 'I should regret the circumstance, but I should still love you, my Lexie. Depend upon it, the old woman was right. You need have no fear.'

'You are such a comfort,' sighed Lexie, kissing the

scar on his cheek. 'Do you know, Fanny wanted us to join them on the Continent to share our honeymoons?'

James's horrified expression confirmed Lexie's view of what his reaction would be. 'You did not agree?'

'I did not! Felix would probably have a fit, not to mention you! She is simply suffering from pre-nuptial nerves!'

'And so are you, my love. In a year's time you will both be contented matrons visiting your offspring in the nursery and neglecting your poor husbands!'

'Never!' Lexie gave a happy laugh, her doubts laid to rest, for the moment at least. 'Oh, James, I can hardly wait for the great day!'

'Nor I. But I am glad we are. Only a week more and I can take you with God's and the world's blessing. And you will have no dark cloud on your conscience to interfere with your pleasure. You know, I never felt you were truly mine.'

'I never felt entirely comfortable,' Lexie admitted.

'But there will be no limitations on our love once we reach Stormaston Park. I am eager for you to see the estate. I love it, and I hope you will, too.'

Lexie did, on sight, despite the lateness of the hour of their arrival. The windows of the house blazed with light to greet its new mistress. The staff lined up and were introduced. So many of them! Lexie wondered whether she would ever remember all their names! But, it appeared, James knew each one by name, knew their position in the household, whether they were married, how many children they had and what ailments they suffered, right down to the yawning boot boy.

She would explore the rest of the house next day. Meanwhile, she discovered that the master suite contained a huge tester bed in which generations of Grahams had been born.

Lexie submitted to Chalker's ministration while Marlow assisted Storm to disrobe. They both took a bath, necessary after the heat of the reception room and the long journey which followed.

'God's blessings on you both, my lady,' offered Chalker as she prepared to leave for her own bed.

'Thank you, Florence. I hope you will be happy here.'

Chalker smiled. 'I can see no reason why not, my lady. Such a household! And you'll be visiting London at least once a year. Don't worry yourself over me.'

Caro had returned to Bruton Street, preening herself on being left in charge. Lexie knew her cousin would keep the place in perfect trim. Merryfield, too, for she had been left with a coach and horses to take her there whenever she felt it necessary.

All in all, things had worked out well. For Oswald Cresswell and Melissa Daventry, too. Melissa had won her campaign to captivate Oswald and had even managed to overcome the opposition of his mama. They were to be wed the following autumn.

But although such thoughts ran along the surface of Lexie's mind as she lay waiting in the bed, her ears were strained for the sound of her husband coming to her from the adjoining dressing room.

He did not take long over his ablutions. As he slipped in beside her, the unhappy intervening months dropped away and it seemed like only yesterday that they had been together. Yet although their voyage of discovery of each other followed a familiar pattern, their emotions were heightened not only by long abstinence, but also by declared love and the new awareness of being joined together in matrimony until death.

The cloud had disappeared from Lexie's mind. And Storm, discovering in himself the capacity to actually enjoy being leg-shackled to his new Marchioness, exceeded even his previous achievements in the matter of expert wooing, combining this with such tenderness that Lexie ended up in tears of supreme joy.

They spent Christmas with the Duke and Duchess in Kent, but returned thankfully to Stormaston Park as soon they decently could.

Lexie had never enquired as to what had transpired between the brothers after Storm had discovered the truth after the duel, but Hugo had returned to his regiment nursing a sore chin and a black eye. They saw nothing of him, although he did visit his grand-parents from time to time.

'To extract money to pay his debts, no doubt,' Storm remarked cynically. 'He knows there is no point in applying to me.'

In May news reached them that Fanny had been delivered, without trouble, of a boy, in Italy. Napoleon, who had escaped from Elba, was back in Paris and an army, led by the Duke of Wellington, was gathering near Brussels to confront him. Viscount Dexter and his Viscountess would perforce remain in Italy until the autumn before attempting the journey home. They had named the boy Peter and the family could announce the birth in late August.

The last of Lexie's fears were laid to rest when she became pregnant some two months after the wedding. The child was born in November. The Honourable Peter St Clare, who had been brought home a week earlier, was, of course, obviously older and much bigger than his diminutive cousin.

With the defeat of Napoleon at Waterloo, where Hugo had unexpectedly distinguished himself, the Dexters had been able to journey home through France. No one outside the family had seen the baby yet. Fanny intended keeping him incommunicado on a remote St Clare estate.

'In a year or so's time no one will notice the difference,' she proclaimed cheerfully when she came to visit Lexie after her confinement.

Felix had poked his head round the door and the couple appeared radiantly happy, which, for Lexie, was all that mattered.

Alone with James, she sighed. 'Perhaps it is as well our baby is a girl. No one will expect her to be so big as Peter. But I am sorry I could not manage you an heir, my darling.'

'I am already deeply in love with Lady Elizabeth,' James told her, touching the baby's silky, golden hair where it had escaped from its cap. 'And I'll wager that our next will be a boy.'

'What do you have in mind as a stake?' demanded Lexie.

Storm grinned. 'Nothing too dramatic or exhausting. Fifty guineas?'

'Done!'

He won the wager, naturally. Lexie parted with her money in a glow of delighted achievement.

And received it and more back again in the form of an exquisite heart-shaped brooch, presented with her husband's constant and abiding love.

LEGACY of LOVE

Coming next month

FAREWELL THE HEART
Meg Alexander
Regency 1815

Accompanying her newly married sister, Elizabeth, to England, Miss Harriet Woodthorpe had no idea what awaited them, but it rapidly became clear that the family thought the Duke's heir, George, had married beneath him. Harriet bristled—more so when their neighbour, Lord Ashby, unaccountably began to take liberties with her person!

If Hugh thought that she would countenance his lecherous ways, he was wrong—but a worse thought intruded. Was Hugh—the man she now loved—responsible for the peculiar accidents that had befallen Elizabeth since she began increasing?

A BIDDABLE GIRL?
Paula Marshall
Regency 1818

Miss Cassandra Merton was seriously worried about her future. The death of Earl Devereux meant she might no longer have a roof over her head, for who was to say what the new Earl, Jack, banished twelve years ago in disgrace, would do?

To her shock, he proposed marriage—the only way to gain his estates according to his father's will. He clearly thought this dowdy mouse would make a biddable wife, whom he could ignore at will—but, once married, Cass would show him how mistaken he was!

Name that Song

How would you like to win a year's supply of simply irresistible romances? Well, you can and they're free! Simply solve the puzzle below and send your completed entry to us by 31st October 1996. The first five correct entries picked after the closing date will each win a years supply of Temptation novels (four books every month—worth over £100).

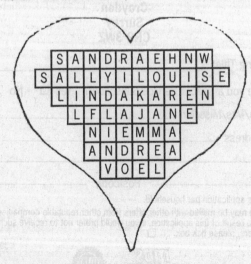

S	A	N	D	R	A	E	H	N	W	
S	A	L	L	Y	I	L	O	U	I	S	E
	L	I	N	D	A	K	A	R	E	N
	L	F	L	A	J	A	N	E	
	N	I	E	M	M	A	
	A	N	D	R	E	A	
	V	O	E	L	

Please turn over for details of how to enter ☞

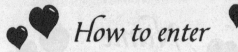

How to enter

To solve our puzzle...first circle eight well known girls names hidden in the grid. Then unscramble the remaining letters to reveal the title of a well-known song (five words).

When you have written the song title in the space provided below, don't forget to fill in your name and address, pop this page into an envelope (you don't need a stamp) and post it today! Hurry—competition ends 31st October 1996.

**Mills & Boon Song Puzzle
FREEPOST
Croydon
Surrey
CR9 3WZ**

Song Title: _____

Are you a Reader Service Subscriber?   Yes ❑   No ❑

Ms/Mrs/Miss/Mr _____

Address _____

_____

_____ Postcode _____

One application per household.

You may be mailed with other offers from other reputable companies as a result of this application. If you would prefer not to receive such offers, please tick box.   ❑

C396
D